MIDLIFE ECLIPSE

DRUID HEIR BOOK 6

N. Z. NASSER

HANORA SKY PRESS

Midlife Eclipse: Druid Heir Book 6
Copyright © N. Z. Nasser 2022
Published by Hanora Sky Press

eBook ISBN 978-1-915151-11-7
Paperback ISBN 978-1-915151-12-4

THE PLAYERS

Alisha Verma - Druid Heir

Echo - Alisha's leopard sidekick

Mirabel (sometimes known as Bel) - a fairy

Marina Ambrose - Alisha's best friend

Ezra Neuhoff - half-werewolf, half-wizard Minister for Justice

Orpheus Might - Vampire, Minister for History and the Today

Robert Jameson - Detective, Shadow Squad

Fei Yen and Faeza - hu hsien, shapeshifting foxes

Joshi Verma - Alisha's father

Sahil Verma - Alisha's brother

Alma Bluejay - Flour seer and Joshi's love

Gaia - Goddess of the Earth

Flinar - an elf

Tielbu - a dragon

Phinnaeous Shine - Shapeshifter, former Prime Sorcerer

Lavinia Drach - Witch, Minister for Defence

Rayna Willowsun - Druid Headmistress of Wildwoods and Minister for Education

Margola Silver - Selkie, Minister for Information

Pan - God of Shepherds, Goats and Pastures

Ignacio - rat familiar
Nightfall - a horse in the Celestial Library
The maker of lightsabers
The blue woman
An apparition

1

There comes a time in a woman's life when she questions her choices and whether she is surrounded by the right people. On one of those counts, I was certain I hadn't messed up.

Marina dipped her hands in a tin of cloudy blue paint, pressed her palms against my chest and stepped back to admire her handiwork. "Oh yes, *that's* the look I was going for."

My eyes widened at the sight of the handprints on my white T-shirt. "You didn't just do that. We're supposed to be redecorating the cottage, not me."

Over the past weeks, my best friend had been the glue that held me together and provided the spark of fun my new foster daughter sorely needed. After I'd refused Marina's offer to heal my broken heart the magical way, she'd stood by my side putting in the hard work without shortcuts. A sister in all but name. Although sometimes she went too far. Which was how I found myself at her mercy as she larked about in my living room in mid-winter, mischief written all over her face.

Twelve-year-old Mirabel's gloomy demeanour evaporated

into giggles. She wriggled her fingers as my rainbow-haired bestie egged her on.

"Let's make it a masterpiece." Mirabel smeared her own prints on me.

I huffed in mock anger, pleased to see her fool around. A month had passed since the fire fairy's parents had died in excruciating circumstances at Wildwoods. I'd replayed the events in my head a thousand times over, working out how we could have rescued them from the goddess Cardea, but my mental gymnastics didn't help. I couldn't turn back the clock.

All I could do was offer Mirabel a place in my heart and my family.

How I wished that family included Ezra.

Ezra was still angry at me for falling for Phinnaeous Shine's games, but he had kept his promise. The cottage, more spacious than my flat, had become my home with Mirabel, and we'd made it our own. With Marina's help, we splashed the walls with colour where there had been drab grey, brought in potted plants to replace the plastic fantastic ones and lit candles to chase away the smell of wet wolf. Ezra's absence still loomed large, but I had someone else to concentrate on. If I didn't sit down, I could almost forget how much I missed him. Who knew children could take up so much time? There was always a rumbling belly to feed, an overflowing basket of laundry to deal with, a screen to drag them away from or a hug to give.

Sometimes Mirabel even relaxed into them.

Sometimes she even let me touch her plush toy bunny without worrying it would disintegrate. The bunny, suddenly favourite again. A memory of home. A crutch. An anchor to her dead parents.

Never in my wildest dreams did I think I'd have a chance to be a mother, but Mirabel's arrival in my life had given me that chance. The roots of our togetherness were fragile and her grief raw, but each day we took small steps that I hoped would make us a family and help her move forward. Of course, her instant bond with our resident big kitty helped too.

I spun around at a touch on my back to find Echo's paw raised aloft and dripping in paint.

He bared his tombstone teeth. "I read an article once about a painting gorilla and thought I'd see what the fuss was about."

"And?" I cocked an eyebrow and stepped towards the two open tins of paint.

Sensing danger, the leopard's emerald eyes narrowed.

Too late. I angled my hands downwards, summoned the breeze and flicked with precision, like a cowgirl rounding on her enemies. Great big dollops of paint landed on Marina's, Mirabel's and Echo's faces. "That'll teach you to mess with me."

Marina squealed at the clumps in her rainbow hair. "The eternal girl's getting big for her boots."

She picked up a tin, her baby blues wide with innocence. Then all hell broke loose.

Paint arced through the living room, swaths of blues and sage greens splattering the walls and plastic covering. Echo pounced on the roller tray with an almighty roar. It spiralled towards Marina, drenching her favourite tracksuit bottoms. Mirabel shrieked and brandished a pair of paintbrushes like a demon child, painting stripes on me and a hissing Echo. With a groan, I gave up protecting myself and erected walls of wind to prevent further damage to the cottage. When the paint tins were empty and the chief mischief-makers sated, we collapsed onto the dust sheets.

"The fairy has made me a tiger," said the leopard in disgust.

"Call it payback for all the times you've tormented the koi in Joshi's pond," said Mirabel.

Marina laughed, joyous and carefree. "I'll get the baby wipes, shall I, Alisha?"

I looked around in horror. The cottage looked like Jackson Pollock's studio. This was how it was. Marina and Echo as the fun-loving aunt and uncle and me as the stern foster mum. "You'd better be hanging about for the clean-up. We'll have to hose everything down, including ourselves. I should farm all three of you out to the grandparents."

"Luckily, Joshi and Alma are in Bulgaria visiting the dragon, or we might fall for your emotional blackmail," said the leopard.

Mirabel's face froze, and she buried her head in her hands. Her shoulders shook with sobs, the bubble of her joy burst.

The three of us surged forward, but I got there first.

I put my hand on her hair, once long, auburn ringlets. Her mother Juniper had always combed her hair. On the day of the funeral, Mirabel had hacked it into a pixie cut. "Honey, what's wrong?"

She lifted her tearstained face, the rollercoaster of her emotions too much for her to navigate without our help. Her disjointed, hiccupping words pulsed with anguish. "You're going to send me away. You're not my real parent. You don't have to stick it out when I annoy you. And I can be *really* annoying."

I knelt before her. "Bel, I'm not going to send you away. Your home is with me now. I don't care about the mess. I was so glad to see you laugh."

Marina motioned to me, a silent exchange passing between us.

I shook my head. Her empath talents meant she could take away Mirabel's pain in a heartbeat. She'd helped Mirabel like this before, but it wasn't a long-term solution. The young girl's emotions mirrored a choppy ocean. None of us knew how a magical Band-Aid would work, but my intuition told me that Mirabel had to process her feelings or they would resurface at some point.

Mirabel opened her cupped hands and revealed an orb of fire, no bigger than a golf ball. Her green eyes stared into the distance. "Why couldn't they stay alive? Fire fairies should have been able to stay alive. They should have been able to extinguish the flames. I'm so angry at them."

I rubbed her knee, ignoring the heat from the fireball in her hands. "Honey, you know that talents vary in the Otherworld. Your parents didn't have as much control as you. It wasn't their fault."

Her almond-shaped eyes met mine. "I know."

"Bel, smother that fire." Urgency in my voice. "We don't want any accidents. Paint is flammable."

Echo emitted a wary growl as the fireball grew to the size of a bowling ball.

"Mirabel," I said sharply, giving Marina a nod.

Marina placed a soft hand on Mirabel's shoulder, and the girl quenched the fire, wracked with sobs.

I pulled her into my arms. "It's okay, honey. It's okay."

A shaky whisper. "I'm so angry at them. I don't know how to make the anger go away. I loved them so much."

I murmured against her hair. "And that love doesn't go away."

AFTER WE HAD all washed up and changed, it was Echo's turn. I brushed the gunk out of his coat following an ill-tempered bubble bath. My middle-aged knees ached from scrubbing the living room. I hauled myself up to make dinner for Mirabel and Echo, before leaving them in front of the television and then sneaking out into the garden. The night was cool, and I pulled my thick-knit cardigan tighter around me, missing Ezra's strong arms.

Marina handed me a glass of wine. "You're doing wonderfully, you know."

I took a deep slug of Merlot. "What if I can't handle it? Maybe she needs more experience. I wanted so much to be a mum, and now I realise I don't know what I'm doing."

"I've seen you with her. She's lucky to have you." She closed her eyes and leaned back, her voice sad. "Mirabel's parents aren't coming back, Alisha. You're the best thing she's got."

My body ached. "What if Rayna was wrong to trust me with this?"

She prised her eyes open. "Rayna's sole purpose is the happiness of her pupils. If you ask me, she did exactly the right thing. The girl has no family, Alisha. You two already had a bond. It wasn't that much of a leap. You'll see. Things will settle down."

"You always know the right thing to say. How was Mirabel's aura today?"

Marina frowned. "Volatile."

"I thought as much. The fire is a worry. I wouldn't be so concerned if her talents were water- or earth- or plant-based. But fire? What if she loses control?"

She twiddled a lock of pink hair. "She won't. Look, I didn't take away all her pain. I eased it just a little to get her out of that funk today before we all went up in flames. But now it's up to you. All you have to do is be her anchor. Just until she's back on her feet."

My finger traced the rim of my glass. "Well, I've got plenty of time on my hands now that Joe Dumfrey fired me from the community centre this morning."

Marina's wine sloshed as she put down her glass. "You're kidding. Why didn't you say?"

"I was waiting for a moment alone with you. I didn't want to worry Mirabel. She has enough on her plate."

"So what are you going to do?" said Marina.

"Fei Yen and Faeza are upset. They riled up the other students and wanted to stage a protest, but to be honest, maybe it's a blessing in disguise. I thought maybe I'd concentrate on Mirabel for a bit. Then there's the Book of Names to find and Gaia to resurrect. I've been having these awful dreams about Gaia stuck in Limbo waiting for me to figure it out."

Marina drank deeply from her glass. "There's only so much you can juggle. And if you need a loan, just say the word. If I can't help my best friend out when she's in need, then there's no reason for me to spend half my working life squeezing out the anal glands of domestic animals or removing their nuts."

I reached across the small garden table to hug her. "You are disgusting and generous, but I promise my bank account is just fine right now. I've built up enough of a buffer."

My best friend's cornflower blue eyes sought mine. "Your finances are fine, but what about your heart? You've been moping around for weeks. Being with Ezra made you happy. You'll kick yourself if you let him slip through your fingers."

"It's quite nice not having to wax my legs. I'm free to go full-on yeti."

She scoffed. "That man would love even yeti you. Have you heard from him since he collected his things?"

I hadn't told her that I'd kept a T-shirt of his from the wash basket. That sometimes, when I missed him, I slept in it and drank in the scent of him. It hadn't been like this with my divorce. That had been a relief. Sad, but necessary. But losing Ezra was a gut punch and all my fault. "He's been busy hunting Phinnaeous. The pack are closing in on him."

Her tired eyes twinkled with delight. "So you're in touch."

Butterflies darted in my stomach. "He's keeping me in the loop so we don't worry about Phinnaeous. He's kind like that. But I'm not worried. Alma used some of Gaia's techniques to protect the cottage before she and Dad left on their travels. That's why there's flour everywhere."

A hard, relieved exhale. "Oh, that's what the powder is. Here was me thinking you have an ant problem and you'd gone all killer on them. Remember when we used to race them up and down our arms at school?" She topped up our glasses. "Seriously, though, Alisha. Ezra's calling because it's not over. Why do you think he let you stay in the cottage? Stop nursing your sore heart and get your man back. He wants what you want. I don't need to read his aura to know that."

The air shifted beside us in a way that was achingly familiar.

"Speak of the devil," said Marina.

Ezra Neuhoff appeared next to us in faded jeans and a white T-shirt, his brown hair flopping into grey, bloodshot eyes and face in need of a shave.

I scrambled up from my slouching position. "Ezra, is everything okay?"

His smile chased the chill away. "It will be."

Echo appeared at the door. He bounded over to Ezra, purring with bliss. "Wolf. I thought I heard your voice. I've missed your manly vibes around here. These ladies don't know how to let it all hang out. It smells of candles, cupcakes and body cream, when it should smell of forest, steak and sweaty muscle."

I rolled my eyes at the leopard. "I've been training hard, as you well know."

Ezra scratched the leopard's ears, but his eyes were on me, copper flaring within their depths. "Have you been training? Is there something on the horizon I should know about."

I dipped my head, the concern in his voice nearly my undoing. Everything had been easier when we were a team, but it wasn't fair to lay that at his feet. "Nothing I can't handle."

"You wear the Jericho necklace and take the sword everywhere, just in case?"

"Yeah. Just to be safe."

"Maybe one day you'll show me what you did at Stonehenge. Animating without your catalogue of creatures."

"I think it was the dormant power that resides there. A sort of magnifier. Or maybe it was being under threat. The rage I felt. Rayna's helping me figure it out."

He raked his hand through his hair, his eyes gleaming. "That's good."

Marina rolled her eyes. "Just cut to the bit where you jump each other's bones."

I glared at her, but she grinned back.

Ezra pushed his shoulders back, pride emanating from him. "Actually, I'm here in a professional capacity, not a personal one. I have to get back to Wildwoods, but I wanted you all to be the first to know. We've brought Phinnaeous Shine in."

I sucked in my breath, knowing how much this meant to him. Not only because of Phinnaeous's crimes against the Otherworld but also because of his cold-blooded dispatch of Gunnolf and his role in our breakup. "You did it. I knew you would."

A frisson of electricity between us made me want to rush into his arms.

"The wolf is the best of dogs," said the leopard.

"Well done, Ezra," said Marina. "Rob said it's been pretty gruelling."

Moonlight flickered across a small cut marring his cheekbone. "It was worth it. That traitor deserves everything that's coming to him."

His appearance had grown more haggard. I hoped now that he'd caught Phinnaeous that he'd go easy on himself. The primal urge to care for him came over me, even though logic told me he could have used his healing charm. "You're hurt. Let me grab some disinfectant."

He shook his head. "It's nothing. The reason I'm here… Phinnaeous will be standing trial at the Court of Wolves tonight. I thought maybe you and Mirabel would want to see justice done."

"Tonight?" My heart rattled in my ribcage.

Ezra nodded. "That's Otherworld justice for you. Brutal and swift. I have special dispensation for the detective to be there too, given he is one of Phinnaeous's victims."

"I have known Phinnaeous was a scoundrel ever since he started sniffing around your grandmother. It took you all a very long time to catch up, but you know what they say about leopards. We're always a few hundred miles ahead." Echo hadn't clocked that the invite hadn't been extended to him. "To put it plainly, not even a haven of pussies in the dock could tempt me to come. I need to stretch my limbs, and tonight promises a magnificent hunt."

"The question is whether Mirabel can handle it." I chewed my lip and did a quick mental calculation. These sorts of decisions were so alien to me. The court sat at midnight. Although it wasn't a school night, I worried Mirabel's fragile state meant it could do more harm than good to see her parents' killer sentenced. She'd had a run of nightmares, and seeing his smug, unrepentant face in real life could add to her trauma.

Marina gave me an encouraging smile. "It might give her closure. I know Rob's been hoping to see justice done. Maybe Mirabel feels the same."

I bit my lip. "I'll speak to her. She should have a say."

Ezra locked eyes with me. "I'll be right here waiting."

2

I rubbed Mirabel's back while she hunched over and ejected her dinner into a dark corner of Crystal Palace Park. I'd missed traversing across the city in Ezra's strong arms, but it was going to take some getting used to for my foster daughter.

"Your body is just trying to get its equilibrium back after teleporting, Mirabel. It gets better, I promise," said Ezra.

Mirabel wiped her mouth with the sleeve of her padded coat. "Next time I'll just meet you here. Even the night bus is better than going through that again."

Ezra opened his mouth to quip something back, but the words died on his lips, as if he wasn't quite sure how to engage with Mirabel. Instead. he led the way towards the yew tree and Wildwoods. "How have you been, Alisha?"

How odd for him to be so formal. My mind flashed to his lips against mine, murmuring his nickname for me, his hands on the small of my back, his shudder of release.

I blinked away the images. "I'm fine. You?"

Shadows spiralled over his face from the bare oaks and soaring conifer trees. "Yeah, me too."

Mirabel gave an audible sigh. "Well, this isn't awkward at all."

I squeezed her. "Give us a minute, will you?"

She sloped off, her purple Converse slapping against the frosted path.

"My aunt's acting Prime Sorcerer and presiding judge tonight," said Ezra.

I raised an eyebrow. "Of course she is. Never one to miss a trick. How harsh do you think her sentence will be?"

He shrugged. "She'll be led by what the crowd wants. Forgiving. Punitive. Sadistic. It could go anywhere. For her, this isn't about Phinnaeous Shine. It's about a cathartic group experience so the Otherworld can start anew."

Wildwoods was only a few hundred yards away now. I frowned, squinting to find familiar stone shapes up ahead. "Where are the sphinxes?"

"They complained that they always miss out, so my aunt's given them permission to attend court," said Ezra. "The coven applied protective wards to the park to make up for them leaving their post. There are more crystals littering this park tonight than empty crisp packets."

I snorted. "I knew that was a crystal I stubbed my toe on."

"The coven will be on hand to visualise a barrier too."

I wanted to speak about us, but my courage fled. "Are you ready for the trial?"

His eyes darkened. "Yeah, I'm ready. There was a lot of time to think while we were closing in on him." The gruff edges of his voice softened. "Are you enjoying being a mother?"

"It's harder than I thought."

"She's a good kid."

"Yeah, she is." I bit my lip. "Have you had your hands full with senate business?"

Ezra came to an abrupt halt. A noise close to a growl

escaped him. "Work's not the most important thing in a man's life."

The air left my lungs. The intent spark in his eyes sent a shiver up my spine.

He reached for my hand. "May I?"

Hope bloomed in me, but instead of rekindling what we had lost, he pushed up my sleeve and traced the new lines of my scar.

Wonder filled his voice. "So this is what happened at Stonehenge. When you said it was a map, I couldn't imagine it." A pause. "This is a sign that it isn't over, Alisha."

I swallowed hard. "I know."

"You've come so far from the woman I first met, the one who had no idea about her magical abilities or her destiny. They're going to come for you, and when they do, I'll be in your corner."

"Thanks." The words almost spilled from my mouth. Begging words. Words of apology and love. Words of loss and desire. But sometimes it was easier to be cowardly, especially in matters of love. Especially as I had been burned before. The lies I told myself since our breakup had unravelled so quickly. That I wasn't lonely without him. That I didn't want his protection or his advice. That his twinkly-eyed smile hadn't made my life better. That a woman in midlife didn't have a libido. But in the quiet of the night, next to the space where he had once slept, I knew the truth.

But my happiness wasn't the most important thing.

A shout from Mirabel. She waited at the yew tree, scrutinising our body language. "You're taking ages."

We hurried towards her, under the nearly full moon and past still trees. Ezra went quiet as we approached the clearing where Gunnolf had been killed.

Ezra pressed his hand to the yew tree rune. Wildwoods emerged before us with its rope bridges and cable cars. This term, its cabins had been decorated like ships in an Armada, with billowing white sheets rimmed with gold, as if to signal the changes now Phinnaeous Shine had been removed from his position as Prime Sorcerer.

"Are you ready?" I put my arm around Mirabel, but her body didn't yield.

Her face crumpled, just for a moment. I hoped she couldn't hear her parents' screams. The ones that still found me in the dead of the night. Then the shutters came down again. "I can't *wait* to make him shrivel under my death stare."

"That's the spirit," said Ezra.

My scalp prickled as we walked towards the arena. Spectators had filled the arena, despite the cold night. Some sat in pews, and others gathered in a semi-circle on the outer boundary. Word of the trial had spread like wildfire, and peculiars wanted to witness the tearing down of a once-great wizard. A decades-long leader who had failed them and had blood on his hands. The dock stood empty.

The seriousness of the Court of Wolves was usually reflected in the austere styling of the arena. Not tonight. Lavinia clearly wanted to leave her mark on proceedings and signal the beginning of a new era. Tonight, the arena shone with the light from a thousand pillar candles, and a gold banner—with a distasteful pink judge's gavel appliquéd onto it—had been erected behind the judge's bench. The sphinxes had taken up position on either side of the bench, freed from their stone bodies.

An impressive sight, said a familiar voice inside my head. *The witch is already campaigning to be Prime Sorcerer when the rest of us haven't even left the starting blocks.*

My eyes snapped to the judge's bench. *Hello, Orpheus.*

To the left of Lavinia's central position, the vampire sat in his Wildwoods robes over a crisp white dress shirt. Rayna occupied the space to Lavinia's right. The remaining senators took the outer seats: Margola, Helio, Cillian, Erelim and

Calypso at the outermost edge. She wore a ballgown, her dreadlocks teased into a beehive and a smudge of red lipstick, as if her evening had been interrupted and she would rather be a thousand miles from Wildwoods tonight.

We would all rather be elsewhere tonight. With the exception of Lavinia, of course. These proceedings don't exactly cover us in glory. The hard lines of the vampire's jaw softened. *It's good to see you, Alisha.*

And you, Orpheus. It's been two whole days.

He'd been a frequent visitor at the cottage and, in his eccentric manner, had gone out of his way to tell Mirabel about her family line so she didn't feel so alone. Like me, Mirabel had discovered that his often sullen, sharp nature could soften for the right people.

My arm tightened around her. I'd attended Gunnolf's trial at Court of Wolves. It had been a harrowing experience, even though I hadn't directly been impacted by his crimes.

I knew what to expect this time around: a drink of truth tonic concocted by the witch Ravynne in her birthday suit, a bare bones summary of the facts, a witness or two, a majority verdict of peers and sentencing by the acting Prime Sorcerer. There weren't any hard and fast rules. As far as I could tell, the options were plentiful: freedom, a draining of magic, the wiping of fortunes, rehabilitation under the tutelage of gentle giants, a wolf escort to the dungeons under the Ritz Hotel or lethal punishment. Otherworld justice was archaic, swift and not always humane.

I clenched my fists. Exactly what Phinnaeous Shine deserved.

Ezra murmured in my ear. "Judging by my aunt's expression, I'd better get to the bench."

Sure enough, she had a constipated look on her face. Next to her, Orpheus spat out his drink, and I knew he'd heard my thoughts.

"Good luck," I said.

Grey eyes on mine. "Will you two be okay?"

I nodded, wanting him to stay with us.

"It'll be over soon, squirt." He tried to fist-bump Mirabel, but she left him hanging.

Then he wove his way towards the senate, incongruous in his jeans and T-shirt. His werewolf nature and orphan history meant he'd always had less airs and graces than the others.

Mirabel screwed up her face. "Squirt?"

"Come on." I hurried her towards the front pew. "Looks like the detective has saved us a place."

Rob shifted along as we reached him. "I was hoping to bump into you. Quite an occasion."

I exhaled. "You can say that again. Any word on Pan?"

The detective shook his head. "He's gone underground. No sight of him at his townhouse or at Richmond Park. He's not even showed up at board meetings for Battersea Dogs Home. I've asked around his usual haunts. There was a sighting in Tooting but nothing concrete when I sent the boys in blue out. Word on the street is that he went into hiding after the gathering of the gods at Stonehenge. He doesn't want to be pulled into this kerfuffle with Gaia in case he's next."

"I need to find him, Rob. I can't let Gaia down."

He rubbed his head. "I know, Alisha. I've got my best guys on it. It's just a matter of time."

"And until then, the Earth goddess is ashes in the wind." I kneaded my temple. "How about the two gods at Stonehenge? The ones I didn't recognise? The one with the poppy and the other with the twin of my sword?"

Rob gave me a grim look. "We're on it. You'll know as soon as I do."

Mirabel nudged me. "Shh. It's about to start."

A triangular head with enormous milky eyes and wispy hair loomed into vision. "Incoming. Any room for a small one?"

"Flinar?" My heart leapt to see my elf friend. "How did you get in here?"

"Oh, didn't you hear? Lavinia gave the elves a pass for tonight. I think it's her way of lording it over the Phinnaeous. She wants him to know she is setting a new direction. I was at the pub, but when I found out, I just had to come." He gestured vaguely to the outer edge of the arena. "I brought my friends with me. Well, are you going budge over, Alisha?"

"Shh," said Rob. "It's about to start."

I shifted to sit on one arse-cheek so Flinar could squeeze in between me and Rob.

Lavinia stood to address the court, dressed in shimmering silver robes. The night sky was devoid of stars, giving a menacing feel to the wintry night, despite the myriad of pillar candles. A scroll and a quill inched up into the air as Lavinia revelled in the attention, her face serene in the candlelight, as if she were an actress waiting for her cue.

Her steely voice travelled across the arena, aided by magic. "Good citizens of the Otherworld, I bid you welcome. There so many of you here tonight to witness this sad day in our history."

Orpheus rolled his eyes. *I expect her army of rats personally hand-delivered invitations.*

She continued. "We have convened here tonight at the Court of the Wolves to address a most grave matter. Tonight, we hear the crimes of former Prime Sorcerer Phinnaeous Shine. We determine if he has broken our laws. The very laws he himself had a hand in writing. The laws that have stripped some peculiars of their freedom, their magic and even their lives."

Excitement rippled through the crowd. It wasn't fuelled by compassion for Phinnaeous's victims and a sense of justice but by the thought of witnessing his humiliation and pain.

Ezra waited by an austere wooden chair, his brow heavy with a frown.

"Bring the prisoner," crowed Lavinia as the quill scratched her words on the scroll.

Mirabel tensed next to me. I reached across to thread my fingers though hers and sent a fervent wish to the stars that what unfolded would not traumatise her further.

Behind a grouping of oak trees, his wolves howled, and scuffling and cursing ensued as Ezra's pack tugged a bedraggled Phinnaeous Shine into the court. He was handsome still. Even on the run, he'd probably had a network of contacts to feed him and keep a roof over his head. His hair and beard were tidy, the tilt of his head as proud as ever. His straight-backed gentleman's posture showed him to be uncowed. But as the five wolves dragged him in, clad in an orange jumpsuit rather than majestic Wildwoods robes, humiliation flickered in his eyes.

A tawny wolf and a silver-white one—that I recognised as Maximillian and Dominic—nosed Phinnaeous into the chair. He collapsed into it. Only the sheen of perspiration that dotted his midnight skin revealed his discomfort. The two wolves circled him, taut with coiled, prowling energy. Frothy saliva hung from their jaws. They sprang back into guarding formation with the rest of the pack.

Lavinia tutted. "Phinnaeous Shine, do you understand why you are here and the charges that have been filed against you?"

The response rung out across the arena, amplified by magic. He kept his eyes lowered. "These customs mean nothing to me."

She gave him a glance so withering it would have felled frost giants. "You understand that the decision we reach tonight will reflect our mutual wisdom and is non-reversible. It will be binding."

This time Phinnaeous lifted his head, and his eyes blazed with barely restrained anger. "I do."

"Then let us proceed." She paused to gather her breath,

and not a pin drop could be heard. "Who is presenting this case?"

Ezra stepped forward, his copper-grey eyes lit with dangerous intent. "I am."

The arena, me included, held its collective breath.

Lavinia bestowed a proud smile on Ezra. Then she swivelled to her colleagues, sloshing an uncorked decanter of truth tonic. "Senators, are you ready to receive this ancient ritual, brewed by the naked witch Ravynne?"

"We are," came the response in unison.

"Then drink." Quick as a flash, she lifted her sturdy, brown umbrella, the one that functioned as a wand, weapon, mode of transport and weather protection for her silver helmet of curls. She pointed the umbrella at each of her colleagues and sent an amber arc of viscous liquid into each of their open mouths.

Orpheus gulped his down, pulled a handkerchief from inside his Wildwoods robes and dabbed his thin mouth. *I can't decide if that was like a baptism, a golden shower or being spoon-fed by Mummy. My humiliation is complete.*

"Mr. Neuhoff, Mr. Shine," said Lavinia, unleashing another round of the truth tonic as they opened their mouths.

Ezra's face twitched at the noxious taste, and Phinnaeous glowered.

She paid them no heed. This was her moment to shine.

"Let the trial begin." She lifted her umbrella.

A spotlight illuminated the dock. A smug expression drifted across her face as she settled into her own seat.

"Phinnaeous Shine, last year marked your third decade as a sitting senator. Of that, you have served almost two decades as Prime Sorcerer." The tension in Ezra's jawline and clenched fists did not translate into his voice. His control was absolute as he laid out the charges. "Yet you stand here today, accused of breaking not one, but five laws of our Magical Constitution."

Mirabel's bottom lip trembled, her hand in mine so hot, despite the cold night. She focussed her eyes on the obelisk in the distance. Like she needed to centre herself just to get through this.

The detective leaned across Flinar to whisper to me. "Maybe you should take the girl out."

Mirabel jerked her head in our direction. "I'm staying here."

Ezra had hit his stride. His quiet confidence and veiled rage echoed around the arena. "Five laws. Five times that *we know of* that Phinnaeous Shine broke the very laws he helped to create. He broke the Judge's Law, disrupting the delicate power balance between magical communities instead of protecting it. His foundation, set up to promote equality between humdrums and peculiars, was instead a front for humdrum supremacy. This is not the first time Phinnaeous Shine has attempted to suppress a group. The elves would attest to this being a character flaw long in evidence."

Phinnaeous looked unmoved until a wave of noise ricocheted around the arena. As if he'd expected the adulation and respect to continue. Instead, Ezra's words had unleashed a roar of approval and stamping of feet from the elves that gathered pace, although other magical cohorts did not join in.

The mood set my teeth on edge. Danger and promise bubbled beneath the surface. A giddy sense of reckoning. Of emotions that threatened to spill out into the open. How heartening to witness justice in progress.

Warmth expanded in my chest. I loved Ezra for finding a way to give the elves legitimacy.

"Enough," said Lavinia. "Or the elves will be evicted from court. This is a place where you may speak only if you are invited to do so."

"Nothing's changed there," called a lone voice from the periphery.

A gasp ran through the crowd as Lavinia somersaulted over the judge's bench, revealing a glimpse of yoga gear underneath her robes. She lifted her umbrella and muttered a spell that catapulted the poor elf over the treeline and out of Wildwoods.

Orpheus rolled his eyes. *She is insufferable. Those who want power should never wield it.*

Next to me, Flinar buried his head in his four-fingered hands and shook his head woefully.

That's why you should be the next Prime Sorcerer, not her, I said to Orpheus in my mind and patted the elf's leg in sympathy.

Ezra pointed at Phinnaeous. "Phinnaeous Shine broke the Pragmatist's Law by colluding with Cardea, the goddess of doors and portals, knowing that she posed a risk to peculiar and humdrum lives. He broke the Protector's Law by targeting the mental faculties of a humdrum, Detective Robert Jameson, a man who has been an ally to the Otherworld."

A ripple of anger ran through the spectators.

Ezra's grey eyes found me in the gallery, and my heartbeat accelerated. "Phinnaeous Shine broke the Founder's Law, by bringing humdrums into Wildwoods, thereby risking discovery and making the humdrums part of a game to undermine the reputation of the eternal girl. On the night of the Halloween Ball, he broke the Monk's Law, by using magic selfishly. By using it to harm others."

He stumbled over his words, and I knew that slain Gunnolf filled his mind. The Otherworld laws didn't consider Gunnolf's death a murder because he had been an escaped prisoner. I also shared his red-hot anger that Phinnaeous had used magic to masquerade as Ezra. That he had effectively ended our relationship.

Ezra blew out his breath. Even with his wobble, he had the spectators in the palm of his hand. "Phinnaeous's dark alliance with the red goddess led to the deaths of two beloved members of this community. Brian and Juniper Elmstorm perished in a horrifying manner. And it was all down to this man. Our Prime Sorcerer. The man charged with leading and protecting us."

A sob escaped Mirabel. She wriggled her hand out of mine and sparked a fiery ball of flame borne from her fear and pain.

My eyes widened. "Bel, please. Put that out."

Orpheus's voice in my head. *Get that under control.*

I'm trying, I said. "Mirabel, please. He will get what's coming to him."

She shuddered and tried to extinguish the fireball. But it didn't work, and her green eyes darted in horror.

Around us, people began to whisper, and Lavinia, too, had cottoned on. She stood, presumably to banish us from the arena, when Flinar opened a black hole the size of a handbag between his bony legs.

"Put it in here, Alisha," said the elf.

I called a breeze and isolated the fireball from Mirabel's trembling fingers, flinging it into the black hole.

Flinar sealed it and blew Mirabel a kiss.

She collapsed against me, whispering sorry over and over.

"It's okay. I've got you," I said.

Nicely handled, said Orpheus. *Losing control of magic is a common side effect of trauma. Keep her away from straw bales and precious items.*

Relief pulsed through me. *I'll bear that in mind. If she can get through tonight, she can get through anything.*

Ezra turned cold eyes on Phinnaeous. "When you so casually break the laws you have written, it makes me wonder—how many other times have you acted nefariously without being caught? So convinced of your own power, your immunity from punishment... I stand here today and speak on behalf of London's Otherworld when I say: your road has ended. You broke our trust. And now we strip you of your power. I have only one question for you, Phinnaeous Shine. Why did you betray us?"

The small red wolf yapped at the prisoner's feet.

Phinnaeous curled his lip in disdain, but the truth tonic meant even if he wanted to be silent, the words would find a way to emerge. "I don't muzzle myself like the rest of you. Peculiars belong at the top of the hierarchy. I was worthy enough to be allied with the gods. What have you achieved in your life, Neuhoff?"

"I have helped people. I have brought men like you to justice. I found the eternal girl, and she will bring about a new world. An equal world. A world of hope."

"Hope is worth nothing," spat Phinnaeous. "Hope only leads to disappointment. It's bare knuckles and closed-door deals that force progress. You will beg for my leadership again."

"No. Your time in the sun is over." Ezra's grey eyes found mine. His mouth drooped in apology. "I call Mirabel Elmstorm to the stand."

3

———————

Mirabel went stiff as rock. She ducked her head, her words barely audible. "I don't want to go up there."

The weight on her shoulders was immense. It wasn't fair. "I know, honey. But it's your chance to tell the story of who your parents were. Do you think you could give it a go?"

Her lip quivered, but she was too stoic to burst into tears. "Maybe. But what if they ask something I don't know the answer to?"

Lavinia cleared her throat. "In your own time."

My head snapped up. "Give us a second."

I returned my attention to Mirabel, anxiety swirling in my stomach. Ezra could have prepared us. Was he thinking of Mirabel when he called her up to the stand or just a slam-dunk in his case against Phinnaeous Shine?

"Phinnaeous Shine is on trial, not you," I said. "Just do your best up there. And take it slow, honey. The truth tonic has a strange effect."

Mirabel stood up, her legs almost buckling. Her wings, which to the untrained eye looked like a shimmering shawl, fluttered, as if she might escape into the night, before Flinar

24

hopped off the pew, grasped her hand and accompanied her to the witness stand.

Lavinia toyed with the decanter of truth tonic. "Open wide, child."

Mirabel opened her mouth and spluttered as the truth tonic hit the back of her throat. She looked so small nestled in the witness stand, an ornate wooden seat with high sides that mercifully blocked her view of the prisoner. Wiping her hand across the back of her mouth, she looked up at Ezra expectantly, her child's frame dwarfed by the magnitude of the proceedings.

"Were your parents good parents, Mirabel?" said Ezra.

"The best. I wanted for nothing. Except maybe a later bedtime. They were always there when I needed them. They wanted more children but were only able to have me, and they were quite old when they had me. Like really old. I was a nice surprise because Dad thought his swimmers couldn't swim anymore." She clapped her hands over her mouth.

Orpheus's dark eyes widened. *Didn't you warn her about the effect of the truth tonic? Poor Brian Elmstorm is probably glad he's dead. What man wants his compatriots to hear about his little swimmers?*

"Just short sentences will do, Mirabel. I'll tell you if the court needs more detail." Ezra gave her an encouraging smile. "Did your parents trust Phinnaeous Shine?"

Her green eyes burned with passion. "Yes. They believed he'd make the world a better place. That's why they joined his foundation. But they started talking in whispers at home more. And then I overheard them the night of the ball. They were going to tell him they wanted to step away from the foundation. They were worried. They realised he was trying to replace important humdrums with peculiars."

"Thank you." Ezra's voice was gentle. "Did you hear the sounds of your parents dying?"

She quivered. "No. The Minister for History and the

Today, Orpheus Might, made sure I could hear nothing. But I imagine it all the time. Their faces just come into my head. And then I can't remember the happy moments anymore. Because all I can think of is their fear. How they must have been scared for themselves and for me." Her voice cracked. "I hate Phinnaeous Shine. He did this to us. He made it so I won't ever see my parents again."

Ezra's chiselled jaw tightened. "Tell the court, Mirabel. Do you want Phinnaeous Shine to die?"

I held my breath.

Her breath hitched. "No. But I want him to suffer. And I don't want his suffering to be over quickly."

The arena reverberated with the stamping of feet.

I didn't join in. My heart twisted. I understood Mirabel's feelings. I just wished life had spared her this experience. That she could be thinking about raiding her mother's wardrobe or her favourite television show or mint chocolate chip ice cream. Anything but her parents', her own or Phinnaeous's suffering. Suffering should never be a child's burden to carry.

She's dark. I like her, said Orpheus. *Much better than a daughter who likes Barbies.*

Girls of Mirabel's age don't like Barbies. They like stealing their mothers' make up, sucking helium from balloons in parks after dusk and snooping on neighbourhood love interests, I said, feeling for once like maybe I knew how to parent Mirabel after all. At least, compared to a centuries-old vampire.

Orpheus smirked. *Mission accomplished.*

"Thank you, Mirabel. I know that was hard for you. You may return to your seat," said Ezra.

I stood as she returned to me, head drooping like a daffodil, blinded by tears. When she melted into my arms, I murmured words of comfort into her hair, but the night was not yet over.

The wolves, until now deceptively still, grew agitated. Their howls made my blood turn cold.

Lavinia surveyed the spectators gallery, as if she were taking a litmus test of their innermost thoughts. Deciphering who craved vengeance and who rehabilitation. Who longed for a macabre end to Phinnaeous's story and who an end that allowed him to keep his dignity or even his position.

Ezra was right, this was more an exercise in politics than justice.

Lavinia pursed her lips. "The wolves have spoken. They have determined we have heard enough. Now we decide. What say you, senate?"

The vote was unanimous, like we had known it would be.

Orpheus, Rayna, Calypso and Lavinia voted guilty. But so did the senators with murkier motives—Margola, Erelim, Cillian and Helio. That was the thing with corrupt leaders. At first, their crimes were hidden behind curtains and boot-licking allies. But eventually, their crimes became so large and their impact so heinous, that nobody could look away. And the axe would fall.

The senate huddled together to discuss the sentence.

"He'll be smashed to smithereens by giants with fists as big as London buses," said a woman in the pew behind us.

"They should let the elves put him in a black hole in the smelliest part of East London. That would teach him. After all, punishment should be about rehabilitation, and us elves can turn the other cheek," said Flinar. "But we'd make the black hole minuscule."

"If the wolves tear him to pieces before the night ends, I can't promise to withhold it from my report to the Prime Minister," said Rob.

Lavinia banged her gavel, and the sound clapped around the arena, silencing the whispers. "Order. Order! We have decided." She patted her helmet of hair-sprayed silver curls. "The senate has decreed that Phinnaeous Shine be stripped of his magic. And that he spend an eternity in the Otherworld dungeons. Furthermore, his entire fortune is to be redirected to Wildwoods School of the Wondrous, where students will be taught how not to emulate his example."

Phinnaeous raged. "You won't get away with this. I made you."

"No. I made myself," said Lavinia. "Oh, the vanity of men." She picked up her dull umbrella by its brass handle and sashayed out from behind the judge's bench, giving the performance of her life.

Orpheus's dark eyes found mine. *She means to be the next Prime Sorcerer.*

I think you would be better suited, I said.

He gave an imperceptible shrug. *It's politics. I already do enough of that. It's time for more important things.*

Mirabel nudged me and broke our connection. "Stop flirting with the vampire."

I frowned. "I'm not."

"He was in your head, right?"

"Yeah."

"*Teen Magazine* calls that head fucking."

I almost choked. "Watch your language, Bel."

Twelve-year-olds were very different in my day. The Mirabel yearning for my admiration when she bumped into me at Wildwoods was remarkably different from the Mirabel who lived in my home. It didn't diminish my love for her, but it did once again remind me that motherhood was a learning curve.

The crowd craned their necks as a spike emerged from the end of Lavinia's umbrella.

Phinnaeous stood, straining against his hand restraints. "After all I have done for you ungrateful swines."

Maximilian and Dominic had the measure of him. His strength was no match for theirs. They bared their grizzled teeth.

With his hands restrained, the wizard could not attack, but he could shapeshift. So he did. He transformed into Lavinia, hazel eyes blazing and defiant.

There was a communal sharp intake of breath as the spectators registered his brazenness.

Orpheus rolled his eyes. *The wizard can't even fall on his sword with humility. I can't wait to write a history of him.*

Not a hair was out of place. Not only did he have her form, but he had her mannerisms. The way she sat with a ramrod back, the jaunty angle of her head, the sardonic curl of her lips, down to the slash of her fuchsia pink lipstick.

The real Lavinia's tinkling laugh filled the air. "Do you really think that is going to put me off my stride? One of my favourite private hobbies is taunting my mirror reflection. It toughens me up. And sugar, I'm tough."

She flicked her umbrella, and a shabby wooden chest landed in the sawdust of the arena with a thump, as if it had fallen from the sky. With a little sashay and a very Dolly Parton jiggle of her pert bottom, she bent to open the chest and drew out a neatly folded item.

"My robes," said Phinnaeous.

"Indeed. You have no need for them now."

I whispered. "This is it, Bel. He's going to get what's coming to him."

Mirabel nodded, eyes brimming with tears.

Lavinia flung Phinnaeous's robes on the ground as if they were filth. With an air of casual violence, she jabbed Phinnaeous in the neck, ejected the blood from the tip of the umbrella into the wizard's heaped robes and swished her umbrella, before chanting a spell. Her witch sisters joined in. Their spell filled the arena, ominous and gaining in power. As if they were words uttered in an ancient cathedral, rather than a makeshift court on the verges of a South London park.

Unlike with Gunnolf, it took the coven to neutralise Phinnaeous's magic, and even then, I discerned the strain on the witches' faces. This was the Prime Sorcerer after all. The greatest peculiar in the Otherworld.

Until you came along, said Orpheus.

Put a sock in it, vamp. You're not good for my ego.

A middle-aged woman's ego can always do with massaging. Like ground so parched that it never runs the risk of self-combusting. Orpheus's face was impassive as Phinnaeous writhed like the slippery eel he was.

Sweat glistened on real Lavinia's upper lip. Her umbrella had a mind of its own. Just when I thought she had lost control of the spell, Phinnaeous's cloak burst into flames.

Phinnaeous wasn't Lavinia. He wasn't even himself. Having treated humdrums with utter disdain, he was now one as well.

He was utterly ordinary. A common criminal.

The sphinxes, whose impressive bodies lay either side of the judge's bench, stood abruptly. Their monstrous otherworldly roar filled the arena, and to me, it sounded like a passing of the baton. The air was electric. Every peculiar sensed the hand of history. The ending of Phinnaeous Shine's era and the beginning of a new one.

Applause erupted in the arena, and Lavinia bowed then hopped on her umbrella to do a lap of honour around the arena, although technically, Ezra had done most of the work. She executed a thrilling mid-air spin and landed cleanly in the sawdust with a benign smile.

"Isn't she marvellous?" said Flinar.

Give me strength, said Orpheus.

"The Ritz dungeons await," said Lavinia as the wolves circled.

Phinnaeous crumpled, his last drops of bravado drained away. His whisper, amplified by Lavinia for the crowd, pulsed with hatred. "You can't control me forever, witch."

"We'll see about that. Do your worst, old man." She skirted around the back of his chair and, with a slice of her umbrella, freed him of his hand restraints, adding insult to injury.

After all, with his shapeshifting skills and wizardry gone, Phinnaeous Shine was no longer a threat.

The pack lifted their heads and howled in the candlelight at the Court of Wolves.

ORPHEUS and I made our way out of Wildwoods. Although hours had passed since our arrival, morning had not yet broken across the park. The night lingered, and a strange heaviness lay across the frosted hedges and trails. A few steps ahead of us, Mirabel chatted to Flinar, relief palpable in the easy swing of her body in contrast to our tension-filled walk to the trial.

The vampire's mood was sombre. "I considered Phinnaeous a friend once. It is depressing to live long enough to see once-good men pollute their souls."

I scooped my thick ponytail off my neck, pushed aside the strap of my baldric and kneaded the sore muscles there. "It should never have gotten to this point."

The vampire's dress shoes clipped against the path. "Phinnaeous was never an easy man, but he didn't start out this way. He merely reached a fork in the road and chose the wrong path. And it took the rest of the senate too long to notice, blinded as we were by his position."

A movement in the periphery of my vision startled me.

I tensed, my hands flexing instinctively to call the winds, my mind thinking up winged creatures that I could animate to protect us.

Orpheus cocked an eyebrow. "You're jumpy."

The hair on the back of my neck stood on end. "You didn't see that?"

"Not everything that goes bump in the night is to be

feared, Alisha. Some dark things are to be pitied. Other ones are just waiting for the light to appear."

I caught a whiff of his cherry-dark chocolate beard oil and relaxed. "I take it you've been reading some poetry recently."

He smiled. "I've been revisiting William Blake, T. S. Elliot and Robert Burns. Not sleeping is one of the upsides of being a vampire. I used to worry about not the lack of time to read all the tomes in my ample library. Eliminating sleep increases my time to indulge my love of words while the rest of the world sleeps."

"Yeah, well, I like face-planting and my duvet too much to forgo sleep."

"I was never a duvet fan. Dreadful things. When I was human, I slept in the nude."

My mind helpfully whipped up an image of Orpheus for me that I quickly discarded. "We were talking about Phinnaeous. I meant what I said before. You should be the next Prime Sorcerer, not Lavinia."

A sigh. "There are other candidates. I rather feel someone unassuming like Rayna would be a breath of fresh air."

"You know as well as I do that Rayna would be desperately unhappy devoting herself to anything other than her plants and her students."

"Perhaps. But I'm afraid a vampire makes a very poor sacrificial lamb, Alisha. The position of Prime Sorcerer may be powerful, but it is essentially a thankless task. There are things more important to me than power."

"Such as?"

"Art, money, carnal desire," he said in a bedroom voice.

I brushed away the feeling that this was a come-on and shoved him playfully instead. "You never follow my advice, Orpheus."

He didn't teeter, immovable rock that he was. "You're one to talk. We're like peas in a pod. A pair of corpses in a coffin. Two halves of the same whole."

I laughed. "Hardly."

"I'm just saying, I listen to you more than most. Even more than my dear dead mother."

"Things get morbid around you so quickly," I teased.

The moonlight lent his chalky skin a milky glow. "Every moment is like a tiny death, Alisha. It's only in embracing mortality that we get a sense of how lucky we are. And I feel very lucky since meeting you."

Slightly uncomfortable, I averted my eyes to Mirabel and Flinar walking the winding path ahead of us. My eyes narrowed as the shadows shifted unnaturally around her.

I squinted in her direction. "Do you see that? Those dense, dark pools around Mirabel?"

Orpheus frowned and following my gaze. "I didn't take you as someone who is afraid of the dark."

I peered after my daughter, my eyes bleary. With the adrenalin of the trial long fled, the winter chill ran through my bones. I pulled my jacket closer around me. "Maybe I'm tired."

"I'm not surprised. You've accomplished feats this year that many would have said are impossible. I think your presence, your decisions, drove Phinnaeous to become careless. Like he couldn't bear the thought of a rival to his power."

I rolled my eyes. "Men. I wasn't competing with him. I'm just walking my own path. Right now, Mirabel's what's important. Everything else comes second."

"Being a mother suits you."

"I look exhausted."

He harrumphed. "You look fulfilled. But your body is tense. I'll arrange some enforced relaxation for you at my place tomorrow night."

I perked up. "Maybe Manfred is free for a massage? But I have no one to look after Mirabel. She's too fragile to be left alone right now."

"Bring her. She can play in the vampire den." His thin lips spread into a smile. "She'll be safe, pinkie swear."

The hair on the back of my neck stood up as Ezra materialised next to us, like he'd just stepped out of a shadow. His expression was downcast. "Sorry to interrupt."

Could it be that he'd overheard Orpheus's invitation? That his old jealousies about our bond still piqued him, even though we were no longer together?

Hope bloomed in me.

Maybe our ending could be rewritten. Maybe we weren't over after all.

We hovered underneath an oak tree. I tripped over my words, eager to make Ezra feel welcome. "You weren't interrupting. Congratulations. That can't have been easy tonight. I would have waited to speak to you, but Lavinia had your ear."

Next to me, Orpheus nodded stiffly. "An exemplary performance, Neuhoff. For a man still fairly new to politics, you do a fine job of it."

Ezra pulled in a deep breath. "I appreciate that. Can I have a moment alone with Alisha?"

"Of course," replied the vampire, although the tone held none of his usual courtesy. He strode off to join Mirabel and Flinar.

Ezra pushed his hands into his jeans pockets. The cut on his cheek had healed already, aided by his werewolf nature and charm necklace, but the shadows under his eyes showed the strain of the night. "I wanted to explain why I called Mirabel to the stand."

I swallowed hard. "It's okay. You needed a victim impact statement to shore up the case. I get it."

He frowned. "That wasn't it. I did it for Mirabel." A vein throbbed in his jaw. "I felt helpless when my parents died. I wanted her to feel like she had more control. That she had put her love for the Elmstorms on the record. That she'd been part of the push for justice. It will help her survive the loss. I just hope I did the right thing. She is okay, isn't she?"

"She needs to sleep, but I think we might have turned a corner tonight. Thanks for looking out for her." My heart expanded in my chest. He didn't have to look out for Mirabel, but he'd done it because that was the kind of man he was. "Do you maybe want to come over?"

Was I offering a hand of friendship, a booty call or undying love? I didn't even know myself. I just knew that I missed him in my life.

Ezra rubbed the back of his neck like he did when he was overworked and the knots built up there. "I have to go. There are adjustments to be made at the Ritz to make sure the cell holds the prisoner. Sleep well, Alisha."

His mouth twisted, and then he disappeared between the worlds, leaving me standing in the spiralling shadows.

4

———————

Faeza swept the counter of Shanghai Moon with the brisk efficiency of someone who didn't want to be drawn into conversation. That is, this particular conversation.

"We're coming." Fei Yen's lips tightened. She unbuttoned her pharmacist's coat with one hand. "You're all wonderful for trying to protect me, but it's not your choice. It's mine."

She was already adapting to the amputation of her left forearm in her remarkable, no-nonsense way. My anger at my brother for hurting her still burned brightly. A month of takeaways plus front row tickets to a K-pop concert for Fei Yen and Faeza didn't absolve him of what he had done.

Behind me, Echo's muzzle burrowed into a drawer of suspicious looking mushrooms.

Ignoring him, I glanced at Faeza with pleading eyes. Surely, she'd chime in on my side?

Instead, she shrugged, but her eyes shone with love. "You think I haven't tried? Fei Yen's more headstrong than ever, however much I try to wrap her in cotton wool." She turned the sign on the door to closed. "So we better be on our way. There's a boxset of a Korean drama I'd like to finish tonight."

Emerald eyes glimmered in the fading light. It was the

time of year when the country barely made it to four o'clock before the curtain of night fell.

"Rajika Verma would say that getting back on the horse is the sign of a true warrior." A tell-tale shredded stem of chestnut mushroom poked out from between his tombstone teeth. The leopard honked with laugher. "Only *hu hsien* don't ride horses, so make of that what you will."

As immigrant women who had moved continents to start a new life together, Fei Yen and Faeza embodied the spirit of change. They leaned into their position as outsiders. They loved fiercely and endured, despite painful experiences. They understood that change could break you into tiny pieces. It could also forge a new person out of you. The glint in Fei Yen's brown eyes showed she hadn't lost her fire. If she was ready to lean into her new identity, we'd support her.

"I'll pay for what Echo has stolen." I pulled out my bank card. "And then we can be on our way."

Fei Yen broke into a smile that would chase away the darkest clouds. While she and Faeza retreated to shift into their *hu hsien* forms, I called an Otherworld taxi, by now well versed in the level of burping required to summon one.

"I'm proud of you, Alisha," said Echo. "That belch signals you would feel at home in a drinking circle of pot-bellied leprechauns."

My mouth twitched. "A compliment that is music to a woman's soul."

We steeled ourselves as the foxes arrived, and all clambered into the claw-marked Otherworld taxi. Neither Echo nor I mentioned the gut punch of seeing the foxes in their changed forms. How their magical forms had added pathos: Fei Yen's amputated left foreleg and the now silver-red coat of Faeza's fox body. Her grief response to being separated from her wife and fearing the worse.

Instead, we sped along the bumpy tarmac to Richmond Park, flying past council estates, Victorian terraces and mansions in this city where rich and poor tumbled in and out of each other's lives. The foxes snoozed tangled up together, leaving me unable to decipher where one ended and the other began. Curled against me, the leopard's breath slowed until he, too, slept.

But I was already on high alert.

Gaia's last whispers—when she was already ashes on the wind at Stonehenge—reverberated in my head. *You must find Pan. He will know how to resurrect me. Find The Book of Names and keep a flask full of chai ready for me.*

We paid the taxi fare of a strand of hair each then slipped through a gate on the south-eastern perimeter. Orange and reds danced in the wintery grey-blue sky as the sun set across the park. In the distance, a walking group, wrapped in winter jackets and colourful scarves, gathered around a map. The foxes darted in the opposite direction, leaping from flat plains to hilly mounds, bushy tails high, their noses close to the ground.

Our group skirted around deer sprawling in the evening sun. The dual tension of family love and work agendas buzzed in my subconscious. I adjusted my sword beneath my jacket and pushed all thoughts of Mirabel out of my mind. Losing focus with gods on the prowl was to have one foot in the grave, and I wanted to get home safely to my daughter. I had so much to live for.

Echo sauntered next to me, tail swishing. "It is a shame to smell all these juicy deer behinds and yet be forbidden from taking a bite."

I gave him a warning look. "The last thing we need is to anger Pan. It'll be hard enough to convince him to help us."

Crouching down, I peeked into a hollowed-out den in the side of a grassy bank.

Nothing. Not even a discarded pipe or scrap of clothing. The gods had roamed the earth since the dawn of time. They knew how to vanish and how to be seen. I understood Pan's need to not attract the vengeance of the other gods. He was only one god, and they were many. I might have convinced him to remember his divine nature once, but he was also half animal.

Fearful animals hid, fled or attacked.

I had no idea what he would choose to do. Dualism ran through his personality. He was a trickster god who revelled in chaos and adapted his actions to his mood. He lacked Gaia's moral fibre and restraint.

Rob's Shadow Squad had failed to find him. But Pan would never be far from his flocks, and as royal gamekeeper, there was nowhere he felt more at home than amongst the herds and flocks at Richmond Park.

Although he was dangerous, I presumably had one advantage. My powers had grown since we had last met. Pan's absence from the circle at Stonehenge meant that he likely underestimated me. I didn't have my dragon at my side, but I could animate at will. And at last, I knew who I was. Not a middle-aged childless divorcee who taught night class but a woman central to a centuries-old prophesy. A woman who had outsmarted and outrun gods. A woman who bedded werewolves, befriended vampires, had travelled to a library amongst the stars and had friends who would put their lives on the line for her. A woman who would no longer let an uncomfortable bra, muffin-top belly or rogue chin hair ruin her day. A woman who could be a mother or a lover or a warrior. Or just simply be.

My future was wide open.

I turned as Fei Yen looped back from across a field, her fox ears alert, emitting an excited cry. Echo raced ahead of me, and when I made it over a small hill, the three of them had encircled a weeping willow, its winter foliage not a patch on its summer glory.

Beneath the droop of its branches, the god of shepherds, goats and pastures tossed in a sweat-drenched dream.

He had stretched out on his stomach on an animal skin, his strong thighs and sticky-out bottom clad in tweed that threatened to split at his arse cheeks. His top hat lay to one side, and his horns poked out through his mop of thick, brown hair. His lips babbled hellishly, though I couldn't decipher the words.

Every cell in my body told me to back away slowly. "It feels intrusive watching him sleep."

"Now is not the time to worry about privacy, Alisha. It is the perfect time to ravage him. I've never tasted god before," purred Echo. "He's already lost one thumb. What's another?"

"Without him, we have no chance of getting Gaia back. Is he having a nightmare?"

"I don't know," said Echo. "But he's out for the count. I know you have an under-developed kill instinct and that middle-aged women are better at getting sloshed on gin cocktails and dancing to the Spice Girls, but Warrior 101 is to press home our natural advantage."

Fei Yen obviously agreed. She pressed a cold nose into my palm, urging me towards the sleeping god. When I hesitated, she darted forward on three limbs, her mouth closing around a long and thin object obscured in the grass.

She lifted up Pan's pipes. The pipes that had allowed him to trigger the movement of herds and flocks to cause tremors across the city.

My heart ricocheted in my chest. I inched forward, hand outstretched to receive the pipes.

The sleeping god opened one pale green eye, before sitting up abruptly. He prised his instrument from Fei Yen's teeth and flicked her away like she was a naughty scamp.

Echo growled in warning, his tombstone teeth ready to protect our tribe.

Faeza urged Fei Yen out of god's reach, the whites of her eyes wild.

When Pan turned his gaze on me, his eyes blazed. "The

last time we met, your dragon scorched the earth beneath my feet and almost barbecued my deer herds. Her Majesty could have beheaded me for that. Luckily, I earned her backing by training her yapping corgis."

I motioned to the foxes to get to safety, but they stayed stubbornly close, along with Echo. My tone was nonchalant, but my body tingled with readiness. "Actually, the last execution in this country was in the early 1960s, and the last beheading was nearly three hundred years ago, so your worries are unfounded."

"Time passes in the blink of an eye for a god. But the time since the heavens crumbled has been long indeed." He grizzled and stood to roll his animal skin up, before placing his top hat on his head at a jaunty angle. "Something has changed about you, druid. Your tone does not convey the proper respect. Why are you disturbing my peace?"

I took a deep breath. "I need your help. Gaia is mere ashes in the wind. With your help, we can bring her back."

His pale eyes glimmered in the dusk, his fingers caressing his pipes. "I sensed her absence in the sadness of the trees and thinning of the soil. But I can't help you, Alisha Verma."

The trees rustled around us in admonishment.

My voice was the quiet before a storm. "You would deny her?"

Pan bleated a mirthless laugh. "I would deny you. A mortal who carries Death's sword is no friend of mine. You might have reminded me of my divine self with the cypress wood from Noah's Ark, but the Custodian collects items borrowed from the Celestial Library, as you well know. And today I am feeling quite the beast."

He certainly smelled beastly. A mix of farmyard muskiness and soured milk.

"Then you have learned nothing at all." I enjoyed the truth that rolled off my tongue. "You do only what is convenient, not what is right."

His lip curled. "You are no longer frightened or in awe of me. But you should be. Once you were a dragon-rider with a vampire and a werewolf at your side. Now, you have two mangled foxes and a leopard pretending to be a Bengal cat."

The leopard bristled, his powerful body with its golden coat of rosetted fur and snowy belly quivering in the evening light. "I am Chanakya Gunbir Hredhaan of Maharashtra. I am descended from a man-eating leopard. I know Western pop songs and the Indian greats. My hearing is so acute that I could hear you blowing off in your tweed trousers while you slept from fifty yards away."

Pan smirked. "That's quite a mouthful. I find one syllable names stand the test of time. You must be tonight's entertainment. A fitting punishment, I think, for Ms. Verma's attempt to steal my pipes."

He lifted his instrument to his lips. It was simple, made from short bamboo pipes of graduated length. The sound he coaxed out from it was sweet and wistful.

Fear snaked through me as Echo and the foxes lifted inexplicably onto their hind legs and swayed, like they were circus acts or puppets without control of their own bodies. The foxes took up a ballroom dance style, Fei Yen's shortened limb resting on the back of Faeza's silver neck. They writhed in time to the music, their faces a ghastly mask of compliance. But it was Echo that made me gasp. Snowy belly exposed, his hind legs stamped the ground unnaturally, and his forelegs flailed in the air. His tombstone teeth chattered and tongue lolled as he tried to resist the pull of the music.

I clenched my fists. "Let them go."

The music continued, a saccharine tune juxtaposed to the unnatural frolics of my friends.

Anger coursed through me. Even a stranger telling me to cheer up made me cross. The cheek of it. Body autonomy was *everything*. Pan had taken my friends' free choice away. For entertainment. To prove he was in control.

Except he wasn't.

"I said, let them go." My self-belief surged. Transcender's obsidian blade glimmered in the half-light as I drew it. I spun the hilt, wielding it like a pro. All my training had paid off for this very moment.

Pan paused on the mouthpiece, scrutinising me. Then he doubled down, picking up the pace until fox legs whirred along with leopard ones and Echo retched with giddiness.

I had thrown a tornado at Pan once, but aided by his pipes, he'd vanished and reappeared just out of my reach. But a grown woman wasn't fooled twice. With my left hand, I beckoned the winds, sensing them gather across the plains of the park and rush to my aid. I curled them around Pan, trapping him where he stood.

His ruddy face twisted in alarm, and the music juddered, like the blip when a record is scratched. "Let this be a lesson to you, druid. A mere mortal has no control over a god's will. I will not enter a fight that is not my own. I won't choose sides."

He pressed the pipes to his lips and regained the beat with surging grace.

I sensed the pull of the music on me, seeking to drown me in sweetness. To make me drowsy or make me dance or make my internal organs grind to a halt. The Jericho necklace burned at my throat. I didn't know how long I could hold out or the strength of his powers.

I had to end this quickly, for all our sakes.

I entered the vortex of winds. They whistled in my ears, a heady rush borne of my own power. My hair, bound in a thick ponytail, whipped around my head. I put the blade to his neck. I wasn't scared to use it. The Otherworld had hardened me. I had seen enough blood to know what it took to keep my loved ones safe.

"The gods aren't as invincible as they once were." Resolve pulsed through my voice.

The music stuttered, finally petering out.

A quick glance through the wall of wind told me my friends had been freed from their ordeal. They lay collapsed on the ground.

The god lowered his pipe. Pale green eyes locked onto mine. "You are strong, druid. Stronger than any druid I have met before. But how long can you survive without Gaia's protection?"

My gut twisted. I wanted to resurrect Gaia because she was my friend, but I'd be lying if I said my own vulnerability hadn't occurred to me. Pan spoke the truth. Gaia was my compass. The twisting path ahead was filled with veiled enemies, and without her wisdom, my chances of success were slim.

The god's eyes widened in terror as I pressed Death's sword against his neck. He arched backwards, wriggling away but the winds at his back prevented much movement. Perhaps he had heard that I had drawn blood and taken flesh from Mami Wata and Cardea. Perhaps he had heard only rumours of the blade's potency against immortals.

Behind me, Echo roared. Not a battle cry but one of warning.

My breath came in quick bursts as I reeled through my options: Kill him. Wound him. Let him walk free. He was a god and I was a mortal, but he hadn't cottoned onto the fact that I was nervy too. That I couldn't stop thinking how much I had to lose if I made one misstep.

I lifted my chin and drew back an inch. "I won't kill you today, Pan. In return, you will help me resurrect the goddess."

He flattened his tweed jacket with jittery hands, still clutching the pipes. "My own skin is more important to me than Gaia's. A menacing darkness comes this way, druid. It's in the trees and in my dreams. It's in my waking thoughts, nipping at my heels."

I let the winds fade, freeing him from their embrace. My

voice was cold. "Remember how I chose to spare you today. Remember how we could have taken your pipe. Remember how it felt to find your faith. There will come a time when you can no longer sit on the fence. You'll have to choose."

The corners of his mouth twisted downwards. Then Pan raised the pipes to his lips. A mournful sound sped him backwards across the plains, towards the dozing deer herds.

Echo padded over to me, slinking around my legs.

"The gods are fickle," I said.

Wise emerald eyes found mine. "He could have killed us, Alisha."

"When Rob said there has been a sighting of Pan in Tooting, I had a hunch. I hope I've made the right decision letting him go. I have to resurrect Gaia before the menacing darkness Pan mentioned comes to a head."

The foxes scampered at my feet, mewling with worry, their fur slick with sweat.

I crouched down to calm them. "Dancing under duress can't have been much fun."

The leopard nudged them out of the way for prime position, purring as I scratched his ears. "Please be advised that I will need a harem of pussies to make me forget what happened here."

I scanned the horizon for a last glimpse of the god, but he was gone. By now, the light had fled. Shadows morphed and grew around us, unlinked from solid forms as we trudged back towards the road, regret and worry drumming in my chest.

5

Orpheus held his belly and laughed, his usually still, emotionless vampire's face animated with delight. "You held your sword to the shepherd god's throat?"

"He's tricky, but he's not the worst of the gods. Without him, any chances of resurrecting Gaia dwindle."

Orpheus chuckled. "You have a predator's instincts, despite all those soft curves. You had a god running without spilling a drop off blood. Shame Margola Silver wasn't lurking in the bushes to record the particulars in *The Otherworld News*. Peculiars should know how fortunate they are to live in the same age as the eternal girl."

Mirabel gave a long-suffering sigh. Proof that familiarity breeds contempt, her adulation of me had taken a nosedive over these past few weeks. Once she'd been a fawning fan. Now my foster daughter pretended to vomit at Orpheus's compliments.

I poked Mirabel playfully in the stomach. "If you must know, I feel rather mocked anytime I'm addressed as the eternal girl, given I'm north of forty years old."

Orpheus gave me an appraising look, taking in the fall of

my simple black dress over my curves. "All that training and the light in your eyes borne of new experiences means you barely look a day over thirty-eight."

Mirabel shook her head. "Urgh. Adults are so weird."

I laughed. I'd only been her foster mother for five minutes, and I was embarrassing her already. "You will be dust, my old friend, before I go fully grey."

Tonight, he wore a hint of colour instead of his usual black. His grey trousers, open-necked blue silk shirt and splash of aftershave were suave, though outdated. Longish, black hair curled over his collar. His goatee was traditional, like a Sweeney Todd barber had groomed it with an old-fashioned blade. His stern Roman nose contrasted with dark eyes that crinkled for me and me alone. A hopeful glint sparked in them, replacing his usual world-weary expression.

What I'd done to win over the most important vampire in London, I didn't know.

You were my friend, said Orpheus. *Plus you're a quick learner. As you know, I can't abide fools.*

I'd accepted the vampire's invitation to his gentleman's club in Charing Cross. His friendship was like a comforting blanket after a fraught few days. He gave artistic Mirabel a tour of his greatest masterpieces, leaving her slack jawed at the Renoir, Constable, Rembrandt and newly acquired Dalí hanging on his walls.

"I have a surprise for you, Mirabel." Orpheus opened a door at the end of the corridor.

Mirabel's mouth fell open as she surveyed a deceptively large cinema room with two rows of reclining chairs. A spotlight illuminated one chair, where a bowl of chips with a side serving of ketchup awaited her.

"I took the liberty of choosing a supernatural teen drama from the 1990s for you to watch," said Orpheus.

"Thank you!" Mirabel spun to give startled Orpheus a

kiss. She flung herself onto the chair and stuffed a chip into her mouth. There, she settled in to watch season one of *Buffy the Vampire Slayer*.

"Shout if you need me. I'm just the other side of the door," I said.

Her eyes were glued to the screen. She didn't even look in my direction. "Uh huh."

With a sigh, I followed Orpheus—and his cloud of aftershave—out of the room.

"You own *Buffy* on boxset?" I asked. "Isn't that show a bit triggering?"

Orpheus gave an enigmatic smile. "I am a reader first and foremost. But most vampires, myself included, find the little blonde girl and her antics with my kind a rousing watch."

I shut the door with a lingering glance, my mama bear instincts in overdrive. We were in a vampire den, after all. Orpheus vouched for Mirabel's safety, but I remembered Seskel, the vampire who had been my first Otherworld kill. A scrawny thing who wouldn't take a no from Marina under this very roof.

Orpheus inside my head was a jolt. *Nobody will harm a hair on the girl's head without my say so, Alisha. They know how dear you are to me.*

A shiver of pleasure ran up my spine. Flirting with a vampire was dangerous, but our friendship had always been based on this, ever since he had first infiltrated my thoughts. He entered my head and soaked up the unsaid, the grey, the secrets of my mind. I liked not having to pretend with him, but it wasn't healthy that he could read my thoughts. Some thoughts were meant to stay in a vault of our own heads. Some thoughts didn't come out fully formed. They were nebulous and needed to be refined. They weren't ready to be heard until they were vocalised.

As usual, I deflected his flirting. "You promised me six-handed Manfred tonight. Just the thought of his chiropractor hands kneading my knotty shoulders is blissful."

His voice had the depths of whiskey, both harsh and soothing. "Actually, I had another idea."

With one last look in Mirabel's direction, I trailed after him into the adjacent room, a vast space under a dusty chandelier. Ambient lighting illuminated various nooks and crannies. Portraits of important men graced the walls. A dusty wardrobe lurked in the corner, no doubt filled with tuxedos made by the finest tailor in London in case a patron tumbled through the doors wearing denim.

Orpheus kept the club fairly tame when I visited, but I was in no doubt about the nature of the dealings at gentleman's clubs. Some came here for a quiet tumbler of whiskey and a game of billiards. It was also a place where indiscretions happened and men lost their dignity and the contents of their wallets. Where they revelled in debauchery. Where deals were made and information exchanged. All behind closed doors.

Tonight, the space was empty of patrons, and the gleaming leather Chesterfield armchairs had been pushed back to create space in the middle of the room. A small, circular table stood there, with a candlelit dinner setting for two and a butler trolley nearby.

Confusion filled me. "Is that for us? It's really fancy."

The angles of his face softened. "I have been thinking about this moment for a long time, Alisha. I didn't expect you to bring religion into it."

His toned chest was visible through the gaping edges of his shirt.

Holy hell, had he unbuttoned his shirt while my back had been turned? This couldn't be a seduction, could it? In my generation, a seduction entailed someone hot-stepping it over to you in a sticky bar and then trying to cop a feel in the taxi home. Of course, I'd noticed him flirting, but I'd put that down to a sign of his comfort with me, not romantic love. Was this a weird aftereffect of the truth serum?

"Perhaps the truth serum has made me braver, but it hasn't altered what I feel." Orpheus pulled out my chair. "You're surprised."

"A little." My belly fluttered as I sat down and smoothed down my dress. Anything to avoid the intensity of his gaze.

His mouth twisted beneath his goatee, and for a moment I imagined kissing those lips, the scent of his cherry chocolate beard oil tickling my nose.

He took his place opposite me. "I couldn't make my intentions clear while Neuhoff was in your life. But I told you months ago that, in a life full of disappointments, you gave me something to live for."

My heart pounded. "I thought you meant the excitement of new adventures. Orpheus, I'm flattered. I really am, but…"

"No. Don't draw a line in the sand just yet. I'm not a stupid man, Alisha. I know you still have feelings for Neuhoff. But have you ever considered how well we could work together? Is it a stretch to think our friendship could develop into something more? We provide balance for each other. A vampire might represent death, but you are vitality. When Mirabel became your daughter, it seemed to me the universe had aligned. I, too, have longed for a child, but procreation is outside a vampire's repertoire."

I flushed. "I love that you have an open mind about Mirabel…"

"I am technically decades older than you, but believe me when I tell you, my organs are in tip top condition. Apart from my skin, that is. But nothing some facial moisturiser and a foot file doesn't fix."

He looked crestfallen at my reaction, so I guided my thoughts to the times he'd protected me. When Pan's tremors hit Wildwoods and we tumbled to the ground from the treetop cabin, his body wrapped around mine.

When his voice had broken my paralysis during the Kraglek trial. When he had sped across the farmhouse meadow in a blur of black and white to block Cardea's attempt to hurt me with his own body. How I had come into the Otherworld and his had been a voice I could depend on. How he had sided with me over the structures and people he knew.

He leaned forward, his lips curving in a soft smile. "All that, Alisha, and more. I can offer you and Mirabel the world. I invited you here to show you. Promise me you will wait for the evening to end before you make a decision."

I knew who my heart belonged to, and so did Orpheus.

Maybe it would have been different if I hadn't met Ezra.

He stood to lift the metallic bell dome covers on the butler trolley and served two piping hot bowls of soup with a flourish. "Et voilà."

I peered into the bowl, breathing its scent. "You remembered I'm vegetarian."

He gave a curt nod. "Roast beetroot soup with caramelised onion topped with a triangle of blue cheese toast. It's not a dish I would choose for myself. I prefer my food with more gore. But I am willing to make changes to make space for you in my life."

It was easier to respond to the first part of his uttering. "Did you make this?"

His laughter was machine-gun quick, as if he'd jinx himself by letting it bubble on. As if he didn't trust himself to be happy. "No, but I instructed the servants on which recipes would be appropriate."

"That's not really a legit term these days. You mean, your staff member."

"I pay them very handsomely. I should be able to call them whatever I want to."

I bit into the toast. "My breath isn't going to thank you for this blue cheese, but it is delicious."

Orpheus chuckled. "Don't think I didn't notice how much garlic you both consumed before coming here."

"A precaution against the rest of your clan, Orpheus. That's all," I said. Ezra had revealed that garlic as vampire defence was a myth. But most creatures recoiled from garlic breath, so a chomping a handful of segments was a pretty good call in my book.

"Neuhoff is right. Garlic doesn't harm my kind." Orpheus picked up a knife, wrapped my hand around its hilt and pressed it to his heart space, his skin cool against mine. "Never be scared of me. This is precise point where you stake a vampire, with an appropriately powerful stake to match the calibre of vampire, of course." He placed his napkin on his lap. "I thought I could teach you how to block your thoughts from me. As a gesture of our friendship. So when I listen to your thoughts, it is your choice, not mine. It's a skill the eternal girl should have anyway."

My stomach fluttered at the thought of this stern man making himself vulnerable for me, but our world values were so different. Take his food source. He'd told me once that he had strict rules about who he could feed on and that the Metropolitan Police and Her Majesty's Prison Service liked to keep the vampires happy with criminals who didn't deserve a second chance. Snacking on irredeemable criminals might be a more efficient use of taxpayer's money than rehabilitation, but everyone deserved a second chance. Even the arseholes.

We would never work as a couple. Our lifestyles, our attitudes.

And yet, I felt a frisson of attraction that could grow into something bigger. I felt safe with Orpheus. He was intelligent and kind, albeit a little sullen in company. He challenged me to grow as a person. He made me laugh and supported my choices. He liked children and had already said that he could imagine Mirabel in his life. He read, collected art, was financially sound and always ready for an adventure. That was one hell of an offer if I was looking for a romantic partner.

If my heart wasn't already latched onto someone else.

And that was the thing about matters of the heart. They weren't ever logical.

His mouth twisted. "Yes, let me teach you how to keep me at bay. Some thoughts, I'd prefer not to hear."

"I'm listening."

"You must evoke your own personal boundaries."

I laughed. "I've been trying to do that all my life, and people spring right over them."

"That's because you haven't been doing it properly." He ran his eyes over me. "Our physical body and mind are connected. All you need to do is project a field of positive energy around you to stop mental attacks. Visualise a cocoon nobody can penetrate without your permission. It takes knowing yourself and knowing who is a threat to you."

I pursed my lips. "It sounds exhausting."

"It can be. For the unpractised. But given your speed of learning, I would have thought this a skill you can easily add to your repertoire. There are ways to enhance the practice. Regularly cleansing your mind in a bath of pink Himalayan salt, for example." He pulled a velvet pouch from his pocket. "Or wearing crystals."

I edged forward, biting my lip as he plucked out a thin, silver ring, adorned with three stones.

He rolled it between his piano player's fingers. "Rose quartz to protect the heart, set between two amethysts to heal the mind. I had my jeweller make it for you."

I shook my head. "I can't accept that."

"It's for the middle finger of your left hand. It's not a wedding band." A dangerous edge to his voice, a dark promise of possession. "You'd know if I was proposing to you." He held it out to me. "Try it on. Try to block your mind from me."

I slipped the ring onto my finger. It was the perfect fit. A sense of calm settled over me.

With a deep inhale, I visualised a white field around me. Not dense but more like a second skin that followed me as I moved. I didn't know whether it was the ring or innate ability, but the magic wasn't exhausting. It was akin to putting on silk stockings. Once I had erected the field, it was like a low-level hum in my head. Like the buzz of a generator.

That didn't mean it worked, but testing out this mind fortification would be fun.

Grinning, I flung a thought at Orpheus. *You're quite the catch for the right woman.*

He stared at me blankly.

My confidence surged. *Can you hear me, you big tampon?*

Orpheus leaned back in his chair, and the glow of the lamplight picked up the hollows in his face. "That worked a little too quickly for my liking. Judging by the glint in those molten brown eyes of yours, you've been making vampire jokes. Am I right?"

"Nothing too under the belt."

"I'm quite sure I've heard worse. Your talents are growing extraordinarily fast." His eyes lingered on my inner arm. He reached across to inspect the soft flesh there, where the map lines had grown between the braille dots of my childhood scar.

The club grew still around us.

No distant stacking of chips in the casino, where vampires entertained the city's rich. No gentle buzz of electricity in the Edwardian building that Orpheus called home. No clink of glasses or scraping of cutlery.

Only Orpheus's light touch on my arm and the promise of destiny.

The wardrobe in the corner of the room rattled.

I cast it a startled glance. "What are you hiding, a wardrobe full of clanking skeletons?"

His enigmatic look didn't set me at ease. "I was going to keep this up my sleeve until later in the evening." He pushed back his chair, offered me the cool grip of his hand and led me towards the hopping wardrobe, where he turned to me. "Go on. Open it. I promise it won't bite."

I was the eternal girl. I was supposed to ward off the coming dark. I wouldn't let a rocking wardrobe in a vampire den get the better of me. That would be silly. Besides, Orpheus wouldn't put me in danger.

Shoulders tight, gritting my teeth, I pulled the handle.

The doors jammed for a second then flew open.

I jumped three feet high. "Holy mother of everything sacred."

Inside the wardrobe, bound to the clothing rail with a pair of handcuffs, was a scruffy blond man wearing nothing but his favourite boxers, a silken handkerchief stuffed in his mouth. His blue eyes were wild with fright.

I pulled the handkerchief out of his mouth, relieved that he didn't appear to have any injuries. Apart from his pride. "Alex?"

"Help! Help!" shouted my ex-husband. "I thought it was my lucky day when that maniac offered me a ride in his Lotus. Then he brought me here."

A rush of maternal feelings came over me, despite our divorce. Probably because I'd spent a lifetime pairing this man's socks and slicing him carrot batons with his dinner because he disliked carrot coins.

"Orpheus, what have you done?" I said.

The vampire's eyes hooded. "I planned to get you a bouquet of flowers, but it seemed such a humdrum gesture. So I settled on capturing the man-child who caused you so much pain. I thought you'd be pleased."

"You're dating this guy?" Alex rattled his handcuffs against the rail. Pores and breath gave of a whiff of stale alcohol.

"You've fallen off the wagon again?" I turned to Orpheus. "Kidnap isn't really my thing. Alex doesn't cause me pain anymore. I moved on from him a long time ago. Let him go."

"That's a shame. I think you might have found the porcupine game very cathartic."

I frowned. "The porcupine game?"

Orpheus nodded. "Toothpicks and nether regions."

I winced. "I think I'm okay."

Alex slumped in relief.

"Very well. If you insist." Orpheus bared his fangs, causing Alex to shrink back in fear. "It is your lucky day after all, discarded husband of Alisha Verma. She has decided to spare you further humiliation." He stared into Alex's blue eyes, his own ones dark pools of forgetting. "When I unlock your handcuffs, you will leave this club, beckon a taxi and go home to your flat where you will sleep peacefully and never touch a drop of alcohol or gambling den again. You will bend to Alisha's will at every interaction and forget all knowledge of tonight's events."

Orpheus unlocked the handcuffs.

Alex lurched out of the wardrobe, massaged his wrists and hoisted his boxers up over his bum crack.

I laid a hand on his shoulder. "Goodbye, Alex."

"Goodbye, Alisha." He gave me a winning smile. Then he walked out of the door without a second look.

"Have you really compelled his alcohol and gambling afflictions away?" I asked.

"You have no malice towards him, so neither did I."

"How's Alex going to make it through the vampires upstairs?"

"They won't touch him. Vampires have their standards, and I'm afraid your ex-husband is in desperate need of a bath." Orpheus held out his arm. "Come, our dinner is getting cold."

I hooked my arm through it but kept up my mental shield.

Orpheus was my friend, but one thing was clear—his kidnapping of Alex only served to underline how ill-suited we were to each other.

We reached the dining table when a distraught moan met my ears.

Then another. And another.

My eyes widened. "Mirabel?"

6
___

Orpheus's vampire speed meant he left me in his wake as he rushed to my daughter. I hurried after him. My primal need for Mirabel to be safe propelled a prayer to my lips despite my atheism, a fear response learned from being the child of parents who had faith.

The room was dark, illuminated only by the scenes on the cinema screen, where the hot English vampire from *Buffy* had gone all bad boy. Orpheus crouched over Mirabel, blocking my view of her, with the exception of her slack arm hanging over the empty bowl of chips, wiped clean of ketchup.

I moved him aside, heartbeat pummelling my chest.

She had curled into a ball on the recliner. Her eyes were open, green pools of fear, and heart-wrenching moans fell like stones from her lips.

I shook her. "Mirabel! Bel, can you hear me?"

Her dead look shook me to my core, green eyes so wide they might have been propped apart by toothpicks.

Orpheus knelt down to her, cocking his head slightly. "Her heartbeat is regular."

The hair on my arms stood on edge. I whipped around,

sensing an Otherworldly presence, but there was nothing there.

Patting her clammy cheek, I fought to keep my panic at bay. "Mirabel, answer me. Orpheus, I need the lights on. Get me the ice bucket."

He responded in the blink of an eye. The spotlights in the ceiling chased away the darkness. I checked Mirabel for injuries. Her auburn hair was mussed. The absence of puncture marks suggested this wasn't a vampire attack.

When Mirabel didn't react to the cold ice cubes I tipped onto her palm, hysteria rose in me like a wave. Buried trauma resurfaced. It seemed like yesterday that I had lost my student Nita at Ra's hand. "I don't understand. I should have brought Echo to keep an eye on her. I should have never left her alone."

His tone was sharp. "If you follow a twelve-year-old everywhere, you'll either be the death of her or end up in a coffin yourself."

"Why is she like this? Could she have ingested something poisonous? Maybe the chips?"

"Fried potatoes are very unlikely to be the culprit in this situation. Those chips are from a well-known high-street fast-food outlet, metres from here. Millions of daily customers would attest to their safety. They can be criticised for high salt intake but not for poison."

How many minutes had passed, when every second felt like an hour? Helplessness clouded my ability to think.

I couldn't tell whether this was a medical or a magical predicament. "We have to get her to the hospital."

"Yes, yes, of course." He bent to scoop her up into her arms.

Mirabel blinked. She gasped for breath, her chest heaving. "Alisha?"

I buried my head in her slight body and helped her sit up. "Thank God. Are you okay?"

Her voice was thin and breathless. "It was awful. Mum and Dad were screaming. It wouldn't end." She trembled. "I am used to manipulating fire, but there was heat in my body like I was burning from the inside."

I stroked her damp hair back from her face. "Bel, it was a nightmare."

"I couldn't move. Someone was crushing my chest. Someone in this room." She clutched me. "Why are there ants running up and down my body?"

I exchanged glances with Orpheus. "There's only me and Orpheus. No one else."

She shuddered, her eyes darting. "There was someone else, I swear it."

Taking off my Jericho necklace, I fastened it around her neck just in case she needed its protection.

Orpheus's eyebrows snapped together. "That is unwise. Mirabel is far less at risk than the eternal girl."

I waved off his concerns. "She's vulnerable right now. I can take care of myself." Humdrum hospitals would only be able to gather half the picture. I knew what we had to do. "We need to get her to Wildwoods so Rayna can check her over."

Orpheus gave a curt nod. "I'll get the car."

I hugged Mirabel. Her tough exterior had gone, leaving a bird-like fragility. "Let's call Ezra. It will be quicker."

His lips twisted. "As you wish."

I rushed for my mobile phone to dial Ezra.

He picked up on the second ring.

"I need you."

As if his instinct to protect me overrode the need for logic, Ezra came without questions, as I'd known he would. I hugged that fact to me in silence, my mind shield raised against Orpheus, for fear of hurting his feelings. We'd teleported together before, but Orpheus's pride had made it an awkward affair. He prized his independence. He was a lone stalker of the night, not a man who needed to carpool with a werewolf.

Still, my nearest and dearest were always there when I needed them, and that love now extended to Mirabel.

Her eyelids twitched as we bypassed the yew tree to emerge in the Wildwoods infirmary. I feared another episode, but once tucked into bed, with the windows closed and a cool sheet pooled over her, she slipped into a peaceful sleep.

Six of us gathered at her bedside in the Wildwoods infirmary: me, Ezra, Orpheus, Marina, Echo and Rayna, who administered Mirabel's care. The druid headmistress muttered inaudibly as she worked, potion bottles clanking on her belt. Marina, with her medical experience, shadowed every move.

Under Phinnaeous Shine's leadership, the infirmary had been a sterilised affair, lacking warmth. But Rayna had stamped her own mark on the space now. The sweet scent of foliage and mature herbs filled the air. The shelves brimmed with jars of garlic cloves, gingko leaves and ginseng roots. The bedding, though still white, was less starchy than I remembered and instead a comforting, smooth cotton.

Echo's head drooped. "I am sworn to protect the Vermas. And since you have absorbed this Elmstorm into your clan, it seems I have failed you again."

"Why is Marina attaching herself to the headmistress? She treats animals—bovines and turtles and goldfish bought at travellers' fairs—not people," said Orpheus.

A vein throbbed in Ezra's jaw as he took in the vampire's unusual attire. "Alisha, what were you doing at Orpheus's club?"

"She was in my private quarters, Neuhoff," retorted the vampire. "Not the club."

I ignored them all. They were background noise to Mirabel's ordeal. She was a slip of a girl, pale against the pillowcase. Every instinct told me to cocoon her away from harm. She had already been through so much.

Rayna took her sweet time, alternating between scientific and magical practices. She used scientific methods such as checking Mirabel's vital signs and examining her skin, gums, eyes and ears. But she also relied on magical practices, placing a drop of turquoise liquid on Mirabel's tongue with a pipette and laying an array of leaves on the patient's chest and soles of her feet.

Eventually, Rayna smoothed the patient's blankets, called us into a huddle in the corner of the room. She untangled her stethoscope from her long, silver hair. "Mirabel is fit as a fiddle."

I slouched with relief. "That's wonderful."

"That doesn't mean she's out of danger."

I chewed my lip, anxiety levels ascending until Marina put her arm around me, her empath skills keeping the wave of panic from overwhelming me.

Rayna peppered me with questions. "You say this is the first time this has happened?"

"As far as I know, yes."

"Is she on any medication?"

"Nothing at all."

She looked pensive. "Good. She's of course dealing with her parent's death and the recent trial. One might expect increased stress levels. You said she woke up gasping?"

"Yes. She complained of a weight on her chest and was worried there was someone else in the room. We checked for intruders. I think she was just disoriented."

The vampire raised a finger to interject. "The girl mentioned heat inside the body. The sensation of ants crawling up and down her limbs."

Ezra harrumphed, and the room suddenly felt too small for both wolf and vampire. I frowned at him, a warning to prevent a repeat of the fisticuffs that they had once engaged in.

Rayna traced her fingers over the sheathed dagger at her waist. "I've seen this once before on a young family member of mine, who suffered with nightmares for years until her parents brought it to my attention. The first time I saw her, it was clear hers were no ordinary nightmares. She would wake up panting for breath, complaining of how her chest had been crushed. Just like my relative, I suspect what we are dealing with is sleep paralysis."

I frowned. "Sleep paralysis?"

She nodded. "In deep sleep, the body's voluntary muscles relax. We might have vivid dreams, but our bodies don't act out physical movements. It's how our bodies protect us from injuries."

"With the exception of sleepwalkers, of course," said Orpheus. "Terrible affliction. When I was human, I used to sleepwalk. I once walked into my mother's bedroom while she was copulating with a stable boy. Quite a relief to find a vampire rarely sleeps."

"Let's concentrate on Mirabel, shall we?" Ezra looped his necklace, complete with his thistle, around Mirabel's throat, where it joined the Jericho necklace.

An overwhelming rush of affection for him came over me, but I averted my eyes in case I let on.

Rayna pressed on. "In sleepwalking, a malfunction means that voluntary muscles move while the mind is asleep, which is why sleepwalkers have no recollection of their actions. Sleep paralysis, which is a probable diagnosis for Mirabel, means that your mind is awake and your body is not so you're trapped. It's only lasts for a few minutes. Essentially, the body has difficulties making the transition from or to deep sleep, and so the sufferer becomes alert but unable to move. It often triggers a panic response and increase in heart rate, which is why Mirabel was gasping and unsettled."

"Will it happen again?" said Ezra.

"It could do. It's quite common in young adults," said Rayna.

Echo growled. "Then I will remain by her side while she sleeps and gently nudge her awake when it occurs."

"I'm afraid that won't work," said Rayna. "Sufferers wake in their own time. It might take seconds or minutes, but she *will* wake. You need not fear. Sleep paralysis isn't pleasant, but it leaves no lasting physical damage. Of course, it might be possible to use your voices as an anchor, but physical intervention is unwise and ineffective."

"There must be something that is possible to protect the girl," said Orpheus.

Rayna brow furrowed. "Record abnormal sleep behaviours. Note down episodes of erratic breathing, panic and nightmares and try to correlate these to her emotional and physical state. Any links will give us something to go on. Exhaustion makes future episodes more likely, so earlier bedtimes could prevent recurrence. Aim to decrease her stress levels. I could prescribe her some herbs. Some valerian root, perhaps, chamomile and passionflower. Perhaps a sprig of lavender mixed in with her evening milk."

"Yes. I'd appreciate that." I blocked the memory of Mirabel's startled eyes and limp body. "Anything proactive to stop this happening again."

"I make no promises, Alisha Verma." Rayna turned back to her patient.

Marina cleared her throat and pulled at a strand of her rainbow hair. "I don't want to step on any toes, but I just wondered..."

Rayna's face softened, warmth infusing her usual no-nonsense demeanour. "Wildwoods is a place of learning, Marina. All voices are heard here, especially following the departure of our most recent Prime Sorcerer."

A flurry of unreadable thoughts drifted across her face.

Marina took a deep breath. "It's just, I think we might be relying too much on scientific explanations. What if there is a magical one instead?"

Rayna pursed her lips. "Continue."

"I think this crop of Wildwoods students proves how valuable adult learners are," drawled Orpheus.

"You're in the presence of a night class teacher," said Ezra. "Alisha's known that all along."

"The wolf and the bat are in a tussle of some sort," the leopard purred. "It's willies at dawn."

I braced myself for innuendo from Marina that never came.

Instead, her voice, usually exuberant, was tentative. "I know you all laugh at me for being superstitious."

"Well, dear, you can't blame us," said Rayna. "You wear a cross, have a clover tattoo, and I found it very odd how at the coven dinner you religiously look people in the eye when you clink glasses."

Marina huffed. "To avoid seven years of bad sex."

"You also knock on wood, won't open an umbrella inside or walk under ladders," purred Echo. "Plus, there was the time you were visiting Alisha at university and she dared you to say Candyman three times or flash her ageing professor—"

Marina's face flamed so brightly I took pity on her. "We've established Marina is superstitious. But she is also a phenomenal scientist."

She gave me grateful look. "When we were examining Mirabel, there was something off with her aura. Usually, it's green tinged with blue. Right now, it's as though another mass is clinging to it. A dark mass. It confused me. I know Mirabel. Even when she's angry, her aura doesn't change this much. It boomerangs back to who she is—a confused but essentially stable pre-teen. My head kept pinging to old mythology books I read at the Celestial Library while I was working on the Jericho necklace. I mean, there was no sex up there sadly and no television, but I managed to read a hell of a lot more than usual. And one of the books was about shadowy figures linked with sleep in different mythologies."

"Yes," said Rayna. "Folk legends speak of malevolent spirits that sit on the chest during sleep, pressuring the thorax. It's why some Otherworld parents refuse to let children sleep with their tummies up. Although I find children who sleep on their bellies often end up with an unsightly sturdy neck." Her swan-like neck had seemingly not suffered such a fate.

"There are many versions of these myths," said Marina. "In Brazil, a crone with long fingernails lurks on rooftops waiting to trample those who sleep. The Portuguese talk of a Friar entering homes through the keyhole, straddling people to give them nightmares. Some Inuits think shamans involved in power struggles cast spells on their opponents, which cause sleep paralysis while they try to separate mind from body. It's possible that we are dealing with a magical entity here."

"That's not creepy at all." I shuddered. "I did sense something back at Orpheus's club."

"That's why we love you, Marina Ambrose," said the leopard. "Your brain is as sexy as your chemical hair."

She rewarded him by caressing his golden fur.

Our attention jerked to the bed as Mirabel tossed in her sleep. Her eyes flashed open, and her body went still. Echo unleashed a roar as we all rushed to her bedside.

"No," I said. "Not again."

"Take heart, Alisha," said Rayna. "We just have to wait it out."

But I could see the trapped nightmare in Mirabel's frozen eyes. I gasped, as her features appeared to twist, rendering her unrecognisable. Gone, her resemblance to her parents. Gone, the plumpness to her face. Gone, the small nose and high forehead. She changed, becoming grotesque, an unknown combination of features that didn't belong to the girl we knew. The Jericho necklace and Ezra's thistle charm glowed around her neck, and suddenly she became herself again.

I stared at her. "Did you see that?"

Ezra cursed, hackles rising. "Yeah. Yeah, I did."

The leopard's ears flattened in surprise. "I will never steal mushrooms from Shanghai Moon again. I must be hallucinating. For one moment, the sweet fairy looked like a goblin and an angry one at that."

"You are right to suspect the work of magic, empath. I should have seen it before. We all saw the distortion of Mirabel Elmstorm's features. I'm afraid her case is more complicated than I diagnosed. I believe we are dealing with some of the most manipulative and trickster creatures in Otherworld history." Rayna drew in a shaky breath. "We're dealing with djinn."

Ezra's Adam's apple bobbed in his throat. "Then I know who we should speak to."

7

Dad's voice rasped down the line, making me wonder if he'd been picking up a bong on his holiday. "Alma's been going mad with flour rituals since this morning. She couldn't work out what was going on, but I just knew something had happened at home. Tell me my sweet granddaughter is going to be okay."

I dropped my voice so that Mirabel couldn't hear. Not only was the cottage a compact size, it also had thin walls. "I hope so. I just don't understand why she would be susceptible to djinn."

"Why are you whispering? Are you and Alma ganging up on me about hearing aids?"

I cupped my mouth to the phone. "Rayna let us come home this morning. Mirabel is watching television in the living room. You know how sensitive kids are. I don't want her overhearing."

Dad harrumphed. "Hmm. The line is awfully echoey, isn't it, Alma?"

"That's because you have it on speaker phone, Dad."

He barrelled on. "Bulgaria is so wonderful that we stayed. Ezra's parents were onto something when they found this village. The peculiars here are like family. They pull together and have done a wonderful job of looking after Tielbu."

Hearing Ezra's name made my gut twist, but I deflected. "Did you check what meals they are giving him? Marina's food plan said he had to cut back on sugar. All those biscuits aren't good for a dragon's teeth. Anyone's teeth, really. I made a bank transfer last week, but it would be good to know if Tielbu's getting the right sustenance."

"Yes, I do miss my studio, Alisha. Thank you for asking. When someone has lived in a house as long as I have, being away from it is like being discombobulated. I very much miss the precise fit of the avocado toilet seat against my bottom. It's my favourite one in the world."

"Actually, I didn't ask about that."

"Oh, didn't you? Maybe some of Alma's flour is stuck in my ear canals. Being in love with a seer does come with its drawbacks…only joking, Alma love." He guffawed.

He'd definitely been smoking something. I'd have to have a word with Alma.

"I don't know how you did it all these years, Dad."

"Did what?"

"Parenthood. It's so hard watching Mirabel go through all this. How do I protect her?"

"I had your mother." He grew sombre. "It's harder for you, doing this alone. There were times that you or Sahil got hurt." He hesitated. "Actually, I remember Sahil getting hurt more than you. Broken bones. A bloody nose. And then there was the time that he fell on his teeth and we had to go to the emergency dentist. After the incident when the birds scratched you, you just seemed to bounce back up as if the earth had protected you."

"That was Gaia, of course," interjected Alma.

A note of surprise from Dad. "Oh, was it? In any case, your mother and I learned that children will fall. You can only be there to hold their hand."

I swallowed hard. I'd felt Mum's presence when I'd trained in the cottage garden with my sword that morning. And later, when I'd trawled through the books on my parents shelves and checked on the koi pond at Dad's house. "Ezra has a plan, but it involves Lavinia. I feel so helpless. I decided to get a head start, just to work out what we are dealing with. First thing this morning, Marina checked the local library, Calypso checked the Celestial Library and I checked your bookshelves for mentions of djinn. But we couldn't find anything to help."

Horror filled his voice. "Djinn?"

"That's what Marina and Rayna think is behind Mirabel's sleep paralysis."

He stammered like he was afraid. "It's best not to think of the unseen. It gives them power."

A shiver ran up my spine. "I have no choice. I have to help Mirabel."

Dad took a deep breath. "Djinn are ancient creatures from the time before men learned how to write and record their thoughts on parchment. There are limited mentions of them across the centuries. In the Qur'an, for example. I know of them through stories and from my Muslim neighbours back home in India. To help my granddaughter, I'll tell you everything I know. But, Alisha, you must deal with this quickly. Once djinn take root, they are hard to dislodge."

His fear was infectious, but I fought to stay calm. "I understand."

"Djinn are born from smokeless fire. They have no original shape. They can be fire or energy. They can take on the shape of animals or humans. Even dead people. They can take on our mannerisms and lifestyles, even marrying and having children. They can inhabit us, running through our blood to give us thoughts. They are strong and fast and live for thousands of years. They can fly and make illusions. But they can be outwitted because they have ordinary intelligence. Not all djinn are evil, but they are all manipulative."

His fear was infectious. I stiffened in terror. "We got away from them the first time. At least now we know what we're dealing with, we can prepare."

He sighed. "My mother wasn't scared of anything, but as a child, I remember her telling me to keep my hair short and not to play in isolated areas or under trees in darkness because the djinn would come."

"Dad, we're always walking under trees in the dark. Wildwoods is in a park, for goodness' sake. Maybe all of this is an old wives' tale." Taking precautions and planning our defence was one thing, but our Otherworldly lives often happened in twilight or after the sun set. We couldn't just grind to a halt.

His tone sharpened. "You need to take this seriously, Alisha. My Muslim friends used to say that prayer is the best protection against djinn, but I know how you feel about that."

Alma piped up, her voice muffled. "Tell her the extreme emotions are a trapdoor for djinn. She should try not to get upset. No anger, fear or worry. Definitely no sex."

"No chance of that," I muttered.

"No perfume or wearing your hair loose," said Dad. "Try to cover your legs and shoulders and no singing. Tell that damn leopard not to sing, especially outside."

Sarcasm rolled off my tongue. "Sounds utterly doable. At least it's not summer. Or else you'd have me going round in a onesie and balaclava."

Dad snapped. "No need to be tart."

"Sorry. It's just been a lot recently, you know?"

"I know, love."

"Any tips on how to fight them?"

There was a kerfuffle that sounded like Alma wrestling the phone from Dad. "I think they're drawn to Mirabel because she is a fire fairy. They seek out heat, you see. But

Gaia told me once that little kernel of knowledge is also key to their death. She said they hate the opposite element. They hate water. Even snow falling on their skin feels like pinpricks."

I hugged the phone to my ear, pensive. Even gone, Gaia still steered me to safer ground. "So rainy and snowy weather means we are safe from djinn. You don't know how helpful this is, Alma. Thank you."

"You're welcome, dear. Your father is giving me daggers. I better give him back the phone," she said in her lilting Spanish accent.

Dad grumbled. "I wasn't giving her daggers. I was practicing my come-hither look. I find it very sexy that she helped you find a solution, and she will be well rewarded, believe me."

I almost choked on my tongue.

He continued, oblivious. "Please be safe, Alisha. I'd feel much better if I were there to protect you both. Or if you had a man to protect you."

Alma called out in the background. "We thought you'd be back together with Ezra by now."

I sighed. "What's that Pat Benatar song that Echo's been singing at me? 'Love Is a Battlefield'?"

Dad groaned. "Tell the leopard not to sing. And try not to worry about Ezra. These things have a habit of working themselves out. In the meantime, your brother's very lonely and he has a shield, so I guess he could do some uncle duties and be Mirabel's protection detail?"

I kept the judgement out of my voice. "Great idea, Dad."

"It does an old man's heart good to see how well you two are getting on. Lovely to hear your voice. I have to go. We're trying out a new routine on Fridays just to shake things up. We wear our fancy dress outfits all day, and if one of us is feeling frisky, the other one is not allowed to say no. Alma's in her maid's outfit already, but I still have to squeeze into my superhero tights."

That mental image was going nowhere fast. "Living your best life, Dad. I'm happy for you. And I miss you."

"I miss you too, Alisha. Give Mirabel a kiss from me."

Alma giggled as he hung up the phone.

I hauled myself off my bed, exhausted from a night of standing vigil over Mirabel plus the dash to my parents' house, and padded over to the living room barefoot and braless, wearing just knickers and Ezra's T-shirt. I held a hairbrush, determined to work the knots out of Mirabel's hair that I'd noticed when she lay against the pillow in the infirmary. With any luck, we'd have a few hours to ground ourselves and recover before we met Lavinia at Baba Yaga's.

Tuneless singing drifted from the living room, where Mirabel snuggled with Echo. Their bond was a joy to behold. The television had been turned off. Mirabel traced the rosettes on his fur as he crooned "I'll Stand By You" by The Pretenders to her.

I felt like a grouch for interrupting them. "Dad says no singing, I'm afraid, Echo. It attracts the attention of djinn."

The leopard hissed. "What terrible creatures. As if it wasn't bad enough that they lurk around, now they are also killjoys. How are we supposed to live without music?"

"How are you feeling, Bel?" I picked up the brush and reached out for her hair. "Let me get the knots out of your hair."

She tensed and shrank back. "No. No hair-brushing."

Heart hammering, I put the brush down, annoyed at myself. It was clearly too early to attempt something so tied up in the memories of her mother. Keen to deflect, I jumped to another topic. "Do you think you might be up to going to school on Monday?"

Echo rolled onto his back in a huff, taking up the giant's

share of the sofa. "It's the Christmas holidays soon. Maybe the fairy should just stay home and avoid the djinn."

Mirabel's moss-coloured eyes found mine, shining with the rebellious spirit her mother had once warned me about. "No way. I'm not staying home. Everyone's already whispering about me since Mum and Dad died. That would make it worse. No one would ever want to be my friend again."

"I didn't realised school has been hard." I dropped to my knees in front of her, but she avoided my eyes. "Do you want to talk about it?"

"Nope." Her jaw clenched, and she blinked rapidly, as if holding back tears.

When her hands grew hot in mine, I held on until the surge of heat subsided. "Bel, we're going to get to the bottom of this, and I'll find a way of keeping you safe without keeping you home from school."

She gave a weak smile. "You promise?"

I froze as particles shifted behind me, giving me the sinking feeling that a wolfish visitor had bypassed the doorbell and dropped straight into the living room. While I was in my knickers. Reluctant to turn around and face humiliation, I clenched my butt cheeks together in an attempt to make my arse looked more toned but which inevitably gave me dimply skin. "Is Ezra behind me?"

"Yep," said Mirabel with a sympathetic pat on my shoulder.

"Can he see my butt?"

Ezra chuckled. "Your tangerine-coloured thong highlights it beautifully."

I cringed, even though he'd clearly seen it all before.

"Welcome, dog, to your home, currently occupied by your ex-lover and her stragglers," said Echo.

Mirabel's eyes were moon-wide, her cheeks flushed with second-hand embarrassment for me.

With the energy and enthusiasm of a tortoise, I tugged down my T-shirt to cover my booty. Then I pushed myself to standing position and swivelled to look Ezra Neuhoff, newly showered and smelling mountain-fresh, in the face.

"That's my T-shirt you're wearing. There was me thinking that I'd picked up all my belongings." His voice rumbled like distant thunder, a promise of danger that made my flesh tingle. His grey eyes twinkled with copper, and desire flashed within their depths.

Heat filled my face. "Oh, this old thing? I found it lying around. I could have taken it down to the charity shop, but it seemed a shame. I mean, it has all its threads. It's not like it's full of holes or anything."

Even Echo groaned.

Echo, who had the sensitivity radar of a block of cheese.

Ezra raised an eyebrow. He wasn't buying any of it. The warmth in his eyes proved he knew I was wearing his shirt out of longing. It served him right if his T-shirt moulded itself to my breasts and he was never able to wear it again without looking like he had man boobs.

"I'm sorry," said Ezra. "Force of habit just teleporting home to the cottage. I should have knocked. Lavinia has a gap between classes and is ready to see us at 11:30 A.M. at Baba Yaga's."

Resolve swept through me. I held out a hand to Mirabel and heaved her off the sofa. "Come on, Bel. Ezra thinks the witches have a spell to prevent harm from djinn. This is how I keep my promise. With any luck, you'll be shielded and ready to go to school with your friends on Monday."

EZRA TELEPORTED us into the cleaning cupboard of Baba Yaga's in Wimbledon, where we crammed into close quarters.

His mouth twisted in chagrin. "I have been told off more

than once for assuming that this gym is full of clientele from the Otherworld, when there is an equal proportion of humdrum members. In a fit of pique, my aunts once told me that I had to teleport into this cupboard. Given their status as family matriarchs, I never did build up the courage to ask them to loosen the rule."

Echo let out a honk of laughter. "It is clear that, although I am but a humble cat, I have the most body autonomy of us all."

"You didn't need to come with us, leopard. Though I'm happy you no longer have the urge to vomit after teleporting," said Ezra.

"I have vowed not to leave the little one's side," Echo purred. "We are a family now."

"I'm twelve, not two," said Mirabel.

"Come on, squirt." Ezra opened the cupboard door.

Although I had teleported alongside Ezra only yesterday, it was easier to enjoy the sensation of being close to him again when Mirabel wasn't in immediate danger. I let go of his hand reluctantly and tripped over a mop and bucket, only just catching a drying rack that threatened to trap Echo.

We followed Ezra out into the bubble-gum pop interior of the gym, only to be met by a wall of musky scent: sweat, jasmine and quite possibly the remnants of rat urine, although Lavinia insisted her house-trained rats would never befoul the place.

My stomach heaved. Given they cooked the coven meals, which I had also eaten, I hoped she was right.

We found Lavinia pulsating in turquoise Lycra at the front of a Zumba class, with age-defying hips that would have given certain pop stars a run for their money. When she caught sight of us, she wrapped up the session and pivoted in our direction, patting her helmet of silver curls that had quite miraculously stayed in place during her high-octane gyrating.

"Hello, everyone." She reached up to press a kiss to Ezra's

cheek. Her inquisitive eyes flicked to the ring Orpheus had given me. "What a wonderful ring, Alisha. Rose quartz set between two exquisite amethysts. To fortify the mind, if I'm not mistaken?"

I avoided the scrutiny of Ezra's stare. "A gift from Orpheus. He's been teaching me how to guard my thoughts."

"A marvellous educator, that vampire. Quite wonderful in his role as Minister for History and the Today," she mused, before turning her attention to Mirabel. "I am pleased you are here. Once I am confirmed as Prime Sorcerer, I won't be as accessible of course. But for you, young Elmstorm, I have cleared a slot in my diary. Don't you worry, my girl. My nephew told me all about your predicament, and we'll have it sorted in a jiffy. The cauldron is already brewing in the basement. I know just what to do."

"Thank you." Mirabel cast me an uncertain look over her shoulder.

"Don't worry, Bel. I'm right behind you." I paired up with Ezra along the corridor.

Echo, reading Mirabel's signals, barged between witch and fairy, a leopard buffer zone.

"Have a good look around, my dear." Lavinia chattered to Mirabel, oblivious to the girl's inner turmoil. As if all that mattered was a tour of Baba Yaga's and Mirabel was not consumed by her traumas. "Twelve years old is too young to be a member, but one day, you may wish to join our illustrious gym."

Mirabel made a noncommittal noise.

Lavinia's pneumatic bottom sashayed ahead of us, like the charm on a hypnotist's chain. "We have a reception lobby, the main gym consisting of three studios and unisex changing rooms, which include massage-jet showers newly fitted with ambient lighting. There's also a relaxation lounge with green smoothies and an array of healthy soups and snacks. No flapjacks or full-fat milkshakes on sale here. Only the best for the clientele at Baba Yaga's."

Mirabel's mossy eyes widened. "Wasn't Baba Yaga scary? Why did you name the gym after her?"

Lavinia cackled. "Oh yes, judging by the tales of my ancestors, she was *very* scary. In fact, we have a lot in common. She was a witch, of course. She guarded the fountains of the water of life. I like to think we have a zest for youth and life here at the gym. Not only that, but she lived with her sisters too." Her hazel eyes were sly. "What she's best known for, of course, is kidnapping, cooking and eating her victims, usually children. Excellent at seasoning, by all accounts."

Echo's emerald eyes creased in mirth at Mirabel's horrified expression. "The witch is pulling your leg, Mirabel."

"Very good, leopard. Don't you worry, Mirabel, dear. I'm very sparing about what goes into my body and prefer a more Mediterranean diet. Please let it be known amongst the Otherworld that I have a sense of humour. It might be a vote winner. Sadly, the position of defence minister has presented me in a rather sombre light in the past."

"She's actually going for it. Do you think she'll win?" I whispered to Ezra.

"She has more ambition in her little finger than anyone else on the senate." He gave a wry smile. "You've never liked her, but there is good in her. In my book, she might be what we need. Sure, she has rough edges, but she usually comes out on the right side of things."

"Stop muttering, you two. In my day, if there were still things unsaid in a relationship, the quickest way to untangle things was a rumble between the sheets," said Lavinia.

I winced. Straight-talking women were one thing, but Lavinia would take a sledgehammer to a butterfly if it suited her.

The witch continued the tour. "The coven flat is upstairs,

of course. Men are allowed there by invitation only, apart from my dear nephew. We usually concoct potions in the flat kitchen, but given that this is a particularly smelly one, I thought it best to work in a corner of the basement. Follow me, dear. And no squealing when you're down here. The rats have rather fragile egos, and if they take a dislike to you, you might find one of them gnawing your ankles."

She threw open the door to the windowless basement, where rats raced on a dozen enormous circular contraptions from which thick electrical wires snaked into the walls.

Echo's eyes lit up at the sight of the prey.

"Be good." I swatted his behind and was thanked by a muted growl.

Lavinia raised her voice above the din of the whirring wheels. "Meet our secondary rats, Mirabel. Here they are, hard at work on our power-generating wheels." She frowned at a scrawny one, who had slowed his speed. "I like to be environmentally friendly. All these politicians pretending that the world isn't burning are a tawdry lot. Each of us has to do our part."

In a shadowy corner of the basement, Ignacio—the rat who had once been Elvira's familiar before her untimely death—had lit an iron cauldron. He bowed to us as we approached, quivering with pleasure when I crouched to give him a kiss.

"I presume everything is ready?" Lavinia peered at a bench laden with ingredients.

The rat's tiny hands jittered with nerves. "Yes, Minister."

She frowned like she had already outgrown that title. "Then we begin our ritual by gathering around the cauldron. To protect against djinn takes a sacred magic, one that I do not practice lightly. Our potion-making requires skill, precision and intent. Ignacio has provided the precision by carefully preparing the ingredients. You will provide the intent by willing the Otherworld community to be protected and the djinn to be defeated at the moment of alchemy. I, of course, provide the skill."

Lavinia inhaled deeply to centre herself, smoothed down the Lycra of her yoga leggings and issued a flurry of commands to the rat. They worked in tandem, the rat ferrying bowls of ingredients and the witch dropping them into the sizzling cauldron.

"Seventy-three litres of water," she said. "A smoke-filled jar of hair strands freely given by a hundred Otherworld creatures. The spit of the gossipy selkie Margola, as a substitute for mermaid spit. No self-respecting mermaid would swim in the Thames. A marigold wreath. A cup of rose thorns. A sprinkle of black salt. A sprig of rosemary. A clove. Next, the prayer of an unbelieving werewolf. That's you, Ezra."

He grimaced but stepped forward all the same, his eyes flicking between me and Mirabel, his sensual lips calling forth soft words that fell like pearls into the cauldron.

"Wonderful, nephew. I sensed your fervency. Next, something of yours, Mirabel. After all, your protection from these beasties is the primary reason we're here," said Lavinia. "A ribbon perhaps. A square of cloth. Oh, yes, an eyelash will do."

Mirabel plucked out an eyelash and dropped it into the cauldron.

The witch gave a satisfied nod. "And finally, four hundred headbands worn in the 1980s."

"You're not serious?" I snorted as Ignacio brought her a tray of headbands that had been taken straight from *Flashdance*.

"On the contrary, I'm deadly serious," said Lavinia. "Ignacio, my umbrella."

The rat fetched her dull brown umbrella from an ornate rack, went down on one knee and presented it to her like it was a sword.

The witch accepted it with a flourish. "Hold hands, all of you. Focus hard on your intent." She muttered a spell as the cauldron bubbled and spat, stirring it seven times in an anti-clockwise direction. "Wait for it…"

The cauldron crackled and popped before emitting a puff of smoke that browned our noses.

Ten minutes later, she had fished out the headbands with her umbrella and instructed Ignacio to give them a whirr in the clothes dryer. When ready, she filled a tote bag with a dozen headbands. "Give these out to your nearest and dearest. Make sure Mirabel takes hers off only when showering. They will give her the protection she needs from the djinn. Her sleep will be peaceful, her thoughts her own. I will arrange for my rats to deliver a headband to every member of London's Otherworld with a warning of what we face."

Mirabel's mouth fell open. "I have to wear one of those? At humdrum school too?"

"It might not be the height of fashion, but remember, child, there's always a price to magic," said Lavinia. "Here's yours, nephew."

"We owe you a great debt, auntie," said Ezra. "I won't forget this."

I couldn't help myself. "Why are you helping us, Lavinia? What's in it for you?"

The witch's hazel eyes gleamed, although by now, her helmet of silver curls had wilted. "Not every kind act is done with a reward in mind, Alisha."

I had the grace not to contradict her, but the truth frothed underneath our tight smiles.

For Lavinia, there was always a hidden motive.

8

———————

Three nights later, with Lavinia's headbands adorning our heads and eager feet pounding packed earth, we crossed Crystal Palace Park without incident. Even though it was night and shadows had fallen, and the trees stood like ominous giants against the sky.

Marina turned to me in a flash of rainbow hair. "Sweet Jesus. Orpheus did what?"

"I didn't want to tell you on the phone. I've been dying to see your expression when you found out." It would be safe to say that right now my best friend had a mouth like a Venus flytrap.

Being the eternal girl elicited stares, but I was getting used to ignoring them. I tucked my arm through Marina's as we melted into the crowds surging over the Wildwoods rope bridges. The throng around us was dense and full of anticipation. All around us, peculiars wore the headbands.

Mirabel, flanked by Echo, bobbed a few metres ahead. We passed the network of cabins, dressed like ships in their billowing white sheets rimmed with gold.

My stomach churned.

White sheets to signal the vanishing of Phinnaeous Shine from public life.

White sheets to signal a new start.

Marina's blue eyes filled with wonder as she admired the ring Orpheus had given me. "He taught you how to guard your thoughts from him. Even though hearing your thoughts makes him happy. How generous of him. Then he goes and kidnaps your ex-husband. All to impress you."

"He was wearing a gigolo outfit, had his chest hair on display and professed his undying love for me. I think he expected me to use Alex as a pin cushion to relieve my stress. It was quite sweet, really."

Her eyelashes feathered her cheeks in the cool evening light. "What a romantic. Rob's been so busy that his idea of romance is remembering to put the toilet seat down."

I raised an eyebrow. "I wouldn't knock that."

"I can read you like a book. You're pining for Ezra."

"I'm going to tell him tonight that I need him. To ask him if we can try again."

Marina nodded. "That's good, Alisha. I'm happy for you…"

I frowned. "I can hear a *but.*"

She pouted. "Part of me thinks it's a shame you turned down Orpheus. I mean, don't you sometimes just want to let your hair down? You've always been so responsible. With your pupils, with your mortgage, with your parents, now with Mirabel. All those years of being married to arsehole Alex. Then jumping into the relationship with Ezra. I mean, you've never even left Echo to fend for himself, even though he can hunt his own food. You always want to be there to fill up his water bowl."

"You're a vet. Aren't you supposed to praise me for looking after my animals?"

"Don't you ever want to just say *fuck it*? Damn it, have a

tumble in the sheets with the vamp. Appealing to your baser instincts could be quite freeing, Alisha. Why do you think I enjoy S&M so much? Always doing the right or proper thing can be exhausting. You have so much power. Don't you sometimes just want to let it all out? You should try giving your animal side a free rein every now and again. And *please* tell me you took the opportunity to kick Alex in the jingle bells."

"Of course I didn't. I told Orpheus to let him go. Although part of me hated taking the higher ground." I did a double take. "That sounded like you wanted me to rough Alex up."

A slight shrug. "Maybe he deserves it a little bit. I'm tired of creeps getting an easy ride. I'm tired of sensing their shady auras then watching their selfish paths through the world."

I laughed. "That's what comes from you dating a policeman. You have crime and punishment in your blood now."

"Ha, our lives have definitely become more interesting since stepping into the Otherworld. For one, who would have thought that, instead of a spiked dog collar, I'd be wearing a sweatband."

We filed into the vaulted cabin along with hundreds of others, the buzz of whispers filling our ears. Inside, silken swathes of gold hung from the rafters, livening up the austere feel of the room with its stone floors and stained-glass windows. Benches had been packed tightly into the space, with a narrow central aisle. High-backed chairs awaited the senators' arrival on the stage, together with a lectern. At the forefront of the stage, there was a curious antique wooden chest locked with a series of padlocks, with jutting carvings shaped like the wings of a soaring bird of prey.

Mirabel's parents had died in this room. If I had my way, I would have torn it down and built it anew to prevent her reliving the experience. But that couldn't be. Wildwoods was a place of traditions.

The vaulted cabin was central to Otherworld democracy.

Today was the day each registered peculiar who lived in London and was over ten years old would vote for the next Prime Sorcerer.

Mirabel and Echo had already saved us a spot.

We joined them, and I leaned into her. "Are you okay?"

"Yeah." She studiously looked away from where the red woman had trapped her parents in the doors and tugged at her headband, conscious of how she looked, although everyone around us sported one too.

Marina reached across. "Would you like my help to calm you?"

"No, I feel all right." She stuck in her earbuds and scrolled her phone for her playlist.

Echo's tail flicked. Mirabel might have been out of the woods when it came to the djinn, but her emotions remained volatile. A wave of nostalgia crashed over me. Though the leopard sat on the bench, he moulded his body to Mirabel's side, understanding instinctively how his softness could lend her strength. Just like he had for me when I had been a girl.

The senate would arrive any minute now.

"Poor Rob. He'd love to be a fly on the wall here tonight. Instead, he's having a takeaway with Fei Yen and Faeza," said Marina. "It's weird for him living and breathing all this Otherworld malarkey and still being a humdrum."

"Dad and Alma are gutted to miss it too."

"And Sahil?"

"You know what he's like. I thought he'd front up with Dad away and pitch in a bit with Mirabel, but he's been AWOL." I sighed. "Maybe it's a good thing Rob isn't here. This many weapons in one room would make even a hardened sergeant from the Met Police break out in a sweat. It's a bit weird they asked those of us without claws and fangs to bring sharp weapons tonight, isn't it?"

"Let's hope it isn't a bloodbath. My period is bad enough. I packed a knitting needle and a scalpel from the surgery."

I dropped my voice to avoid eavesdroppers. "Did you see that bit on the six o'clock news tonight about the new craze in London, the comeback of the *Flashdance* headband? Lavinia that did that."

Marina giggled. "You know she'd give anything to live in a Jane Fonda aerobics video."

"Wouldn't we all?" I said. "Seriously though, you know what's coming tonight, don't you? Those headbands the rats distributed were akin to a campaign leaflet. No wonder she helped us. It gave her a chance to shine. She's been the talk of the town. How, at a moment's notice, she concocted a potion to neutralise the power of the djinn. How her powers are more formidable than any other witch in Otherworld history. How, in this time of encroaching darkness, it makes sense for the defence minister to lead the senate. No other candidates stand a chance."

"Lavinia's aura is so complex I have trouble reading it." Marina waved to Flinar in the centre of an elf contingent, a few feet away from the sphinxes. "Maybe crowning a queen is what the Otherworld needs after Phinnaeous Shine. But I like that she invited the elves back into the heart of Wildwoods. It's a step in the right direction."

I blew Flinar a kiss. "I think Rayna's had as much to do with that as Lavinia, with purer intent. It suits Lavinia to take the credit. That way she can shore up her support. But will she do anything meaningful to help the elves? Will she let the elves have a seat on the senate?"

"Who knows? At least we can tell from Baba Yaga's that she enjoys living amongst humdrums. She steps in when humdrums need protection. Unlike that psycho Phinnaeous Shine." She hesitated before ploughing on, her words a jumble of passion. "You've been taking a back seat since Mirabel moved in. I know how important being a mother is to you, but have you noticed since we sat down how many people here look to you for leadership?"

A ripple of excitement surged around the vaulted cabin as the senate entered.

I tapped Mirabel's knee. "Take out your earbuds."

Tonight, the senate didn't enter from behind the stage. They chose instead to parade down the central aisle in pairs. In they came, faces sombre, chins lifted. Rayna and Helio, Calypso and Erelim, Margola and Cillian, Orpheus and Ezra and finally Lavinia Drach, as if she had already been crowned queen. They had dressed in purple robes like royalty, with the Wildwoods crest stitched above their hearts—only the ill-matching headbands made them ridiculous.

Once the senators had taken their seats, Lavinia approached the lectern, candy-pink lips curved in a benevolent smile.

I sighed as the crowd burst into spontaneous applause.

Orpheus couldn't help himself. He rolled his eyes so hard he must have cricked his neck. I missed his sardonic commentary in my head, but I kept my mental shield up, wanting to protect him from my involuntary thoughts about Ezra. How I missed him. How I didn't know how to find my way back to him. How conflicted I was about giving room to my desire when I had Mirabel to care for.

The remaining senators on the stage, including Ezra, stared straight ahead, their faces studied masks. The Bestiary Minister Helio, whose hair was unkempt at the best of times, seemed to have burned the front of it. Perhaps a mishap with one of his creatures.

"Isn't it favouritism that she gets to open proceedings and address the crowd?" I muttered.

"She is Acting Prime Sorcerer. It's part of the role," said Marina, but her incessant rubbing of the clover tattoo on her wrist revealed she was just as nervous about tonight.

Lavinia's hazel eyes scanned the room. "How wonderful to see so many of you gathered here to make your democratic choice. A choice that, given the lengthy tenure of the previous incumbent, has not been put to the vote in generations. What a delight to have our elf friends here to be part of this historic evening."

A smattering of applause drifted across the room.

"You saved us, Lavinia," called out a fallen angel in the row behind us.

The witch giggled in delight. "Very fetching you all look in your headbands too." Every syllable she uttered quivered with excitement. "As per our laws and traditions, we waited until the night of the full moon to remove the Chest of the Fire Falcon from the Wildwoods vault."

"Cool." A note of sadness filled Mirabel's voice. "My parents would have got a kick out of seeing this."

I reached for her hand.

"Each senator who covets the position of Prime Sorcerer visited the chest during the night. There, they sat in silent repose before seeking to unlock it using all magical abilities at their disposal. Four candidates attempted the feat. One was unsuccessful and felt the full force of the Fire Falcon." She pointed a manicured finger at the bestiary minister's singed hair. "Helio Woodwink is out of the running."

A communal gasp from the crowd and the swelling of anticipation.

Lavinia had them in the palm of her well-creamed hand.

Rayna stepped up to the lectern, her quiet manner a world apart from Lavinia's preening. "It now falls to me to conduct the remainder of the ceremony. Would the three candidates for the position of Prime Sorcerer, as marked by the Fire Falcon, arise."

Three peculiars stood: a witch, a vampire, and a selkie.

Marina snorted as frantic whispering erupted around the vaulted cabin. "The selkie better not win it. That woman's a vacuum into which anything might rush."

I slumped. It was hard to call. In her own way, as the voice of *The Otherworld News*, Margola had as much clout as Lavinia and Orpheus.

Rayna raised her arms in a balletic movement. "Lavinia Drach, Orpheus Might and Margola Silver, show us your marks. The marks that indicate you may enter the ballot."

They lifted their wrists. A feather had been etched into the thin skin there. Margola's was blue like the sea she swam in, Lavinia's sparkling grey like her curls, Orpheus's crimson red for the blood that nourished him.

"The candidates may now speak to outline their vision for the Otherworld. As per our laws, you may use seven words only, seven for the falcons who used to guard these hallowed halls," said Rayna.

Margola's face glistened with a sheen of sweat. Clearly, she disliked being under the lens. She adjusted her cat-eye glasses, smoothed down her chignon and raised her feather. "My voice shall speak for you all."

Orpheus next, his eyes dark with intent. His crimson feather emphasised his dangerous nature. "Our history will guide our future."

"Huh," said Marina. "I was kind of hoping for more from him."

My heart sank. "Bless his cotton socks and his love of history. Not sure it was a vote winner though."

Lavinia held her feather mark aloft. "I will defend you to the death."

The crowd roared in approval and stamped their feet, producing a monstrous wave of sound that made my toes curl, but they were no match for Rayna's skill as a headmistress.

She raised her voice above the din with the authority of a woman who kept wolves at bay and bloodthirsty vampires in check with ease. "It is time to vote. All that is required is a single drop of blood, and Wildwoods will do the rest."

The headmistress unsheathed the dagger from her waist.

I gasped. It was easy to forget the dark underbelly of the Otherworld. To forget the sneaking rats and sharp-beaked crows, the octopus tentacles and dragon fire, how every peculiar here had a skill that could shred your mind or tear your flesh. How, unlike the humdrum world, violence was often the default, not restraint.

Naturally, the vote here would use blood, not paper.

All around us, peculiars responded to Rayna's call. I gawped, awestruck. Out came daggers and kitchen knives, swords and scythes. Long and thin, curved and thick, dual and single edged, razor sharp and rusting. But not all peculiars required weapons. There were hidden familiars and snapping plants. Out came menacing fangs, bark-like claws, protruding bones and greening nails in desperate need of an expert manicurist.

Marina had armed herself with both her knitted needle and scalpel. Mirabel brandished the dessert fork I'd allowed her to take and Echo's fleshy gums had peeled back to reveal the full majesty of his tombstone teeth.

I drew out Transcender, my heart in my mouth.

"Now." Rayna pierced her own palm with her dagger.

A drop of blood emerged and floated to above Orpheus's head, remaining there. As each Otherworld member extracted their blood, crimson pearls floated up into the rafters, journeying to their choice of Prime Sorcerer, until each candidate had a cloud of blood above their heads.

I cut my palm and winced as Mirabel did the same, and our globules of blood joined the rest. Mine, like hers, hovered above Orpheus.

"Gross," she said. "Is that going to drop on them? They could have worn rain jackets. Lavinia has her umbrella, I guess."

"I cast my vote for the vamp," said Marina.

"As did I." The leopard licked his paw. "He is a man of

great wisdom and a little ridiculousness. That is a combination I can vote for."

I frowned. "It's hard to tell from here, but it looks like Ezra voted for his aunt."

Emerald eyes narrowed. "The wolf seems to be in alignment with the majority. The sphinxes and the elves cast their votes for the witch too. She seems to have been running her campaign far longer than the others. A master chess player if I ever saw one. Perhaps wily enough to lead us through this turbulent age."

"Shh." Mirabel fussed with her headband. "Or we'll miss the announcement."

Rayna bounced lightly on her toes. "As determined by the volume of the blood cloud over the candidates, I declare Lavinia Drach the first Prime Sorceress in this great city's history." She raised Lavinia's arm in victory, unleashing a rush of euphoria amongst the crowd.

In the front row, Lavinia's coven sprang up in delight. The crowd followed suit, braying and whooping their joy as if Lavinia's reign would be one of hope. As if the prophecy didn't speak of the coming darkness. As if the Earth would continue to turn through the seasons, despite Gaia's absence. As if a changing of guard at the city's top magical institution could right all the wrongs of the past.

All around us, peculiars recorded the historic moment on mobile phones.

Orpheus, whose cloud had been second largest in size by quite some margin, gave a nod of acceptance. He hadn't had the appetite to run the senate anyway. More's the pity. Margola, however, squirmed with humiliation as her cheeks flushed red. It took courage to put yourself above the parapet, where all could watch the fall. Tomorrow's headline had already been written, though it wouldn't be the one she had dreamt of. Orpheus held out an arm to her, and they returned to the rest of the senate.

"Be seated and quiet, citizens of the Otherworld," said Rayna. "The ceremony is not yet completed."

The air left my lungs as the Chest of the Fire Falcon shuddered before us. Its jutting wing carvings quivered and seemed to expand in length. The locks on the antique chest rattled and sprang apart. I gasped when the lid creaked open just as the three crimson clouds of blood, still floating mid-air, joined together in the shape of a falcon and swooped into the chest. It clamped shut, its padlocks magically locking and its wings becoming inanimate once more.

"Well that was a trip," said Marina. "Who needs drugs when we can watch this shit?"

"Our vote is bound by blood and cannot be easily undone," said Rayna. "There can be no thwarting of a just Prime Sorceress's will. We pledge to be led by her until the Chest of the Fire Falcon is taken from the vault to deem another worthy. As per tradition, our ceremony concludes with the new incumbent of the role issuing her first and only decree that is not subject to approval by the rest of the senate."

Rayna stepped back, leaving the stage to the Lavinia.

The new Prime Sorceress smiled with the radiance of a thousand suns. "I decree that the Sorcerer's Senate be renamed the Peculiars' Senate to signal how we work for the benefit of all."

The vaulted cabin echoed with thunderous applause.

Marina's droll voice in my ear. "She's quite the reformer."

I rolled my eyes. "Let's hope she puts the apostrophe in the right place."

The witch knew how to play to the crowd. She whipped off her Wildwoods robes and picked up her dull brown umbrella. Her lips moved silently as she murmured a spell. The silken swathes hanging from the rafters rippled like the sea, eliciting gasps from the crowd as they turned from gold to pink.

Heaven help us. I knew instinctively that the white Armada-like drapes of the Wildwoods cabins had been turned pink too.

Echo shaped his fearsome jaw into something approaching a smile. "The witch and I have much in common. She, too, likes to mark her territory."

Lavinia turned to her senate and beckoned Ezra to her side, as if she was anointing him as her deputy. Their djinn-defence headbands looked like wreaths. Ezra bent to press a kiss against her cheeks, and together, they stepped off the stage and walked through the cheering crowd to the great doors. I searched for Ezra's eyes, craving the warmth of their copper grey, the knowledge that we were always on the same side, even if we were pulled in different directions.

When he walked past without a second look, the pit of my stomach churned.

Flinar bounced over us, his sail-like ears quivering with awe. "Isn't it wonderful? A new chapter in Otherworld history. How marvellous to have a Peculiars' Senate. The elves can rest easy knowing we have an ally right at the top of the senate."

He darted off to join the torrent of peculiars surging behind them into the moonlit night where canopies of trees and pink fabric swayed in celebration of the new Queen of Wildwoods.

Calypso appeared in the throng, towering above us in her blade runners, resplendent in blue-tipped dreadlocks and her Wildwoods gown over a trouser suit. She murmured in my ear. "So another chapter begins. How glad I am to be tucked away amongst the stars in the Celestial Library so I don't have to witness all this nonsense. Although, I do have a mind to visit my family in the Caribbean. Perhaps you have time for that swap day in the library, so I can entrust my Custodian responsibilities to you for a short while?"

"I wish I could. But Mirabel's finding things hard since

her parents died. It's not the right time." I pushed down the niggling feeling that I was breaking my promise to Gaia to find the Book of Names.

But Mirabel needed me. I couldn't go gallivanting around the universe.

"Very well." Calypso's lips tightened. "Another time perhaps."

Together, we craned our necks to catch a glimpse of Lavinia and Ezra. They rode the first cable car down to the level of the arena, where an Otherworld taxi waited to ferry them onwards. When the rope bridges rocked precariously and the crowd jostling became too much, we said our goodbyes to Calypso and moved away from the bustle.

Mirabel tapped my shoulder, her fairy nature piqued. "I don't understand, Alisha. Why didn't Ezra teleport them away? Or they could have ridden Lavinia's umbrella. It's weird to bring a taxi into Wildwoods. It disturbs nature."

I shrugged. "Lavinia likes the hoo-ha. I'm surprised she didn't plan fireworks to mark the occasion. That Otherworld taxi is like her version of a bridal car. I wonder if Lavinia realises that, just like marriages, politics can easily go wrong."

Echo's emerald eyes gleamed. "What's our plan now? It's not like we have ever fallen in line with the Prime Sorcerer. We might be an ageing crew, but we are still rebels."

I took a deep breath. "We start fixing everything that is broken. And that begins by resurrecting Gaia."

Marina shook her head, whispering so Mirabel couldn't hear. "I thought you were going to come clean with Ezra tonight and lay it all out on the table, like every damn thing. Your naked booty on the kitchen table so he can eat you up like you're a slice of tiramisu."

A stab of pain in my chest. Maybe he'd leap out of the car. Maybe he'd feel the need to see me too. A swell of disappointment came over me as the Otherworld taxi as sped off into the night, kicking up a cloud of sawdust in the arena.

"Oh, honey, I'm sorry," said Marina.

I put on a brave face for Mirabel. "It's okay. It wasn't the right time."

Part of me had expected the night to end like this. I had my duty to Mirabel, and Ezra had his duty to Lavinia. I'd tussled with her over him before. I knew how determined she was. Take tonight. Every cell in that woman's body, from her pink-tipped toenails to her glossy helmet of hair, had been coded with purpose. There had never been any doubt that Lavinia was destined for the greatest heights. I'd seen time and time again how, during the slippery climb to power, moral values and compassionate intelligence mattered less than pure ambition.

I wished I didn't have reservations about her.

But I couldn't help thinking that the Otherworld had chosen the wrong person all over again.

And that she was dragging Ezra along for the ride.

9

When the crowds had dispersed, the four of us rode a cable car down from the treetops to ground level. By now, the clock had struck two A.M. My body had grown accustomed to adventures while the city slept, but the fragile skin around my eyes didn't thank me for it. I had more fine lines than crushed velvet.

I pulled my jacket tightly around me, edging up the collar to ward off the cold. Our breath, even the leopard's, was a fog of condensation. Mirabel blew shapes with her frosty breath. I marvelled at the snapshot of her innocence, when free from the quicksand of grief.

"It feels different out here." Marina scanned the vista of the park.

The trees curled unnaturally, but I shook off the frisson of fear snaking up my spine.

"Try to relax. We can't wear the headbands forever, but we're safe enough." The voice at our rear made me jump. A shadowy figure loomed into vision, dressed all in black, his pale skin making him look like a floating head to bleary eyes.

"Orpheus!"

"Were you intending to leave without saying a word tonight?" said the vampire.

"I was so glad you decided to run as a candidate. I would have said goodbye, but it's late. I need to get Mirabel into bed."

He nodded. "I heeded your advice. Someone needed to challenge the witch's ego. A Lavinia-Margola match up would have been akin to Muhammad Ali fighting a scrapper from the schoolyard. I did my duty and put myself forward, although it was a great relief not to win. However this ends, the fault cannot be laid at my door."

Marina giggled. "Said with a vampire's true optimism."

But he only had eyes for me. "You have yet to give me an answer, Alisha. A man like me doesn't often put his heart on the line."

Marina whistled. "I don't need to be an empath to sense those unresolved issues. I'm going to catch the night bus."

I reached out for her. "Wait for me. We'll go together.

"You take your time. Rob will be waiting up for me," said Marina. "Give her a ride home in that sleek penis extension of yours, will you, Orpheus?"

I waited until she was out of earshot then bit the bullet. "Orpheus, I'm sorry. You're always there for me. I value our friendship so much, and maybe, there could have been something between us but..."

"You're still in love with Neuhoff."

I nodded. "I am."

"Well then, Alisha," he said stiffly. "Forgive me for my unwanted affection."

"Orpheus, I'm flattered. I really am."

He frowned. "Kidnapping your ex-husband diminished my chances, didn't it?"

"Actually, as horrified as I was in the moment, I love that you did that for me." I ached for him. "You're important to me, Orpheus. As a friend and colleague. I was hoping we could put our heads together tomorrow to help me figure out how to resurrect Gaia with or without Pan's help. There must be something I'm missing."

Orpheus pressed his lips tightly together. "Back to business then. Only with an eroded friendship because I no longer have access to your thoughts."

"Not diminished. That was an act of generosity." I pulled the amethyst-and-rose quartz ring he had given me from my middle finger. "You should take this back."

"I bought it for you. It is yours to keep." His face shuttered, as if he had reverted back to the formal, friendless vampire I had first met. "I will take my leave. We should avoid each other for a time. Goodnight, Alisha."

He spun on his heels and veered in another direction, as if he couldn't bear to spend a moment more with me.

Replacing the ring on my finger, I watched his retreat with a heavy sigh. Time to get my troops home.

The quietness of the park settled over me like snow over a mountain. I stiffened, intuition pinging. I heard neither chatter from Mirabel nor rustling as the leopard climbed the trees. My chest tightened, and my awareness of my environment deepened as I spun in a slow circle.

Dense creepers clinging to a pine tree on my left. The withered canopy of a willow tree. Moss-covered lawn beneath my feet.

A deafening silence, as if even the creepy crawlies had gone underground.

Mirabel, kneeling on the ground, picking mushrooms by moonlight, with Echo dozing next to her.

Her headband lay discarded at her side, earbuds in her ears. A typical pre-teen blocking out the world.

"Bel, put on your headband," I cried out to no avail. "We are not alone."

My stomach rock hard, I pulled Transcender from my

baldric and dashed towards her, dropping my mental shield. *Orpheus, we're in trouble. I need you.*

A scream built in my throat as a creature appeared beside Mirabel, made from an ephemeral substance that solidified before our eyes. As if it came not from the real world but from embers of nightmares.

The creature wasn't clothed and had a primordial power such that the very trees seemed to prostrate. Its body was a compact mass of fiery bones and smoky, sinewy flesh, with monkey-like limbs and two stunted, protruding wings. A muscular horned head turned in my direction. A decaying soul glimmered in the darkness of its pupilless eyes. Smoke escaped curved nostrils set within a gaunt nose, and a ridged tongue darted out.

It edged towards Mirabel, its thick tail twirling behind it, each movement scraping the soil.

"It's the djinn," I shouted to Echo, but still the leopard slept, as if caught in a fairy-tale slumber.

Too late. Too late for Mirabel to put on her headband. Too late for me to protect her. Too late for me to tuck her into bed, away from all the things that went bump in the night.

I couldn't give up. A mere three feet remained between them.

I called the winds with my left palm and pushed Mirabel and her errant headband away from the fairy ring of mushrooms. Horror painted her face as she slammed backwards, out of the reach of the djinn, her earbuds scattering across the soil. I did the same with Echo, praying I didn't damage his spine as his body arced and slid down the bark. I held the sword aloft in my right hand, an involuntary battle cry tumbling out of my dry mouth as I drove the sword into the djinn.

Suddenly, Orpheus was at my side, fangs already finding their place in demon flesh.

You came back for me, I said.

Of course, he replied.

The djinn's slanted nostrils gave out intense heat I could feel on my skin. It screeched.

Not in pain but in glee.

My sword didn't meet the resistance of flesh. Instead, Orpheus and I stumbled into each other, mouths aghast as our target evaporated and formed again a few feet away.

"Echo's not waking up, Alisha," called out Mirabel.

But my attention was fixed on the creature, aware that any false move could cost us our lives.

"I am Morpheus." The creature's mouth cracked open into a smile of introduction as a dozen djinn gathered around him, each a mirror of his original form.

Time skewed as my breath burst in and out.

We were so exposed out here, outnumbered, with my daughter at risk. The sphinxes weren't even back in position. I had no choice but to brandish my sword like a loony to scare off the djinn, but they stayed in situ, awaiting Morpheus's orders.

Light flared as Mirabel lit a ball of fire in her hands. She struggled to control it, before throwing it at the closest djinn.

Panic gripped me.

"Stop!" Dad and Alma had told me that djinn were attracted to fire.

The djinn absorbed the fire into its black skin and grew larger.

Mirabel recoiled. "I'm sorry."

"It's going to be all right, Bel. I promise," I said.

"That's debatable. I'm not sure you should be making a promise you can't keep," said Orpheus. "That group of horrors is enough to make a vampire pray. I'm a little sad that I didn't go out on a high of bedding you, Alisha, before I crumble into a pile of dust." He stared at the leader of the creatures with disdain. "You can't be Orpheus. I'm Orpheus."

The creature thrust out its chest. "M-orpheus. With an M.

The world has indeed gone to shit if you have to stop mid-attack to explain one's name. Oh, what the hell."

It grew in form, elongating, until its horns and wings disappeared and its face grew flatter and more human-like. Shadows slipped around it, until it became a bearded man, clothed in a silver catsuit, with a gaunt face, ginger hair and a poppy pinned to his breast.

Behind him, his army of djinn fidgeted, pupilless eyes turned in our direction like some sort of misfire of a zombie apocalypse.

The vampire's tone was droll. "Orpheus with an M. Are we supposed to fear you in that get-up? You look like a misjudged entry into an ABBA competition at a local fair."

My eyes narrowed. "I recognise you. You were at Stonehenge when Gaia died. You're the god of dreams."

Morpheus played with his poppy. "Indeed I am, as your leopard has found out."

My gaze flitted to Echo, being nursed by Mirabel. My heart wrenched at his flailing limbs, caught in some nightmare of the dream god's making. Mirabel had mercifully put her headband back on, at least.

I returned my focus to the god.

You're quicker than me, I said to Orpheus in my mind. *Get Mirabel back into Wildwoods.*

This god can make his bodily form evaporate and reform. We don't even know what other forms he has or if the yew tree can keep him from Wildwoods. What makes you think Mirabel will be safe there or that I'd leave you alone with him when he possesses an army of grotesque creatures to do his bidding? said Orpheus.

Morpheus waved his spangly arm. "Helloooo. I can hear your thoughts, by the way. But carry on. I'm a patient man. I'll wait."

I shot Orpheus a look, hoping that he would do my bidding while I distracted Morpheus. "You weren't wearing that outfit at Stonehenge."

Morpheus pouted, pulling it off surprisingly well through his ginger beard. "Death prefers a more sombre look than disco diva. It was different when she dated Gaia. Their love story was so grand that Death embraced colour. She even wore sequinned saris and glittery Indian bangles on her many arms. But you know how it is when one partner in the couple is so blinded by love that they lose their identity. It was bound to end in disaster." He winced. "It made Death even more psychopathic than before. So here we are. With the Father of the Gods dead and Death as the grand dame of us all remaking the earth in her image. Far easier now Gaia's out of the way, of course." The god made a show of yawning at Orpheus. "Your kind are curious things. Your minds are closed off to me unless you are in your deepest sleep. It took me some practice to gain access even then, but in the 1920s, I discovered a practice subject in the basement of a castle in Madrid. I spent a few weeks boring into his mind while he slept in his coffin. Right now, I can't see into your head, but as we both know, behaviour patterns are an easy thing to predict when you live as long as we do. I suspect right now you're considering using your unnatural vampire speed to strongarm the girl and the leopard out of here and then return to your lady friend."

The vampire glowered at the god and his djinn army, fangs at the ready.

"I'm afraid you'll be unsuccessful. But do have a go, dearest. I promised my djinn army some fine viewing tonight. They're very excited to see me in action." The god's tone hardened. "I ask again, druid. Aren't you curious to know what I want?"

Planting my feet in a wide stance, I deepened my breath the way Rayna had taught me to do before a significant draw on my druid skills. I lifted my chin, disdain filling me. "I already know what gods like you want. I know from your place in the Stonehenge circle that you mean me and my kind harm. That you lust after power and that whatever form you take, Morpheus, you don't have a compassionate bone in your body. Or else you'd know better than to accost a woman and her child in the middle of a park late at night."

The god played with the zipper on his silver catsuit. "The thing is, as the god of dreams, I tend to operate at night. It's part of my whole"—he spread his hands in a wide circle as if he was a showgirl—"shebang."

Alma had told me that djinn were made from fire and how water was the key to their destruction. Now was the time to put my research to use. The research I'd done late at night, when I'd sacrificed reading a novel and instead picked up one of Marina's veterinary textbooks or my parents' mythology books, to soak up all the knowledge I could find about all the winged creatures under the sun. Real ones and ones from the imagination. Ones that could be found on different continents, ones that existed in the here and now and others long extinct. Because as surely as the sun rises, I had known the day would come when another rogue god would cross my path and being prepared was my ammunition.

It wasn't like I could unleash a pterodactyl or a phoenix on the world without breaking the Founder's Law and rousing the suspicion of every humdrum in London about the existence of magic.

But every iota of learning helped fuel my imagination and my resolve.

I inhaled deeply and wrenched images from my mind. I'd been able to animate multiple creatures since my surge of powers at Stonehenge, but I had to pace myself. That much creation made me weak. It was not something I could do over and over again, though the Jericho necklace at my neck helped me to recover sooner. It was a battle tactic that I had to employ at the right time.

But I had learned a new skill, practiced in the garden of the cottage. A skill I had never attempted under pressure.

Tonight, it could save our lives.

My heartbeat accelerated, and my fingers twitched in mid-air as I called thirteen waxwings forth, assigning them a clear purpose. The birds emerged from the firing synapses of my imagination, not directly in front of me, but on the banks of the lake in Crystal Palace Park. I felt them claw their way out of my thoughts into the threads of the world.

Then I collapsed onto my knees to the sound of Mirabel's cry of terror and a flurry of cursing from Orpheus as he rushed to my side.

They came, a flock of waxwings, their arrival heralded by the rolling bell-like trill of their call. As they journeyed towards us, they each carried a beakful of water from the lake. In the dense night, their beauty was hard to discern, but when their plump bodies swooped above the djinn, I picked out their striking crests, the reddish-brown plumage and black throat, black eye masks that reminded me of superheroes on morning television in my childhood and bright displays of yellow on their tails.

A flash of surprise crossed Morpheus's face as he looked up.

The waxwings poured the water from their beaks onto Morpheus and the djinn. The djinn shrieked as the water hit their fiery bones and sinewy flesh. They writhed, their grotesque faces dissolving before our eyes, their wings snapping and shrivelling as the mischievous waxwings circled overhead, trilling in celebration that their purpose had been fulfilled.

All apart from one, whose trilling had a mournful note.

Because Morpheus still lived.

I wanted to be angry at you. Orpheus helped me to my feet. *Now I find myself in love with you all over again. It's most inconvenient.*

Morpheus's gaunt face flickered with emotion in the

moonlight, the lock of ginger hair on his forehead drenched, a trickle of water running down his nose.

In it, I read irritation and incredulity. What I didn't read was fear. My chest tightened as realisation dawned. We were still in danger. A djinn wasn't Morpheus's original form, merely a form he adopted.

He couldn't be killed by water droplets rained down on him by a waxwing.

But a woman in midlife wasn't one to sit down and give up at a setback. A woman in midlife had learned that life wasn't always smooth sailing. When things went wrong, as they always did, cursing was a great stress reliever. Likewise, a decent brew of tea in your favourite mug, a bubble bath or an afternoon nap. Singing along to a Madonna song at high volume often helped too or dancing in the rain, even if your boobs went in different directions and you were soaked through to the skin. When things went wrong, there were always coping mechanisms.

But the end result was always the same. You dusted yourself off and had another go. And if all else failed, kicking an annoying man in the nuts was always a good last resort. Even if he was a god.

Especially when that god was distracted.

I took a running leap and dropkicked Morpheus's family jewels, simultaneously slashing with the Death's sword, capable of wounding an immortal. Orpheus joined me, his fists raised, pummelling with vampire speed, fangs out. I howled with frustration as again our onslaught did not land.

The god dissipated, disappearing from sight, and re-emerged frighteningly close to Mirabel.

I didn't know how to end this, and the fear of failing my daughter ate me up from inside.

Morpheus smirked and stroked his ginger beard in a way that screamed weirdo. "I suppose I can give you some credit for your perseverance tonight. It was quite innovative how you managed to deal with my djinn, but I can summon a hundred more to me to replace the ones that perished."

Orpheus smoothed down his clothes, dishevelled from our attempt to overpower the god, and adjusted his cufflinks. "I would have thought that the god of dreams wouldn't cavort with djinn, especially djinn of malicious intent. The gods are above such small creatures, are they not?"

"My dear boy, I'm afraid these days all sorts of creatures cavort with one another. Since the big guy in the sky fell, there's no one to put on the brakes." Morpheus looked at me in surprise. "Oh, those thoughts of yours are a wild ride. You think that He is alive. And that Gaia is saveable."

I spat the words. "She is."

"Is she though? That's the thing about believers. They're often delusional. It's why we like them. Take you and your sweet belief that your tiny sword could damage me. It has, of course, cut a pound of flesh from lesser gods. But how can you kill me if you can't even meet the target? You can keep it, as far as I'm concerned. You see, I'm more dangerous than the gods you have met so far. I can't influence the harvest or the seasons. I can't manipulate heat or electricity. I can't control the herds or cause earthquakes. I have no powers of seduction and can't determine a man's fate with an inking. Neither can I open portals or spread disease. I hold no dominion over death. But I, druid, am so much more. I can decipher the very nature of your dreams and fears. I can enter your head until no essence of you remains. And that makes you putty in my hands." He levelled a superior look at me. "Now will you ask me what I want?"

"What do you want, Morpheus?" *I* didn't want him anywhere near my girl. I met his eyes, glacial pools, with one blue and one green iris, and held my breath.

He folded his arms across his sinewy chest. "I want you to stop looking for the Book of Names. Or I will be forced to take the person you dreamt of."

My blood turned to ice. I glanced at Mirabel, a stupid reflex when I should have known better.

Morpheus smiled. "Yes, Alisha Verma, you understand now."

I glared at him. "She is protected from you. You can't hurt her."

He snorted. "Are you serious? Is she really going to wear that fashion monstrosity all her life? What about when she washes her hair or goes to her first disco or has her first kiss? Are you going to demand she always wear that luminous witch-manufactured jerry cloth? Judging by tonight, the moment you turn your back, the girl will take a risk. Gods live long lives, Alisha Verma. I'm quite ready to wait until the perfect moment to destroy her happily ever after. Poor poppet. How sad would it be for it all to go wrong after she has lived through her own nightmare."

Never bargain with the forces of evil, said Orpheus. *He can't be trusted.*

My mind raced, working out my options. The headband had been a solution that Lavinia had cobbled together at the very last minute. Maybe she could improve upon it. She could find a less obtrusive way to protect against the djinn. A small piece of cloth stitched into our underwear or a crystal stashed in our clothes. And I wouldn't have to worry about Mirabel discarding her protection, and with every day of increased maturity, she would understand how to keep herself safe.

Morpheus ejected a hearty laugh as he wiped glittering sleep dust from his eyes. "You really fell for that elaborate spiel? It's quite amusing that you are the Otherworld's only hope. A gullible opponent is my favourite kind. Did you *really* think that a headband could keep me out of the girl's head?"

I called out in anguish as the god discarded his physical form, becoming a stream of glimmering moonlit particles. I raised my hands to disrupt their passage with a current of wind, but the particles simply separated and reformed, adjusting their course, flowing into Mirabel's nostrils with sickening purpose.

The girl gasped, and her features distorted as they had in the infirmary, losing their softness and youth.

When she spoke, her voice wasn't hers. It was lower in range, brittle and mocking. "See how easy it was to leap into this head, disrupt her thoughts and plant the seeds of nightmares? The choice is yours, Alisha Verma. You can surrender this tiresome overreach of yours and forget the Book of Names and any attempts to meddle in immortal affairs. Be a happy family or imperil your new charge's safety. It's up to you. I will be watching, and I will be ready."

Mirabel slumped as the dream god left her body in a whoosh of particles that surged over the treetops.

I was at her side in a heartbeat, cradling her face as it became hers once more.

Echo roused from his sleep. His body slackened with relief at the sight of us and raced off in the direction of the god with a roar, causing the waxwings—loitering in a nearby tree—to trill in fright.

Mirabel flinched as her consciousness returned. "What happened? Is he still here?"

"He's gone, Bel." I exchanged glances with Orpheus. Could I turn a blind eye to the rogue gods to have the family I'd always wanted?

Her pale, tearstained face broke my heart. "Is he going to come back?"

It was a mother's job to shield her children. "Let me worry about that. Come on. There's a rowan tree in the car park the waxwings might like. They're partial to berries. Then we need to get you into bed."

I only hoped that the nightmares didn't follow.

10

————————

A woman with a difficult decision to make required a close circle of family and friends around her. Those loved ones might simply listen, ask provoking questions or offer their own wisdom. That didn't mean the woman failed to rely on her own intuition but that a circle of collaborative support meant success more likely than being a lone cowgirl.

So I did the only thing a woman in the modern world could do when her child slept but she needed help.

I arranged a video call with my nearest and dearest.

At the appointed time, I beckoned Echo to my side and set myself up in the cottage living room, far enough away from Mirabel to keep the delicate conversation from her ears and close enough to the router to prevent the internet connection from crashing out. Six squares of loved ones populated the screen of my laptop: Dad and Alma, Marina and the detective, Fei Yen and Faeza, Ezra, Orpheus and Sahil, who had texted out of the blue with news to share. It felt like my very own senate.

Only Gaia was missing.

Dad's nose loomed large on the video screen. He found it difficult to know how to position his face in relation to the camera. His moustache twitched with emotion. "Wonderful to see you all. Thank you for the package of medicines you sent, Fei Yen and Faeza. They arrived yesterday. I've already seen a difference in the size of my verruca."

"Of course, Joshi. We are happy to look after you," said Fei Yen.

"Perhaps I can speak to you about my dry skin affliction," said Orpheus.

The foxes nodded, synchronised as ever, like two halves of one soul. "It would be our pleasure."

"Anyone else want a consultation for minor ailments?" Echo purred. "The rest of us are finding this conversation thrilling."

"You mock me, leopard, as you have always done, but it's hard being a pensioner when adventure calls," said Dad. "I'm lucky you can prepare my prescriptions of course, Fei Yen and Faeza, but there are difficulties. Exploring the world is a great privilege, but there is always a yearning for familiar places and faces."

"He misses his studio," said Alma. "He pines for it like a newborn baby pines for its dummy."

Dad's brow furrowed. "Nonsense. I miss my son and daughter's faces."

I smiled. "We miss you too, Dad. Don't we, Sahil?"

My brother cocked his head. "Yes, I think of you as soon as my eyes open in the morning. Even when I have a hot blonde in my bed."

"Sahil, maybe angle the camera away from your package," I said.

He grumbled. "I was showing Marina what she is missing."

Marina gave the camera a tongue-in-cheek thumbs-up, while Rob directed a death stare at it.

Echo barrelled on, not reading the room. "What kind of

bed were you talking about? A bird nest or a king-size four-poster? Pigeon or human sex?"

Alma frowned. Clearly, only she and Dad were allowed to go public with their bedroom shenanigans. "So Lavinia Drach is Prime Sorceress. That figures. She's always had her eye on the prize."

Marina, her laptop stacked on a pile of books, had her lighting just so to show off the sheen of her newly dyed hair. "She's living her best life, Alma. She's taken to travelling in a fleet of Otherworld taxis and gets an office at Wildwoods now too."

"Dad, can you mute yourself when you're not speaking? There's a lot of heavy breathing going on there," I said.

"Sorry, love."

Ezra looked exhausted but gave Dad a fond smile. "She's stamped her mark on it too. Phinnaeous's office held a desk like an altar, a map of the galaxy, books of pressed butterflies, lamps everywhere and a flickering candle that never went out. Lavinia's tossed it all out. She has an Ikea desk and chair, a pink futon, an exercise bike, a stack of umbrellas and an ashtray of cigarette butts, even though she doesn't smoke and has always chided me for it. You know how health conscious my aunt is."

"I've got to say, mate, after the rollercoaster with Phinnaeous Shine, I couldn't be more relieved," said Rob. "Your aunt and I have had a rapport for years, going right back when I started visiting Baba Yaga's as a junior member on Shadow Squad. I can do business with her."

Ezra frowned. "Alisha, are you okay? You're very quiet."

God, I missed him. "Actually, I arranged this call because I need some advice."

They listened as I filled them in on the previous night's events, mouths aghast, with the exception of Orpheus, who'd lived through it with me.

Dad was the first to speak. "Alma, we need to get back to

London. Alisha needs us. Or better still, come to Bulgaria with Mirabel. We'll protect you. We have the dragon. Alma can throw flour in the dream god's eyes if he tries to get lairy. I'll keep a pocketful of chilli with me in case things go really south."

I frowned. British women were limited in their choice of self-defence weapons. A can of deodorant, holding keys between our fingers or a knee in the sausage and eggs were options. But Dad's advice had been to throw chilli in an assailant's eyes. "I don't need a knight in shining armour, Dad. I just need your counsel."

Ezra was grim-faced. He pulled off his headband. "So these things my aunt concocted aren't a solution after all?" He swore under his breath, crassly enough for Alma to flush red. "You could have been hurt, Alisha. Mirabel too. We can't take this lying down."

Orpheus snapped. Their scuffle at the cottage had left a simmering distrust between them. "I was there, Neuhoff. We didn't take it lying down, but our magic has limited impact on the dream god and Mirabel is at risk."

"I'm not sure the camera is getting my best side, Alisha, and I want to look my best when I make my apology." The leopard let out a fart so squeaky it sounded like the release of air from a balloon.

I looked at him in disgust, but his majestic face looked so unmoved that it seemed like my rear end was the culprit. Sahil sniggered, and Orpheus raised an eyebrow that seemed to suggest I needed pharmaceutical help from the foxes too, while the rest were too polite to mention the offending sound.

"What I was trying to say when I was so rudely interrupted is that I'm sorry for sleeping through my protection duties," said Echo. "Let me assure you that it was no restorative sleep. I was submitted to a recurring nightmare in which the butcher's was always closed and you couldn't get those freezer steaks I so adore, Alisha. Still, it is an oversight of Shakespearean tragedy. I will submit myself to the currents of the river Thames if you deem it so."

"Actually, Echo, I suspect even your sleeping body next to Mirabel made her less likely to give up in that moment because she had to take care of you," said Marina. "Otherwise, she could have felt alone out there."

"Mirabel's already lost so much," I said. "I don't doubt my abilities to take on the dream god, especially with all of you at my side. But now I have her, my priorities have changed. She comes first. I need you all to tell me that I'm doing the right thing. That it's okay to hang up my sword and the Jericho necklace and just do what's right for me and Mirabel."

Their silence clawed under my skin. I tugged my sleeve down over my scar, the map that reminded me of my gutlessness. The one that would forever symbolise how I had abandoned my duty for personal gain.

"Is anyone going to say anything?" I prompted.

"I would choose family over the world," said Orpheus quietly.

"As would we." Fei Yen and Faeza smiled at one another.

"And me," mouthed Dad to the camera before unmuting himself and giving us a close-up view of his nose hair. He backed away and put his arm around Alma. "It's enough for me when the world shrinks to a point, as long as my loved ones are safe."

Alma sighed. "I am sorry, my love, but I disagree. Nothing is ever that simple. Our relationships with loved ones and with the world are symbiotic. Can we be happy if the world burns? I think not."

Echo's green eyes were solemn. "I agree with the flour seer. The great Rajika Verma laid down her life for the world, and I learned by her example. I am sorry, Alisha. But sometimes it is necessary to sacrifice personal happiness for the good of all. Like when a leopard accepts to wear the glamour of a domestic cat."

Marina bit her lip. "I know you don't want to hear this, but you're dragging your feet because you're scared of losing Mirabel. But what if, by doing nothing, you lose her? You remember the school playground. We learned pretty fast that, whenever anyone gave us an ultimatum, we'd tell them where to stick it," said Marina. "Why would it be any different now?"

Dad groaned. "No wonder you two were always in trouble."

Bitterness filled my mouth. "What about you, Ezra? What do you think? Do you feel this way? That I could be doing more?"

He ran a hand over his face, sighing. When he faced the camera, his eyes were molten grey and copper and oh so true. "You can't abandon your identity as the eternal girl. It's who you are. The identity you fought to uncover. But that doesn't mean you have to sacrifice your dreams. You can have whatever you want. You just need to be willing to fight for it."

Rob nodded. "We have a responsibility to the world, or our families won't be safe. Let me find out all I can about Morpheus. He has to have a weak point."

Sahil put his hand up. "I know no one's that interested in my opinion, but I have something that might tip the decision one way or another. I didn't disappear off the radar because I was being a wanker. I swore I'd make it up to you all, and I meant it."

Faeza gave a heavy sigh. She'd never truly forgive him for attacking Fei Yen.

"There are so many pigeons in this city that I thought, why not take advantage? So I went undercover to spy on the gods. I had to be careful, of course—"

Dad loomed towards the camera. "You're so brave, son."

"Ra could easily turn me into barbecue wings. Hermes knows his birds and would see through me in an instant. Mami Wata's essentially half fish, so she was hard to track.

But the dream god. He stands out in his spangly silver catsuit. Not many men who strut about in that get-up. Even with my distorted pigeon vision, I was able to track his repeated visits to a nightclub on Old Compton Street."

"What did you find out?" I said.

"That the dream god can't resist disco music."

My irritation swelled. "That can't be all?"

Echo honked with laughter. "Well, that's one bit of good news. We're past the point of no return regarding attracting djinn, so I guess it's okay for me to sing again. It might even win us favour with the disco diva dream god."

My brother cocked his head to one side. "Don't you all see? You can't kill him with Transcender because he dissipates, and you don't have the Book of Names yet so you can't control him. But you can distract him with disco music."

"Huh," Rob stared at his phone. "Looks like a man matching Pan's description has popped up Gaia's flat in Tooting again."

Alma feigned upset. "Oh, that's terrible. With us abroad, you must go and check it out, Alisha." Former actress that she was, she almost pulled it off, had it not been for the sly look in her eyes.

"I would have thought that was a job for the Shadow Squad," said Dad.

"No dear," said Alma, firmly. "Gaia's home is sacred. It's no place for red-faced men with dirty feet and truncheons. No offence, Detective."

"None taken," said Rob. "I can tell the team not to engage, if that's what you want, Alisha?"

"I'll go with you," said Orpheus. "If you need a wingman."

Ezra's voice was a possessive growl. "No, I'll take her. It'll be quicker to teleport. That way, we stand a chance of working out what Pan is up to."

Echo nuzzled my shoulder. "I'll watch over Mirabel and defend her to my dying breath. You can count on me."

"That's settled." My ears caught a rustling from the bedroom that indicated Mirabel was awake. "Whatever my next steps, one thing is certain—I can't bow out to a quiet life until Gaia is back where she belongs."

I POURED Mirabel some chocolate cereal and pushed the chipped bowl and a spoon towards her. "I'll be back before you know it. Do you remember I told you about my friend Gaia? I just have to check on her home so it's intact for her when she comes back."

The fairy stabbed at her breakfast with the spoon, eyes narrowing. Her short hair was more knotted than ever. "What if the dream god makes an appearance?"

"You don't need to worry. Ezra and I have all the skills we need to make it home safe in one piece." Still, I heard the dream god's warning in my ears, telling me not to meddle in immortal affairs. But I had no choice. After all Gaia had done for me, I had to help her.

Ezra teleported into the living room, calling out his arrival. "Hello? Everyone decent in here?"

Mirabel placed her cereal spoon on the counter and eyeballed him. "Bring Alisha home, or I'll dislike you forever."

Ezra held his hands up. "Whoa, what have I walked into? You dislike me?"

"You broke her heart, didn't you?" said the girl.

My breath caught in my throat as I laced up my trainers, wriggled into my baldric and adjusted Transcender on my back. I opened my mouth to defend Ezra, but he responded first.

"No, Mirabel. She broke mine. But that's okay." He met

my eyes, and my belly flipped. "Because broken hearts mend, and sometimes, they signpost what is important to us so if we get a second chance, we can grab it with both hands."

I swallowed hard as I stood to hug Mirabel, and her arms tightened around me. "Marina and Orpheus are on speed dial on the kitchen phone if you need them," I said. "Echo's not going to leave your side."

Humming the tune to "I'll be Watching You", Echo slinked into the kitchen. "That's right. I'll be an inch away, even when you are doing a peepee."

Mirabel's groans followed us as I stepped into Ezra's arms. When we disappeared between the folds of the world, my head rested against his chest and the air squeezed out of lungs, and I didn't know whether it was being with Ezra or the pressure exerted by the forces of teleportation that made it so. His arms around me weren't polite. He held me low on my waist—not a friend's grip—but a lover's. As if I was precious cargo entrusted solely to him.

We materialised in Gaia's front garden in Tooting as the midmorning sun hid behind a stack of smoking terracotta chimneys.

It pained me to find her magnificent garden dead and wilting, when once it had bloomed even in unseasonable weather. Now, flower heads drooped, overcome by weeds and devoured by snails. The deterioration had accelerated even faster than naturally should have been possible. As if the garden itself were in mourning. As if it couldn't bear to be beautiful without the Earth goddess there to admire and tend to it. As if her absence had been a death knell.

Ezra unclasped his hands from around my waist and whistled low and long. "She's really gone, isn't she?"

"Not for long, I hope," I said. "You didn't have to come with me."

"The hell, I didn't." His voice was gruff, his gaze

searching. "Is there something going on between you and Orpheus? You wear his ring."

"A gift from a dear friend, that's all." I chewed my lip. "Did you mean what you said to Mirabel? About second chances?"

The hard lines of his face softened. "I did." He squeezed my hand, calloused skin against mine. "Let's talk about it after this, okay? I need to keep my head straight, and you, hellfire, have a way of turning me inside out."

I nodded, heart in my mouth at his use of his name for me. The one that I had once railed against but which now was a reminder of the quirks of our relationship, the things that only he and I shared. We traced the path through the weed-ridden garden to Gaia's sunshine-yellow front door. It was closed, but when Ezra put his hand to the doorknob, it turned with ease.

"Stay close," he mouthed, although I was supposed to be the eternal girl and he shouldn't have worried about me.

Though it was nice that he did. After all, a woman of my age appreciated equality, but we knew it shouldn't come at the expense of tenderness or gentlemanly manners. A man holding the door open of a café, giving up a seat on the tube or offering to drive through the night didn't mean that he was protecting the weaker sex. It simply was his way of showing care, and chivalry done well was an aphrodisiac potent enough to wet a ladies' gusset, granny pants or not.

We tiptoed through the hallway, senses tingling, on high alert for the shepherd god. He might have been harmless enough, but he was still a trickster god. With the curtains drawn and the shutters closed, the flat was shrouded in darkness, despite the light outside. Ezra touched a finger to his moon charm, and a soft light illuminated the room. The difference was stark from the last time I had visited. No neighbourhood children tumbled through the door after us or loitered in Gaia's kitchen. No delicious smells—of spicy curries, freshly baked rotis, cinnamon cookies or cardamom chai—wafted up my nose. No wise words or knowing eyes coaxed my troubles out of my mouth or solved them without judgement. The magnolia walls and framed photographs of local children stood intact, but the warmth had fled the place. Even Gaia's succulents had languished, turning brown at the edges.

Still, although she had gone, Gaia's lingering presence held a sense of home.

We glimpsed the trespasser sitting at her kitchen table, enjoying a *laddu*, a guilty expression on his face. As a mark of respect, he had removed both his shoes and his top hat, allowing us a peek of hairy toes and smooth horns.

Relief flooded me. I'd hoped when the detective had told me about potential sightings of Pan near Gaia's home that, contrary to his protestations, he'd felt more for her plight that he had let on. Listening to my intuition had paid off.

Pan sighed when we approached, patted his mouth with a paper napkin and brushed the crumbs from his maroon tweed suit. "She knew I loved these. I think she kept a batch in the freezer especially for me."

"She had a way of knowing things," I said.

The god sniffed. "Or knowing people. The Tupperware box even had my name on it." He picked a yellow Post-it note out of his breast pocket, dark eyes filled with melancholy as he stared at it.

The language was indecipherable to me. It could have been Aramaic or Hebrew. Who knew what the gods spoke to each other. I knew so much about them and yet so little. Watching this god, here in Gaia's kitchen, I couldn't begin to fathom what shape their relationship had taken over the centuries. Only that Pan seemed to have been touched beyond measure by a bit of her cooking and that food— though presumably not essential sustenance for immortals— had emotional value.

Ezra indicated the panpipes that lay on the table, next to the god's top hat. "Don't get too close."

"It's okay." I pulled out a chair and sat down opposite the god.

"She was always kind to me. Even when I acted out," said Pan.

"Sounds about right," I said.

He frowned. "You want to resurrect her."

I leaned forward. "I made her a promise."

"I am not as strong as her. If they come for me, I might not survive. Without me, the herds would perish. No beef burgers or goats cheese for mortals. What a loss that would be." He picked up his panpipes and twiddled it between his thumb and forefinger.

Ezra shot forward, hackles rising.

I held up a hand, reluctant to interrupt Pan's flow of thought. The poor god seemed incredibly lonely. First, we'd found him sitting in solitude in a dead woman's kitchen, stuffing his face with Indian sweets, made all the more pathetic because they were supposed to be eaten during communal celebrations such as Diwali, Eid and weddings. I mean, if he wanted to eat alone, the proper thing to eat was surely a microwave pizza, followed by a packet of Hobnobs and a large slice of regret. Second, he didn't seem to have anyone to talk to. His isolation from the other gods and Gaia's absence seemed to have made him a gibbering wreck.

Pan glowered at the hilt of my sword, just visible above the collar of my leather jacket. "You didn't kill me."

"No, I didn't."

"But you could have."

I sighed. "I believe so, yes."

"You are different to other mortals who attempt to thwart the gods." His nostrils flared. "You have a humility about you. A softness to your strength."

"It's hard to maintain a tight core at middle age. I like crisps too much."

Ezra rasped. "Christ, Alisha. Accept the compliment."

Pan pushed his shoulders back. His belly protruded through his shirt, no doubt the result of far too many *laddus*. "To the wolf and you, I entrust a secret, Alisha Verma, one you must take to your graves. Because it is dangerous to know the secrets of the gods, and to administer them, and mortals who bear witness to these secrets endanger themselves and may easily find themselves upon the funeral pyre if the fates deem it so."

My stomach hardened with knots. I spun to face Ezra. "Leave. I can do this alone."

His grey eyes flashed copper. "Not a chance, hellfire. We're in this together."

The god turned his dark beady eyes on us. "So be it. Listen carefully, mortals. Since the dawn of time, there have been sacred places and objects that regenerate and restore the gods and their favourites. The Holy Grail, the Fountain of Youth, the Tree of Life, the Garden of Hesperides, the Pyramid of the Sun, the Ka'bah, the Lake of Avalon, the sacred stone Alatyr, to name but a few. To the naked eye or faithless, these places may seem ordinary. But places and rituals hold great power to those who know how to access them. They can heal injuries, wash away sorrows and make what is old new again. They can also bring back a soul from the brink of death or reverse death altogether, as long as too much time has not passed. What Gaia requires is the Rejuvenation Pool in the basement of Shakespeare's Globe Theatre."

11

"You can't be serious." Incredulity coloured Ezra's voice. My heartbeat accelerated. "A Rejuvenation Pool in the heart of London?"

"Some of us did kick up a fuss when the building was constructed on top of it, but you know what theatre types and their patrons are like. Once they get an idea in their head, there is no stopping them." The god glowered. "Of course, there are a number of Rejuvenation Pools dotted around the earth. Gaia told me as much herself when we last discussed it. For some, one must trek through the wilderness or fight off battalions of armed monkeys, so we're quite lucky to have one nearby where quiet reigns once the curtain falls on the performance."

I rubbed my clammy hands on my jeans. "I've been to the Globe. It's a substantial space. Where exactly is the Rejuvenation Pool?"

"Opposite the stage in the middle of the central yard. To those without true sight, it seems to be a puddle. The caretakers of the building have been irritated by it over the years. They have sometimes dug up underground pipes in order to discover a leak. Why should there be a puddle in the middle of the yard on a rainless summer's day? But at the Globe, there are a thousand building maintenance aspects to worry about, and they soon forget."

"So we'll find it easily?"

"Yes, Alisha Verma. I'm afraid you will never again be able to visit the Globe without seeing the Rejuvenation Pool. You will have to sit in the stands at the farthest place away from the central yard, or you will sense the change in humidity around the pit. The slow currents, the rising steam and a slight whiff of sulphur. For when a person with true sight finds the Rejuvenation Pool, it is not a puddle at all. It is a body of water as long as a full-sized bathtub but with limitless depth, potent with possibility." He quivered with excitement. "You will need to submerge Gaia's remains in the Rejuvenation Pool and utter these words: *Shamayim-perakh-ahava-chayim-neshama sheli.* And then wait for her rebirth."

I spluttered, frowning at Ezra rustling behind me. "Come again?"

Pan tutted. "It is Hebrew, druid. You're a languages teacher, aren't you? I have a great hatred of repeating myself, so absorb every flowing phrase, guttural syllable and consonant of harsh grace. *Shamayim-perakh-ahava-chayim-neshama sheli.* Did you get that?"

"Uh huh." Crossing my fingers that Ezra had a good memory, I repeated the words in my head, fearful of forgetting them.

"One word of warning," said Pan.

"Yes?"

"The goddess may suffer some delirium upon reconstitution. This is quite normal with such a delicate process. She should recover, given time. How long, I cannot predict."

I groaned. "What exactly am I supposed to immerse in the Rejuvenation Pool, given that Gaia became ashes on the wind?"

"My dear girl, I'm not a miracle worker." He winked. "But rumour has it you are a wind druid. I would have thought you had that particular problem under control. Indeed, I suspect it's one of the reasons Gaia chose you as the eternal girl."

Anger darkened Ezra's face. "The Earth goddess chose to put Alisha in this position? But the prophecy—"

A bleat-like laugh bubbled out of him. "The Otherworld is so precious about prophecies. But they are nebulous things. Prone to rewriting and reinterpretation. The Earth goddess had a list of mortals who could have been her right-hand woman in this crusade of hers. Alisha Verma merely had the right ingredients in her character and skillset to make her a good option in this grand game."

I laid a hand on Ezra's arm. "It's okay. I'm ready for this."

"I hope so, Alisha Verma. The final battle is only just beginning." Pan placed his top hat back on his thick, brown mop of curly hair. "You may yet wish we had never met."

AFTER PAN HAD GONE, we stood in Gaia's garden, our breath visible in the cool air, while I called the box office of the Globe Theatre and an overly talkative administrative assistant revealed that there were no performances, practices or school visits scheduled that afternoon.

"I'm very sorry. But you'll have to make a booking for another day. Dress warmly when you do come. Remember we operate in all weather scenarios." She snorted with laughter. "As they say, there is no bad weather, only bad clothing."

I hung up. "Well, that's a stroke of good luck."

Ezra's grim expression reignited the fear in my belly. "Let's get this over with."

He clung to me as we zipped across London, through

swirls of monochrome light and substance, the pressure of teleportation bearing down on our bodies before we mercifully surfaced left of the stage of the Globe Theatre.

I caught my breath as he touched the binary code charm on his necklace.

His grey eyes glinted with satisfaction. "That should disrupt any CCTV cameras. Wait here while I double-check we're alone."

Ezra faded from sight as I took in the empty open-air playhouse, a twenty-sided polygon with standing room for seven hundred audience members in its roofless central yard and sheltered gallery for eight hundred more. With its oak beams, lime-plaster walls, water-reed thatched roofing and zodiac signs painted over the stage, the building seemed rooted in the past. In its third incarnation on its original site, Shakespeare's Globe had been home to the country's finest playwrights and actors. It was part of the city's fabric. I had taken my immigrant class here a number of times. I'd seen *The Tempest*, *Othello* and *King Lear* on this very stage.

And had never known that I stood mere feet from the Rejuvenation Pool.

Air particles oscillated as Ezra materialised next to me.

"The coast is clear." His hands rested on my waist, a bittersweet moment of respite. There was so much unsaid between us. "Are you sure about this?"

I nodded, and we stepped off the stage into the central space where, just as Pan had described, a wet patch glistened in the winter light, though there had been no rain and no audience to spill their drinks. I neared it, the hair on my neck rising in anticipation. The puddle widened and lengthened with every step closer. It had neither the clarity of rainwater nor the cloudy dark palette of the Thames. Instead, it was thick, syrupy and brown. My nose wrinkled at its putrid, sulphuric stink.

Ezra gagged. "And I thought Maximillian's back passage emissions after a kebab were bad."

"Do you know how fairy tales present magic as a glittery delight? I'm starting to realise how that is false advertising." I sighed. "Now we've found it, how are we going to summon Gaia from the ashes scattered at Stonehenge? It seems an impossible feat."

"I believe in you," he said, simply. "And so did Gaia."

I swallowed hard, and when I closed my eyes, the stirring winter winds seeped under my skin and into my very bones. I pictured the Earth goddess: her plump frame and cherubic wrinkled face, her dark knowing eyes and parched Cupid's bow mouth and her long earlobes like centuries of gravity had taken their toll. Her characteristic came to mind too: her grandmotherly warmth and love for the earth, her constant faith and sage advice, her prowess on the battlefield and her tendency to solve problems with food.

My fingers stretched out as I reached for her with that vivid image in my mind's eye and a yearning in my soul. My body moved involuntarily, undulating hips, a bending and a turning of my limbs, a flinging back of my head and a prayer on my lips for Gaia's safe return.

Somewhere, I heard Ezra call my name, but the meaning didn't penetrate.

Winds buffeted around me as I focussed, whipping my ponytail high up behind me, power pulsing through me.

Was this what it meant to be the eternal girl?

To forget the aches and pains of my middle-aged body and be rejuvenated by this flow of energy through me? To forget all doubt and rediscover the innocence of youth when I believed I could do anything? To forget my damaged womb and know that I could still be a mother and I could still create? That I could be the conduit to the rebirth of the Earth goddess.

My belief in myself had never been as strong as in this moment.

I lost all sense of time and space as my palms opened and I sent forth the winds that swirled around me. Gaia's name rang in my head. A bell. A beacon. A chant in my head that filled all corners of the known universe.

And then I yanked the winds back to me, prised my eyes open and directed them at the Rejuvenation Pool.

The debris floating in the wind could have been decomposing leaves or a clutch of soil or fragments from the surface of the river Thames, mere inches away. But I knew it was her ashes by the curious mix of gratitude and peace in my heart, which I had only ever truly felt in the Earth goddess's presence.

We watched, open-mouthed, as the ashes dove into the Rejuvenation Pool.

"You did it." Ezra lifted me up and spun me in a circle, under the open roof of the Globe Theatre.

I giggled and stole a kiss from him, soft and filled with yearning.

He kissed me back, and everything felt okay in the world.

The winds died down. We drew apart and monitored the Rejuvenation Pool for a moment. It was still and silent as if nothing had change.

"The words. We have to say the words. *Shamayi—*" I sank to my knees beside the pit and fumbled to recall them, heart sinking. Shaking my head, I tried again. *"Shamayim* or *shamani?"*

"Shamayim-perakh-ahava-chayim-neshama sheli." He crouched at my side. "Three years of Hebrew School on a Sunday has to count for something."

My heart burst into a thousand colours. "I love you forever."

"Easy, hellfire." He growled. "I'll hold you to that."

Ezra grabbed my hand, pulling me back as the

Rejuvenation Pool bubbled and churned, both of us disquieted by what unfolded beneath the surface, masses forming, a silhouette writhing. The grim liquid's pungent odour made me retch, and I trembled, fearful that what emerged would be a monster, not the goddess.

When a hand broke through the surface, I screamed.

"Shh, sound travels from the amphitheatre over to the riverside." Ezra covered my mouth. He glanced at the hand, horror writ large on his tired face. "Oh what the hell." He reached across and pulled.

Inch by inch, a woman slithered out of the pit.

She cowered on the floor, unrecognisable for the gunk and goo that covered her, then opened her wise, brown eyes. In them, I saw the turn of the globe, the fiery core of the Earth and the soaring birds. She looked younger than she had when I'd last seen her. Her skin smoother, her breasts higher, not a streak of grey in her hair.

"Alisha?" said the woman, before vomiting out gunk.

I rushed to her side, covering her with my jacket. "Gaia."

The goddess looked up at me, flinched and screamed like a banshee. A gunk-covered banshee with a scream that could wake the dead. Or at least attract the attention of the hundreds of office workers on the embankment, braving the wintery weather to grab their lunch from one of the riverside shops.

"What the hell is wrong with her?" shouted Ezra over the din.

Bewildered, I tried to hug her. "Gaia, please. Let's talk about this."

She shoved me away, her screams increasing in volume, soaring up the octave. As if her mind had unravelled in that unnatural pool. As if it would take time to build up the cells and memories of who she was again.

Pan had warned us about delirium, but I had expected a

sedate, pliable goddess, not an unhinged one. This version of Gaia scared me.

The voices of men shouting floated over the outer wall of the theatre. We had to keep her quiet, but her screams made every thought impossible. I reacted instinctively, lifting my palms to stun the goddess into submission with a wall of wind.

She rooted her feet to the ground like a tree, and swerved my attack with ease, before running at me with the rage of a wild boar.

My bladder almost emptied with fright.

I had a whole toolbox of skills to defeat an enemy, but Gaia wasn't an enemy. She was my friend. My mind in disarray, I wasn't sure whether to brace myself, draw my sword or run for the tube.

"I'm going to regret this." Ezra balled up his fist.

Seconds before the goddess charged into me, he swung his right hook and took her clean out. She dropped into his arms like a sack of potatoes—her screams mercifully silenced—leaving him covered in gunk from the Rejuvenation Pool and shaking his head in disbelief.

"What a ruckus," said a man's voice. "Kids playing with a wind machine and screaming at the top of their lungs, the nut jobs. A kick up the backside and a few hours in a cell will sort them right out."

"Hurry," said Ezra, expression grim. "Hold onto me."

I wrapped my arms around his waist as he carried us and the unconscious Earth goddess to safety.

12

We reeled through the monochrome world, three bodies glued together by the currents of the universe while teleporting, and by fate. Ezra manoeuvred us through the hidden folds of the world, bringing us to the home we had once shared together. We emerged in the living room, to cries of surprise from Mirabel and Echo.

I hastily threw a blanket over the sofa, and Ezra laid the goddess on it.

"Are you okay?" I hugged Mirabel, tracing soothing circles on her back.

Her thin arms clung to me. "I was so scared you weren't going to come back."

"I'm here now, but I need your help. Are you up to that?"

She gave a tearful nod.

Echo nudged Gaia's slack arm, his emerald eyes fearful. "The Rejuvenation Pool covered the goddess in a heinous fluid that smells like sewers on a hot day and killed her. Life will never be the same again." He slumped in despair. "But in a strange sense, it both stole and gave back her dignity. She smells like sewer, but her youthfulness has returned. In this way, she has fulfilled a secret but common goal shared by the vain amongst us. To look good in death."

"Echo, the goddess isn't dead." I checked the slight rise and fall of her bare chest to be sure.

"Thank the stars," wailed the leopard. "I was trying to hold it together for Mirabel, but my insides turned to jelly, like when I listen to Celine Dion."

Ezra shrugged off his filthy jacket. "Maybe I should have taken her to the Wildwoods infirmary. Or to her flat to jolt her memories of who she is."

I shook my head. "Her flat's being watched. You did the right thing bringing her here. Let's keep this to ourselves for now until she comes round and is back to herself. Pan said it could take time."

"I don't know, Alisha. Time is something I'm not sure we have much of."

A feeling of expansion in my chest as my thoughts cleared now we were safe. "When I heard Gaia's voice on the wind at Stonehenge, she told me to keep a cup of chai ready for when she returned. There's a café in Tooting she invited us to—you know the one I mean. She goes there as part of her nightly ritual and swears it has the best Indian tea in London. Chai with sweet milk, cardamom, cinnamon and cloves, stewed until it hits just the right note. Do you think you could bring her a flask?"

His grey eyes glowed with copper as he faded into the threads of the universe.

Echo licked the goddess's feet and spat out the gloop on the wooden floor. "You make a good team."

I ignored the fluttering in my belly and fetched a bowl of soapy water and a sponge from the kitchen and knelt beside the goddess. "Mirabel, rummage in my wardrobe for some clothes for the goddess. There's a green punjabi suit at the back and an unopened matching set of Marks and Spencer underwear in my drawer."

Mirabel darted off while I mopped Gaia's brow. Washing her made me emotional. She could have been my mother or grandmother. There was something holy about caring for someone like this, even though I wasn't religious. This was a silent contract between two individuals. A recognition of vulnerability and humility. An honour. A labour of love.

Soon, the water in the bowl grew as murky as the Rejuvenation Pool. When Mirabel returned with the punjabi suit and stripped it from the hanger, I sent her to exchange the bowl of water again and again until Gaia looked like a semblance of herself. Together, we dressed the goddess. When I reached the final gold button at the neckline and was thinking about whether to dry shampoo her hair, a hand gripped my wrist.

Gaia's eyes reflected the fury of the cosmos, wild and empty with flaming sparks that could sear planets. "Where am I?"

Echo's growl reverberated around the room, drowning out Mirabel's whimper. "Let her go."

I met the goddess's gaze without fear. "You are at my cottage, goddess. You are safe."

Her grip tightened, nails like rose thorns, drawing blood. "Then why is your heart drumming in your chest faster than a hummingbird's wings."

There was no warmth in her face, no traces of the wise, kind goddess.

My mouth went dry. I had wanted to keep Mirabel safe, but what if this woman would never be the goddess I knew again? The gods had many faces. Gaia had told me herself that she had caused Vesuvius. What if I had brought her to the cottage and she burned it all down? Heat flared at my back, and I knew without turning, without hearing a word, who it was.

"You heard the leopard," said Mirabel quietly. "Let Alisha go."

The goddess's gaze clouded. She sat up, retaining her grip on my wrist all the while. She poked a tongue into her cherubic cheek. "I know that name."

Years of kickboxing classes had made it second nature to wriggle out of an opponent's move. I swivelled out of Gaia's grip, heart heavy with sorrow, Transcender heavy on my back. The goddess was weakened now. It wouldn't be easy, but with Echo's help, I could take her. There was no other way. I couldn't let her hurt Mirabel. If I had to choose between goddess and child, there was no contest. Still, Mirabel nursed her ball of flame, while we waited for Gaia's next move.

The goddess touched the base of her neck. "Alisha. Yes. That name is buried in the recesses of my head. With other names. Rosalie and Rajika and the face of a beady pigeon." She stood, beautiful as the rolling hills in my green punjabi suit, eyes blazing. "Who am I?"

The particles shifted as Ezra returned balancing a flask, a chipped cup and a saucer in his hand.

"You are a woman who enjoys chai." He poured out a cup of chai under Gaia's suspicious eye. Then he offered it to her, as the heat and spices from the tea dispersed into the room and into our nostrils.

Gaia accepted the cup and inhaled the scent of the brew.

I edged towards Mirabel, who extinguished her fireball. We held our collective breath.

The goddess sipped the tea then slurped it with the relish of a parched woman. She emptied the cup and met my eyes. Her smile was like a new dawn.

THE EARTH GODDESS hugged the flask of chai as she took her leave, eager to savour another cup in her beloved flat and put on her favourite sari. When she had gone, Mirabel and Echo curled up together in the window seat of the front bay window, while Ezra helped me wipe down the mess from the Rejuvenation Pool. We worked side by side, sponging down the sofa and the floor and throwing open the windows to get rid of the sulphuric stink that Gaia had brought with her to the cottage.

I scrubbed a stubborn mark on the sofa. "I knew it was really her when she started telling us off about not watering her houseplants."

His brow furrowed. "All that stuff about her hearing them crying from dehydration. She was pulling our leg, right?"

I shrugged. "Who knows what a goddess hears? Marina's thought that plants are sentient for years. Maybe there's something to it. What was it she said about my punjabi suit? I didn't quite catch it. My head was still processing what we managed to achieve."

Ezra laughed. "That she was grateful for the loan of it but the calibre of the needlework wasn't befitting a goddess." He plucked his top and sniffed it. "Speaking of clothing, I have to get out of these. I reek."

Sauntering to the kitchen, he peeled off his clothes, until he wore only his boxers. A half-smile playing on his chiselled face, mischief written all over it.

He knew his effect on me.

I bundled his jeans and T-shirt into the washing machine, together with the gunk-ridden blanket. Pouring in the detergent, I averted my face to hide my creeping blush and the fact that every part of my body reacted to him.

Putting his hands on my waist, he turned me around and cupped my chin.

My lips parted, and the world went still.

He traced the line of my cheekbone.

"I have waited so long to do this properly." His grey-copper eyes danced with intent as he searched my face and leaned in, exquisitely slowly, nudging my nose in an eskimo kiss.

The delay made me weak with desire.

We had kissed before, a hundred times, but never with such longing. I swayed in his arms, knees buckling. He scooped me up, his hands on the butt of my jeans, my legs tangling around his bare ones. And then his lips were on mine, his stubble on my cheek, the taste of mountains and whiskey in my mouth. Teasing and tender. His face blurred, and I quivered with need, dizzy in his arms, never wanting to let go.

"I need some juice," said Mirabel, somewhere far away.

Groaning, I wrenched myself away from Ezra. "We can't. She'll see."

"Then we go outside," he said, gruffly.

He teleported us to the back garden, where the afternoon light spread across the lawn and through the bare boughs of the trees. I was still clothed and in my socks, but the cool air chased goosebumps up his skin and his bare feet must have been ice blocks on the hard ground, despite his wolf nature.

"You're cold," I said.

"We'll soon warm each other up." He threaded his fingers through mine and led me the small grove tucked away along the boundary of the garden, where his mother had once had a picnic spot.

It was so overgrown that barely any light reached in. The picnic table had long deteriorated and been chopped for firewood. His mother's fairy lights were here still, decades old and entwined with ivy, their battery source long depleted. More than once, I'd considered giving this part of the garden new life, but it hadn't seemed right to go ahead without Ezra having a say. I knew how much this place meant to him, how every stone and pathway held a memory.

But then he placed his finger lightly to his moon charm, and the fairy lights lit up.

"I'm starting to love your aunties for giving you those charms."

"Shh." He put his forefinger to my lips. "I don't want to think of them. Don't spoil it." He raised a questioning eyebrow and tugged at my T-shirt. "May I?"

I looked up at him from under my eyelashes. "Yes."

He didn't need telling twice. I giggled as he whipped off my T-shirt and unbuttoned my jeans, impatient as he pushed them down over my hips, heat gathering between my legs. Feeling silly in my bra and knickers with my socks still on, I ripped them off. Already, he dipped his head to the lace of my bra, his teeth finding and tugging at my nipples. Then he let go of me.

Bereft, blinded by longing, I moaned in complaint.

Ezra lay down on my discarded clothes and long, tatty blades of neglected grass and pulled me down on top of him so his body took the brunt of the elements. He circled his arms around me, pressing me against his hard chest and concave belly.

"Alisha," he murmured against my mouth. "We should talk."

"This is talking," I said. "Just with our bodies."

He drew in a ragged breath. "I think what we have is real, but after last time, I need to hear the words. Just once."

I pulled back a fraction, distracted by his hands at the base of my spine. I didn't need to focus hard because these words had been ready for weeks. I might have held them back while I was prioritising Mirabel, but that didn't mean they hadn't burned to get out ever since Phinnaeous had pulled the wool over my eyes and fooled me into believing my insecurities.

"I'm sorry, Ezra. I should have trusted you with my doubts, not let them prise us apart."

His eyes were molten embers. "Those aren't the words," he said harshly.

I went quiet inside and said what I knew to be true. "I love you, and I never should have let you go."

Ezra pulled the hairband out of my ponytail and tossed it aside. Calloused fingers ran lightly down my arm, skirting over the lines of my scar. Then he threaded his fingers through the back of my hair, kneading my scalp, before pulling me in for a bruising kiss. "That's better. You're mine, hellfire. From the minute we laid eyes on each other."

I sucked in my breath as he undid my bra and my breasts spilled onto his chest. He bent his head to them as I arched against him. He throbbed against me. I was helpless in his arms. I'd yield to all his demands, open myself up to him in the ways I'd never opened to anyone, run away with him, beg him to stay with me always.

We rolled over, his weight on me as the space around us evaporated. I forgot the world. I forgot my daughter. I forgot the gods. There was no one except me and him in this moment. He bit my bottom lip, drawing blood. His first kisses had been all giving. These sought to conquer me. To make me his. Pushing my knickers aside, I clawed my nails down his back, urging him inside me.

He growled, low in his throat, holding back for a moment.

But his eyes told me that it wouldn't be long. He needed me as much as I needed him.

When he entered me, I bit his shoulder to stop the moans. We rode the stars together.

Afterwards, when we were sated, we lay back against the earth. He nuzzled my shoulder and swept back my damp hair, the curls that had gone wild in our stolen moments. He winced at a chestnut poking him in the back. I rolled it away from us and fussed over a patch on his back where the prickles had left their mark. We both still needed to be close to each other. Reaching behind, he pulled me around so my back lay against his chest and wrapped his arms around my waist.

His voice vibrated against my ear. "Next time, we do this in our own bed."

Warmth radiated through my chest. "Our bed?"

"I thought I could move back in. If that's okay with you and Mirabel?"

My pulse jumped in my throat. He'd mentioned Mirabel, like we were already a family. "Won't the pack miss you at the farmhouse?"

"I never unpacked my bag. They know my place is with you. You are my home."

I kissed his hand and held it to my face, feeling at peace. Was this what it felt like to belong? Gaia was back, and we were a family. We'd have to speak to Mirabel, of course. Our bond was so new. I didn't want more change to unsettle her. I'd make her understand that Ezra living with us meant more happiness. That it meant another person to care for her, just like Echo and I did.

"We should get inside before we catch a chill. I need to get back to Mirabel." I hesitated. "Ezra, are you sure about this?"

His kiss was all the answer I needed.

"I've never been more certain of anything in my life than you, Alisha Verma. We're on this road together." He untangled himself from me and retrieved my clothes from where they had been strewn across the grove. Handing them to me, he pulled on his boxers and brushed a kiss across my forehead. "I'm going to head back to the farmhouse for some things."

The dream god's ultimatum pinged into my head. I opened my mouth to make sure we were both on the same page about the life we wanted, but I didn't want to rock the boat.

For all my criticism of my parents' decision to bind our magic in childhood, I now understood why they had done it. I, too, would walk away from the Otherworld to keep my family safe. All this talk about me being the granddaughter of the great Rajika Verma, when it turned out I was more like Dad after all. Magic was important to me. But I could be happy without magic.

Without Ezra and Mirabel, my world would shrink to a point.

Now wasn't the right time to rock the boat. Ezra would understand. His experiences, too, taught him that family took sacrifice.

Instead, I clutched my clothes to me and leaned in for a lingering kiss. "I'll have a wash and then pop a lasagne in the oven for dinner."

His grey eyes danced. "Domestic bliss already."

He vanished between the folds of the world, and though he had gone, the fairy lights still twinkled.

13

I slept like a baby, with my head on Ezra's chest, and woke with the sun, basking in the feeling of belonging. The evening with Mirabel had been awkward, but that was only to be expected. New arrangements took time to get used to, but we'd soon fit together like pieces of a jigsaw.

It was right to walk away from my delusions about taking on the gods and put motherhood first.

I silenced the niggling voice in my head that reminded me that my parents' decision had only worked for so long. Eventually, Mum had been forced to take another path. I silenced the doubt about whether I would be happy living a humdrum life and if Ezra would be as attracted to me if I was plain old me: a middle-aged, night class teacher who closed her eyes to the Otherworld.

He would understand. It wasn't like I wanted to forget our magical identity, more that the time had come to stop chasing danger and turn our focus inward to protecting our loved ones.

"Morning." His arms reflexively tightened around me as his eyes opened and he pulled me in for a soft kiss, our breath mingling.

"Hi." I shivered with pleasure, hypersensitive to every touch and texture: the stubble on his face against my cheek, the kneading of his fingers at the small of my back, the warmth of his soles on my calves.

Disappointment clouded his face. "I have a meeting with my aunt first thing. She's excited about her vision for the senate and has asked me to help."

"She's definitely anointed you as her deputy."

Ezra tickled me, the mattress bowing under his weight. "I hear an undercurrent of disapproval. Is that a complaint? Most women find it an aphrodisiac when their man goes up the ranks. Besides, I like my favourite ladies to get on."

I laughed. "You go do your thing."

"And you'll be waiting here just like this for me when I get back?"

"Actually, I have some new school shoes to order for Mirabel, a CV to send out for a new teaching job, and then Marina's coming over for a chat before we go and check on Gaia." I sneezed. My escapade with Ezra resulted in a rotten cold, but it was worth it.

"You caught a chill last night."

"I'm holding you responsible."

He laughed. His spirit was lighter, like in the days when we were first getting to know each other, before Gunnolf's crimes and his killing and the hunt for Phinnaeous. He scratched his jaw. "I thought you were planning to take a break from the teaching, just until the dust settles with Mirabel and the Otherworld?"

I avoided his gaze. "I'm just going to dip my toe in again. I miss the classroom. Fei Yen and Faeza have been nudging me about it."

"There's a lot on your plate, hellfire. Pace yourself, okay? I better jump in the shower." He rolled away from me and grimaced. "Just one more thing. Don't tell Gaia I punched her lights out."

"Yes, sir."

His eyes darkened. "I should take you straight back to bed, except my aunt's sending an Otherworld taxi for me."

I gave him an incredulous look. "A bit much, isn't it? Given you teleport."

"She says appearances matter when we're on official business. She wants to set us apart from Phinnaeous Shine. To be seen and to prove we are doing the work." He shrugged. "All a bit unnecessary if you ask me, but I'm not complaining. Those mattresses in the taxis can restore my aching body after our night of—" He waggled his eyebrows.

I grinned. "Go on, shoo. Stop distracting me."

Thirty minutes later, Mirabel and I had made ourselves presentable and agreed on a new pair of school shoes online. I scurried about the kitchen, slicing salmon into cubes as a treat for Echo and mopping up the counter. The domestic work lulled me into a meditative state like it often did, the repetitive patterns allowing my thoughts to crystallise more clearly than when caught in the whirlwind of life.

The wheel of time turned faster the older I got. Sometimes, when I spotted an old lady walking down a London street, back crooked, skin saggy, hair uncombed, I searched beyond cataracts for the light in her eyes. It buoyed me when I found that spark. Ageing didn't have to mean dwindling hope, stagnation or loneliness.

The future was wide open.

I could make mistakes, and I could recover from them. I could have passionate love in my twenties, thirties, my forties and beyond. Life was what we made of it.

When the doorbell rang, I pulled a eucalyptus-scented tissue out of the box to blow my nose and hurried to greet her, feeling a pang of loss for Mum. Funny how family, domesticity and things as simple as choice of tissue brand could trigger an avalanche of memories. But grief was funny like that. It made you look backwards but also forwards. I mourned all those daily conversations that had been erased from my future when I would have told her about what challenges I faced.

Marina came in, and we retreated to the kitchen for a natter over a cup of tea.

She peeked into the living room, where Mirabel and Echo watched Saturday television. "Echo's very attached to Mirabel. Fascinating seeing their bond develop."

"He's been on the prowl across the city less and less recently. That incident in the park with the djinn really shook him up. It's like he needs to prove himself. He doesn't want to leave her side in case it happens again."

Her cotton-blue eyes exuded sympathy. "He's protective by nature. It's his whole purpose in life. Alisha, you don't need his protection anymore. You're powerful in your own right."

Maybe she was right. Maybe Echo's protective feelings towards me had been transferred to Mirabel. I didn't mind. She needed him more than me. His presence at my side had always made me feel safer, and now he did that same kindness for her. But I missed him all the same.

"I'm proud of you." Marina smiled at how the two kitchen chairs had become three. "You and Ezra found your way back to each other. Not only that, but you risked chilblains and voyeurism by neighbours to do it outside in the cold. That is a middle-aged fantasy, right there." She slurped her tea. "Have you told Orpheus about Ezra moving back in?"

"I've not reached out in days because he said he needed some distance. I called yesterday to fill him in about Gaia, but one of the vampires told me it was a busy night at the casino and he couldn't come to the phone. The background noise sounded more like a raucous harem of women."

"Could be a case of rebound sex," said Marina. "Predators don't take kindly to other people having what they want. I hope he doesn't get fangy about it."

I worried that we'd crossed a line and our bantering, generous friendship would suffer. "He'll come round. How was your week at work?"

She tugged an errant lock of rainbow hair. "Oh, you know how it goes. Tired feet. Blurry eyes. A rabbit with the shits. Maybe we should take a dip in the Rejuvenation Pool and cure all our woes."

"No more hot flushes or perimenopause. No more dyeing our roots, straggly chin hairs or crow's lines around our eyes. No more comparisons with younger women, panting or holding our boobs when we run for the bus."

Marina expanded the wishlist, on a roll. "No more reading glasses or fanny farts. No more underwired bras or saggy jaw lines. No more knee-jerk purchasing of all the multi-vitamins under the sun or expensive skin creams. No more needing a wee two minutes after a visit to the loo."

I clinked my mug cup with hers. "Sounds heavenly."

Something shifted in the corner of my field of vision. It wasn't the oscillation in particles I recognised as the precursor to Ezra returning home.

It was something else entirely.

Fear crawled up my spine. I turned my head, heart in my mouth, to find shadows materialise into a solid form in the third chair. The dream god casually crossed his legs in his spangly silver catsuit and twirled the poppy on his breast as if he'd dropped in for a cuppa.

Marina stifled a scream and leapt for the iron saucepan on the stove. "Who are you? Bjorn from ABBA circa 1970?"

She swung the saucepan through the air.

The dream god cast her a dismissive look and blew the seeds of the poppy in her face.

Acting on pure instinct, my palms flew up to redirect the path of the poppy seeds away from my best friend, but they snaked back around and found her face, glistening as they settled there. The air left my lungs as Marina slumped to the floor, taking the clattering saucepan with her.

With a cry, I rushed to her side and checked her pulse. Her breathing was laboured but regular. I put a chair cushion under her head and stood, shielding her body. I took on a combat stance, legs planted for maximum stability, fists raised but the winds a whisper away.

"Why? Why did you do that?" I said to the god.

His cold smile showed his contempt as he sprawled in the chair. His relaxed posture made me even more fearful, so secure in his belief that I posed no threat to him. "You didn't listen, druid. Cheap words when your actions don't match. Did you think I wouldn't sense the stirring of the earth? Gaia is born again at your hand."

My thoughts cartwheeled. I hadn't attempted to find the Book of Names. But I had helped Gaia to return. Her resurrection wasn't an attack on him. I just had to make him believe that. "I will walk away from it all. Leave my loved ones alone. The gods can do as they please."

The chair scraped against the floor tiles as he stood and smoothed the catsuit over his bony hips. He lowered his bearded chin to look down on me. "Dreams are such fragile things. Vivid representations of unanswered questions. Nebulous wishes oxygenated by slumber. A cleansing process of our lived realities. A window into our unconscious minds." He stepped closer. "You enjoyed a taste of your dream. Now I will turn it into blackened ash."

My blood ran cold. I didn't second guess my decision to help Gaia. But I cursed myself for leaving the sword in the bedroom. For my vanity in thinking I could just walk away, when Marina and Rob, Alma and Echo had warned me that Morpheus couldn't be trusted. When Ezra had counselled me not to abandon my identity.

He was inches from Marina. Mirabel and Echo were only on the other side of the wall. Surely they had heard the din? I wished with the fervency of this darkest night that the leopard would take Mirabel far away until the god had gone.

The god wiped sleep dust from his eyes. His sneer told me he could read every thought.

How did I fight against an enemy that can fade to nothing, that could enter my head and read my thoughts, regardless of what trinkets I wore?

I grounded myself, there in the kitchen, though it was always easier outside with the swirl of the wind and the soil beneath my feet. Always easier when not in a confined space, when my anxiety at my loved ones being in immediate danger didn't crash over me like a wave.

Regulating my breath, I tried to remember I wasn't alone. I had friends and family. I was the culmination of two druid lines. I had power and grit, and a life I wanted to protect.

I could handle this.

He didn't seem to have a weakness, but he kept wiping sleep dust from his eyes.

Sleep dust gave me blurry vision, but what if Morpheus suffered from it without respite?

My stomach in knots, I searched my mind for a creature to animate en masse. Fast, reactive, deadly creatures that the dream god would find it hard to get a handle on. That he would struggle to see if my hunch was right. That might buy me a chance to retrieve Death's sword and put an end to this.

I saw the creatures in my mind's eye, not just one but a crowd of them. My pulse leapt as I brought a swarm of wasps to life and assigned them their purpose.

Hundreds of them surged at the dream god in their yellow-and-black jackets, wings flapping, antennae twitching, stings at the ready. He startled, raising his hands, and melted into his invisible form, but whenever he solidified, the wasps were there again. Persistent, clever little insects.

I rushed out of the room, at loathe to leave Marina but determined to grab my sword. I groaned at the sight of Echo and Mirabel readying their attack. The leopard had clearly been biding his time, unwilling to be outwitted by the dream god again. They should have run, but it was all happening so fast. Marina lay on the kitchen floor, unprotected.

"Echo, guard Marina," I said.

He bristled with rage at Marina's plight and charged past me into the kitchen, snarling and spitting. Vicious intent strained in every sinew of his muscular body. "Disco diva dream god. I've been waiting patiently for a rematch."

The leopard leapt at the re-materialising dream god, his jaw wide, and took a chunk out of the silver catsuit and, presumably, the god's flesh underneath.

I didn't wait to see what happened next. Urgency filled me. I needed Death's sword.

"Bel, with me." I grabbed her wrist and tugged her after me to the bedroom, where I opened the window. "Go, now. Hide in the meadow. Keep running until you can't see the cottage anymore. We'll find you when it's over."

She shook her head. "Let me help."

I dove under the bed for the sword. "It's you he wants. Go."

A ball of flame illuminated dark shadows under her eyes. Her forlornness registered even in my panic. "I already lost my parents. I'm not losing you too."

I clambered to my feet, sword in hand, horror filling me.

"Put the fire out. He works with djinn. They are drawn to it." My scalp prickled.

They came. Twenty of them, maybe more. All squeezed into my bedroom, which only that morning had been my love nest with Ezra. Great filthy creatures of fiery bones and malice, naked and sinewy, with horns and smoking nostrils and protruding wings, leaving trails of grey slime on our white Laura Ashley bedding that I wouldn't be able to bleach out.

"Run," I screamed as they surrounded us.

I drove my sword into three, slashing at their heart space and their heads, determined to do maximum damage. I killed them in a frenzy.

This was my life now. Blood and gore and grim reality.

Humdrums had no idea this existed when they watched their horror films with popcorn overflowing from their bowls. I jabbed and tornadoed the shit out of the djinn, even though the battle ruined our home. Curtains falling, wardrobes cracking, a burst pipe in the bathroom, my most comfortable bra ripped in two. Sometimes, there was no choice left but to fight. When I spotted the water jug on Ezra's side of the bed, I tossed it at the last group of djinn blocking the door, Alma's advice about their incompatibility with water ringing in my head. They shrank back and sizzled, and we squeezed past them, Mirabel's hand in mine, my mothering instincts in overdrive but also my sisterly ones.

I couldn't leave Marina to fend for herself. I couldn't leave Echo.

I led the way into the kitchen, where my swarm of wasps had depleted, my sword's obsidian blade ready to strike.

There, Marina was still out cold, and a snarling Echo faced off against Morpheus. A roar ripped from his throat as he sank his teeth into the god's limb, shaking his head from side to side. But Morpheus shifted, becoming smokeless fire, causing the leopard to shrink back, head cocked in confusion, whiskers singed.

My mind whirled. I had to protect Mirabel. I had to get Marina out of there. Echo couldn't take the brunt of this fight. Every cell of my body yearned to save him too.

When Morpheus re-materialised, his catsuit looked worse for wear, his backside bled and his ginger ponytail was dishevelled. His hands had reverted to his original demon form, with talon-like claws. He didn't seem to have many offensive strengths—apart from the mind-dickery, the disappearing act and the talons—but he'd still done a number on Echo. His talons had shredded Echo's ears and left tiger stripes down the leopard's left flank.

The leopard remained valiant still.

"This time, you won't be the only one who leaves his mark." Echo lifted his leg to spray urine on Morpheus.

But the dream god had enough of games. Gaia had once told me that the gods tolerated mortals for entertainment. They liked to trifle with us, make us pawns in their own inter-god wars and increase our suffering so we would boost their own powers with our prayers. When their patience ran out, they would crush us like ants beneath their boots and not feel a pang of regret.

Our lives, our dreams and our minds were disposable.

He needed to be stopped.

I had been wrong to think I could walk away. Wrong to think Morpheus would leave us alone. Wrong to waver from my mission. The only way for me to have a quiet family life wasn't for me to hide from danger.

It was to settle it once and for all.

The dream god could see me coming—literally and mentally—unless I acted unexpectedly while Echo still distracted him. I threw Transcender up in the air, raised my palm and used the winds to plunge it through Morpheus's chest.

He dissipated, and the sword arced and skidded across the floor to the skirting board. Eyes like liquid gemstones as he solidified. "It has already ended."

My heart hammered in my throat, body shielding Mirabel behind me. "You're lying. You didn't expect us to put up a fight. You thought it would be easy."

"Look behind you," said Morpheus.

It was a trick. He wanted to take my sword. The hair lifted on the back of my neck. I didn't want to turn around, but a hiss from Echo changed my mind.

Stomach quivering, I spun in a slow circle.

Mirabel stood there. Her colouring and height remained the same, but her bone structure had changed entirely.

I cried out, sick to my stomach. "Mirabel!"

"Djinn are tricky creatures. Shapeshifters, scheming, patient." He sneered. "All that time you battled them in your bedroom created the opportunity for one of them to slip right into the girl's mind and fill her with doubt."

Clutching Mirabel's hands, I rubbed my thumbs over her hot skin. She was shorter than me and so small, still. If I had to carry her to safety, I would. "Please. Find your way back to me. I'm right here."

Her mouth twisted. She ripped her hand from mine and jabbed a finger at my chest. Her eerie voice was robotic, an abomination of the sweet, troubled girl I knew. She was my foster daughter, but her words frightened me more than anything I had ever heard before. "You only wanted me because you can't have your own babies. You regret offering me a home now you and Ezra are back together. You would rather I didn't exist so you can spend all your time with each other instead."

"Bel, that's not true," I pleaded.

"You don't love me. You'll never love me as much as my parents loved me." A stream of poppy seeds flowed over my shoulder and into her nostrils.

Mirabel dropped like a stone in a well.

The dream god materialised in front of me and caught her in his arms. He sniffed her auburn cropped hair, eyes gleaming. "Sleep paralysis makes bodies strangely heavy. Such a fresh young thing to take to the dream realm. On the night of the eclipse, it's curtains for her." A pause. "This will break you."

Despair rose like a wail in me as he and Mirabel became translucent, fading from sight.

I grasped at them, but my hands went clean through.

A growl sounded behind me, and I twisted round to see

Echo leap clean through the wrecked kitchen and into the fast-vanishing dream god and his victim.

Then my leopard too was gone, and all was quiet.

I sank onto my knees on a carpet of fallen wasps and cradled Marina.

Her lips parted, and her eyes slowly opened to take in the carnage around us. Her voice was parched but thankfully, mercifully, utterly hers. "What happened?"

"They're gone, Marina. He took them. The dream god took Bel and Echo, and I'm going to take them back before the night of the eclipse."

14

Lavinia sent a clean-up crew. Her rats surged all over the cottage, armed with cleaning utensils. They worked in teams, bagging corpses and rubbish, hoovering, spraying disinfectant, mopping down surfaces and, finally, giving the cottage a spritz of air freshener and a whirl of cleansing incense.

"There you go. All the bad juju is gone." The witch nosed around our home with beady eyes. "So, this is the love nest my sister shared with your father, Ezra. I turned up on the doorstep many moons ago with a carrot cake, and she invited me into the kitchen but no further. A prime example about how Morena and Levi's love excluded all others. Funny how Mirabel feels the same about you and Alisha."

I bristled, wise to the tug between us for Ezra's affections. Lavinia wanted him at her beck and call and preferred not to share. But Ezra was his own man, and we had gone through too much for me to roll over for another woman's ego trip.

Ezra put a comforting hand on the small of my back and snapped, "Lay off it, Aunt Lavinia. Alisha's going through enough. And I think you'll find that my parents' love didn't exclude me. I was at the centre of their circle. It was only after they died that the coven and the pack made me an outsider for both werewolves and witches by fighting over me like a pile of meat."

"There, there, nephew." Lavinia patted his shoulder. "I didn't mean to upset you. It's a fraught time for everyone. Truth be told, I feel mildly guilty that my headbands didn't do a better job of protecting the child, but then warding off djinn is a different matter to warding off djinn supercharged by Morpheus himself."

I huffed out an angry breath. If I were a betting woman, I would bet my life savings that Lavinia only cared that her stunt with the headbands had given her the momentum to become Prime Sorcerer. "There must be something we can do."

Lavinia leaned on her dull brown umbrella with a sigh. "How I wish that were true. Sadly, even with all the power of London's Otherworld at my fingertips, the dream world is beyond my reach. We will make sure that Mirabel Elmstorm and Chanakya Gunbir Hredhaan of Maharashtra's names are never forgotten. Though they will be unable to receive burial rites, we will erect a memorial stone for them at the heart of Wildwoods."

Ezra pulled his brows together and shook his head. "Unbelievable."

I recoiled and lashed out at her. "We're not giving up."

Grim-faced, I turned back into the kitchen, leaving him with his aunt, and rubbed my throbbing head. My phone call with Rayna had been difficult enough—she had entrusted Mirabel to my care, and I had utterly failed—and now there was Lavinia needing an empathy transplant.

I missed Orpheus. He never would stand for the ludicrous thought of abandoning family.

Marina paused helping Rob to collect up splintered pieces of the kitchen chairs and gave me a hug I wanted to lose myself in. How lucky we had been that the dream god's reckoning hadn't left her with any lasting damage. But even Marina's warmth couldn't dampen my horror.

She squeezed me and then drew back with a shuddering breath, her pink-and-turquoise hair frazzled about her heart-shaped face. "We'll get them back."

I kneaded the back of my neck. "I should have let her keep wearing the Jericho necklace. She might have stood more of a chance on the dream plane with it."

"You were in your own home. You can't expect to have your guard up even then," said Marina. "Bel has Echo. She will be all right. He will look after her."

A wail in my throat that I suppressed, barely holding on to my control. "I'm the eternal girl. I should have known better."

"Get that out of your head. The guilt's not helpful," said Marina. "You may be powerful, but you're only human."

Rob rubbed his head. "I've been piecing together more about the dream god's background. He was a travel agent specialising in exotic locations. You know the ones I mean. White sands and scuba-diving and those wooden huts on stilts in water. Then in the 1970s, he became a board member of EvolveTech."

I shook my head in despair. "What was I thinking? The gods have been intertwined with my family for so long, he never would have let go. I've been such a fool."

Marina sighed. "We'll put this right, Alisha. I promise."

Rob continued. "There's was outrage when, at the height of the AIDS crisis, he was quoted in a business broadsheet saying that EvolveTech had built a FTSE 100 company on the backs of the dreams of sick people."

I glowered. "Can he get any lower?"

"The board voted him out after that." Rob raised a wry eyebrow. "Then George Lucas came along, and he saw an opportunity in making lightsabers. Nowadays, the top-notch ones go for hundreds on eBay. He's been making quite a killing and has a reputation for bespoke, personalised lightsabers that he personally hands over to the customer with no delivery charge. Of course, that crossover point is dangerous for the customer. The Shadow Squad has opened up a whole case on it, thanks to you. There's quite a market for lightsabers amongst kids and grown men. And those dreamers are fertile ground for mischief. We have to go slowly. Making a watertight plan is our best chance of bringing Mirabel home."

I inhaled deeply through the nose and exhaled through the mouth. My throat scratched as though it held shards of glass. No paracetamol would fix this. This was the pain of letting down those who depended on you. Every cell in my body urged me to tear down the fabric of the world to bring Mirabel and Echo back. "No, Rob. We're not going slowly. I don't think or weigh up. I just want to do. I just want to get my girl and my leopard back and never let them go again."

The detective frowned. "Alisha—"

Marina rubbed her four-leaf clover tattoo, compulsively, a sure sign of her anxiety. "The eclipse is three days away."

"Three days. Three days to save them." I rubbed the middle of my forehead, eyes closed, blocking out everything but my internal voice. "There's only one person who can help right now. She's known Morpheus for centuries, and she'll know how to access the dream world."

Footsteps sounded towards us. Then Ezra's arms closed around me, his voice steely with determination. "Grab what you need. I'll take you to see Gaia." He dropped his voice a notch in volume. "Rob, when you're finished here, just make sure the Prime Sorceress leaves with you. She's already twitching to go through our underwear drawers, but her time will be better spent preparing for tomorrow's senate meeting."

Marina clutched me. "I'll come with you."

I shook my head. "You took enough of a knock. You're staying here."

"She's got me. I won't let anything happen to her," said Ezra. "We're going to bring our family back home."

After a brief hesitation, I texted Dad, Sahil and Orpheus about what had happened. Dad would light a candle at a shrine and pray to Ganesha, Sahil would twiddle his thumbs and Orpheus would turn to his books to see what solutions might be possible. It didn't matter if none of it helped. It only mattered that, in their own way, they all cared for Mirabel and Echo, and their combined good thoughts for us might tip the balance of the universe in our favour.

Once I'd fetched Death's sword and the Jericho necklace, Ezra wrapped me in his arms and spiralled us through the universe to Gaia's flat in Tooting. Ezra rapped his knuckles against the open door, and we hurried inside, our senses awash with the aroma of curry: pungent turmeric, fried onions and garlic and roasted aubergines.

We found her at the stove frying poppadoms, dressed in a green, white and yellow *bandini* sari. Her bingo wings had returned, as if the Rejuvenation Pool's boost of youthfulness had worn off. "Alisha, Ezra, I had a feeling you might stop by. Just a minute. The children will be here soon, demanding food for their empty bellies and a listening ear for their troubles. Then there are nut stashes to share amongst squirrels and hibernating animals to check on."

I murmured something nonsensical, impatient for her attention to turn to us. But the Earth goddess had many loves and many needs to meet, especially after her absence. I'd wanted our reunion visit to be full of joy. Instead, here I was in the middle of another unholy adventure. I paced while she finished up, panic rising.

"But of course I'll make time for my favourite druid and her wolf. I owe you both a great debt. Thank the heavens you remembered the chai, Alisha. Or it would have been centuries of carnage before I remembered my true nature. I might have triggered an extinction-level event or forgotten who I love and who I despise." The air smoked in the kitchen, but still she pressed on, the gas ring burner roaring as the stack of poppadoms grew. "That Marks and Spencer underwear you put on me was a revelation, Alisha. I have made an appointment with the Bromley branch to get myself refitted. After my dip in the Rejuvenation Pool, my breasts have changed somewhat. I'm a bit sad they're not pointing upwards, but that's the way of the world. Sometimes a balloon loses its air. It's all quite natural."

Ezra stiffened, distinctly uncomfortable, his foot drumming in his impatience to get to the purpose of our visit.

But the Earth goddess could never be rushed, such was her belief in the seasonality of all things and the virtues of patience and the alignment of the stars. Finally, just when I couldn't bite my tongue any longer, she scooped the last poppadom out of the oil with a slotted spoon and laid it on a piece of kitchen paper, before breaking off a piece that crunched in her mouth.

"Not the same without a dollop of mango chutney, of course," she said, "but it will do."

"Gaia, we need your help," I blurted out.

Her eyes darkened with the knowledge of the cosmos, and her crow's feet deepened. "You have come to ask me how to access the dream realm. But you fail to account for why you didn't follow my instructions in the first place." She wiped her smeary hands on her sari and poked the scar on my arm. "You have a map ingrained in your arm. A map that has been in the making since you were four years old in your parent's garden and the birds attacked you, drilling the first dots into your skin. A map that culminated in the lightning strikes at Stonehenge that burned the path into your flesh." She beat her chest with her fist. "A dying goddess used her last breath to tell you to retrieve the book that would allow you to control the gods, and you did *what*? You decided because you had your own personal happiness that you could walk away from your duties? After all the gifts and knowledge I bestowed upon your family?"

I shrank before her anger, wordless and ashamed.

Ezra sprang to my defence, his eyes lowered. "You ask too much of her, goddess. She has bent herself into unfamiliar shapes, taken her dwindling courage and forced herself into situations no mortal should endure, to help you. To finish this path that her grandmother began."

Volcanic fire in the Earth goddess's eyes. "Then finish it she must. Because a prophecy was written long ago that you both seem to have forgotten. *When Death opens the door, only the eternal girl may stop the coming Dusk, together with a disintegrating tome lost to the world.* Death is coming to us all, unless you act, Alisha."

I lifted my chin and met her gaze. "Tell me what to do."

Gaia softened. "I am a mother first and foremost, and I have a fondness for the leopard. I don't expect or want you to abandon your beloveds, Alisha. Your nurturing feelings are what is going to help us win this fight. Your spirit might feel broken right now, but those cracks you feel in your heart… they let in the light. They keep you humble. They show you care." She steepled her fingers and blew out her cherubic cheeks. "You will need a detour before finding the Book of Names. Try not to get killed in the process, that is all. It is a longshot, but it is doable."

"How? How do we find Mirabel and Echo?" said Ezra.

Desperation prickled at my skin. I tucked my hands under my armpits, a self-hug. "There are three days until the eclipse."

"That is when Morpheus will be at his strongest. You must find a way to get them out of the dream world, and then, if they haven't yet fallen prey to their doubts, your love will save them." Gaia rocked on the balls of her bare feet, her toes just visible under the folds of her sari. "But accessing the dream world is tricky without Morpheus as a guide. Not even

I can do it. It's easy for the mind and body to become unlinked, triggering certain death." She indicated to Ezra's charm necklace and my Jericho one. "No trinkets can help because they can't pass into the dream world. There is only one solution."

My mouth went dry. "Yes?"

The goddess exuded calm. "You must find a spirit gallant enough to rescue the fairy and the leopard without your involvement. A spirit who has been waiting for the right quest to heal himself and reach fulfilment."

I frowned. "And who is that?"

Her brown eyes had the richness of fertile soil. "You must go to the artefacts vault of the Celestial Library, accompanied by a person who will risk the heat of fire for you."

Ezra squeezed me.

"There you will find a worn brown saddle. If you touch Transcender to the saddle, you will find what you seek, but the task of persuasion will be up to you. In that, I cannot meddle. The earthly realm is my arena, not the spirit one." She blinked rapidly as if she was unsettled, but the moment passed so quickly I could have imagined it. "Now, where is my flour? Pan helped himself to all my *laddus* and will be here soon enough asking for more."

On a whim, I pressed a kiss to her paper cheek. She smelt of the sun and the soil and the salty sea. "Thank you, Gaia."

She nodded. "It will not be easy, and you must use all your wiles and grit, with a sprinkling of belief. And when you return, we will feast, dust ourselves off and battle again."

I was so tired. I wanted to curl up with Ezra, Mirabel and Echo on a king-size bed and doze for days, only waking to look at their faces and then drift off again.

But we didn't choose our trials. They chose us.

All we could do was put one foot in front of the other and walk on.

15

Dusk had fallen by the time we reached Shanghai Moon. The sign on the door read *Closed*, but Fei Yen and Faeza sat in the dim light of the shop, polishing off some chow mein, their chopsticks skills deft as they fed one another. Sitting opposite them, with the slumped demeanour of someone who obviously felt like the third wheel, was my brother.

"What's he doing here?" Ezra trilled the doorbell and gave a tight smile.

Sahil unlocked the door, while the foxes headed into the back of the shop to tidy away their dinner. "So you lovebirds are back together? I'm happy for you, sis. At least one of us is lucky in love. Neuhoff's a dozen times the man Alex is."

Ezra shook his hand, his eyebrow raised a touch. "I appreciate that, Sahil."

My brother's ruffled hair, werepigeon-style even in his human form, gave me pause. It was an age ago that he'd left his suited, booted, Saville Row self behind. His deep voice had a nasal undertone. He had sprouted tufts of nasal hair that were in dire need of a wax, as if his werepigeon side was winning over his human one. I doubted he found it easy to attract women in the nightclubs these days.

"I know what you're thinking," said Sahil. "I'm losing my looks. It's a hard pill to swallow. But then, most men are balding by middle age, and here I am spouting new hair, even if it is from weird orifices. And there are other pluses too. I sold my Range Rover the other day. I made a pretty packet."

"You love that car," I said.

"Yeah, but it costs a fortune to run a diesel car in the city these days, what with the Mayor of London's new policies. And instead of getting a Tesla like every other rich wanker or sweating my man boobs off on a bicycle, I can pretend to have exemplary eco-credentials by ditching a car altogether and just pigeon it everywhere. Plus, it's healthier for my lungs because I can fly above the smog."

He always did this. Justifying his life decisions into a neat little package so it made him seem clever. Compassion filled me, knowing how he had always preferred order to chaos and how none of us could escape our magical identities. Magic was a dark body of water with fierce undercurrent. At times, it dragged you down to the silt on the bottom of the riverbed. At others, it allowed you to glide, a heady sense of liquid freedom.

Those moments made it all worthwhile. I only hoped I could pull it off once more for Mirabel and Echo. What I couldn't understand was why Sahil was here.

I left the comfort of Ezra's side and hugged my brother. It made me feel good when we were on the same page. I wanted it to continue. "What are you doing here?"

"Continuing to make amends. And then I received your text." His face fell. "I can't believe it."

Fei Yen and Faeza approached, still in their white pharmacist's coats. They bowed their heads in sorrow. "Your brother told us. We are so sorry. Mirabel and Echo are our family too."

Sahil cocked his head. "That girl allowed me to hang out with her with no judgement when the rest of you were still angry at me. And that bloody leopard has been a pain in my arse forever. A mocking, scratching, skulking, stalking creature, who highlights my flaws with such gusto, I sometimes wonder if he would prefer to see me face down in a ditch. But he is as much as part of my life as Mum and Dad's house, and I can't imagine our family without him. So if I can help in any way, I will."

"You're going soft," said Ezra. "I like this new you."

"Hard being a dickhead when you're surrounded by heroes," said Sahil.

I ignored their unlikely bromance, my muscles tightening in readiness for the challenges ahead. Every passing second sounded like a gong in my head. "We have work to do. Gaia has advised me to travel to the Celestial Library for an artefact. It's the only way to rescue them."

The foxes nodded. "We'll ready the tarot table."

The three of us followed and took a seat at the table. The foxes removed a wipe-clean tablecloth and replaced it with a maroon velvet one more befitting the ambience of a tarot reading. They switched off the shop lights and turned on the table lamp instead and finally lit an incense stick.

"It's scented with holly," said Faeza. "To protect you on this perilous journey."

"No need to rub it in," said Fei Yen. "They are aware of that already."

"Yes, but it is better to go into these things with eyes wide open. Missing limbs are nasty surprises," said her wife.

Fei Yen caressed her amputated arm. "Everyone has their challenges. I'd argue the werepigeon has more than me, even though he is technically intact."

Sahil blanched. "Ouch. It feels like I wasn't supposed to overhear this conversation. A bit blunt, you know?" He drew in a deep breath. "I'm going with you, Alisha."

I grimaced, thoughts whirring. I hadn't thought he meant anything concrete when he said he'd help me out. I'd assumed Ezra and I would go together. As much as I loved my brother and we had found a way to show our love that I was thankful for, we weren't an easy partnership.

"It's ill advised for three people to go through the tarot portal," said Fei Yen. "Too much DNA floating around. The results could be unpredictable."

Faeza's eyes widened. "It doesn't bear thinking about. You could end up with a werepigeon head, Alisha. Sahil might end up with your animation skills, and Ezra might get wind."

I snorted. "He has plenty of that already. Listen, Sahil, I appreciate what you are trying to do, but you'd have to do a trial to prove your worthiness to the Celestial Library. It would hold me up."

My brother eyeballed me, gleaning that I was making excuses. That he was my second choice of wingman. "Ezra hasn't done one either. He'd hold you up too. And flying could really help you out up there. It's different to teleporting. Wouldn't having a bird's eye view of the Celestial Library help you get the artefact you need more quickly?"

Ezra pressed his lips together. "He's right, hellfire. Your brother's got the precise skillset to help our girl and the leopard."

My heart hurt. I swallowed hard. "Okay. Let's do this."

Fei Yen pulled the midnight-blue curtain around on the circular ceiling rail, enclosing us in soft, velvet folds that glittered with sequins. When she had reclaimed her seat at the table, Faeza shuffled a simple Ryder Waite tarot deck with the proficiency of a casino attendant.

Faeza leaned forward, her voice a whisper that sent chills up my spine. "There is nothing unusual about this deck of tarot cards. In fact, it couldn't be more ordinary. It houses twenty-two Major Arcana cards and fifty-six Minor Arcana cards across four suits: Cups, Pentacles, Swords and Wands.

But when you tap the cards, everything changes. That's when the journey begins. Tap the deck, together as one, Verma siblings."

Sahil and I exchanged glances, counted to three and tapped the yellow-and-blue deck.

A rush came over me, as if we had really infused the cards with our energy. As if the air around the tarot table had been charged by us.

Fei Yen gave a happy sigh. "There is magic that happens when families work together." Her voice became more urgent. "But the window won't be open for long. Now you must ask a question, Sahil, as your sister has done in the past. An open question that will take you closer to the library and give it a sense of who you are."

"Remember, the library only accepts those who are pure of heart," said Faeza.

Sahil gnawed the side of his thumb. "Can you show us a girl and a cat?"

Ezra grimaced. "That was properly shit, mate."

"An open question, Sahil. Hurry," I said.

His nostrils flared. To his credit, he tried again. "How can a brother make up for his past mistakes?"

"Yes," said Faeza quietly. "That's a good a question as I've ever heard." She cut the deck and folded it into one again, before spreading the cards across the table with an artful swish. "Choose two cards, Sahil."

My brother deliberated for a long moment and chose two cards next to each other at the edge of the spread, one tattier than the other.

Faeza sucked in her breath as she flipped the cards and held up the first one, which depicted a man on a throne with a city behind him, balancing coins on his body. "Sahil chose the Four of Pentacles. It represents an abundance of material desires consuming your existence. The second card is the Six of Cups. The child on the picture is offering the young girl flowers in a courtyard. This card is full of nostalgia and memories of innocent days gone by. It is a reminder to cherish those who have stood by you."

"Only one of these cards is a gateway to the Celestial Library. As a first-time traveller to the stars, Sahil must choose. If you choose poorly, both you and Alisha will be barred from another attempt at the passage tonight," said Fei Yen. "Each subsequent attempt shrinks the odds of success until a time you complete the journey or are barred from the library forever. Of course, you might also perish while in the ether."

Beads of sweat broke out on my brother's forehead. He drew a series of quick breaths, followed by a long one, panting like he was in labour. "I don't know. I don't know. I don't want to let you down."

"Pick one," I pleaded. "Bel and Echo need us. You've got this."

I hoped he had this.

His body jerked as he sprang forward and tapped the Six of Cups.

Relief flooded me. It was the card I would have picked. The lamp flickered, sending demon shadows across the table. Where the cards had been, a pool of blackness opened.

"Go quickly," said the foxes in unison. "The portal won't be open for long."

Sahil gave me a look of horror then stepped into the portal, yanking me after him.

Ezra's voice followed us into the ether. "Take care of my girl, Sahil Verma. If it's the last thing you do."

The channel took us, dark and black and full of searing heat, with no stars to guide our path. In my mind, a mantra, over and over, that this would not last, that it would be over soon. That I would ensure any pain for my family to be safe. But it was hard to keep calm after a leap into the unknown. Harder still when travelling with a companion.

Sahil and I no longer held hands, but when I forced my eyes open, there was almost touching distance between us. The gravitational pull on our bodies stretched my bones as I jerked after him, struggling to withstand the crushing heat. There was no water as respite, only dense air and fiery rock. Was this what Mirabel and Echo experienced in the dream god's nightmare realm? Magma, dying stars, lava and supernovas. My tear ducts were obsolete here, and sandy residue clogged my eyes and the creases of my skin. Sahil's agonising screams abruptly stopped, and as his limp body surrendered itself to the forces, I worried that our complicated sibling love would end here in ashes.

The ether spat us out in the great hall of the Celestial Library. The marble floor was mercifully cool, and we lay on our stomachs, our skin and mouths parched, our cheeks soothed by the stone.

Sahil was the first to move. He staggered to his feet and brushed the debris from his skin. His mouth went slack with awe as he took in the paintings of angels and cherubs dancing on the ceiling in the flickering light of stars and planets. "This is where Rajika worked? Shit, and I thought a London penthouse was cool."

"You have no idea." Sitting up on my knees, I cast an eye around the great hall.

A cool water fountain bubbled between two armchairs, and a ring of fire blazed above it. The map on my arm stung, and the hall echoed with the sound of hooves. I dragged myself to my feet, anticipating the arrival of Nightfall and Calypso. Every thought now centred on the saddle Gaia had spoken of, the key to my family's safety.

"Hot damn." Sahil whistled in appreciation as Calypso entered the great hall riding Nightfall side saddle.

She wore a coconut-shell bikini top threaded with flowers and straw hula skirt, under which we caught a glimpse of her favourite daggers strapped to her thighs. Her dreadlocked hair had been fasted in a thick, high ponytail. She slid off Nightfall's satin black flank and landed lightly on her blade runners.

Her clear, melodious voice echoed through the great hall. "Welcome grandchildren of Rajika Verma. The library told me you were coming for the swap day."

I crossed the floor to envelope her in a hug. "Actually, I was hoping you'd stay and help. We have a saddle to find."

Nightfall whinnied and tossed back his head.

"Don't be throwing one of your wobblies," said Calypso. "She's not talking about you. Everyone knows that you are a bareback creature. We wouldn't dare to put you in a saddle."

Nightfall snorted and turned his back on us.

"A bit moody, is he?" said Sahil.

Calypso frowned and addressed me. "I'd say it's a coin toss whether your brother passes the trial. Still, the library trusts the Verma line enough for me to go on my holiday. It says between Nightfall and you two, it has all bases covered, and it's been so long since I've swum in Caribbean waters and eaten my mother's rum cake." She spoke fast, with no pause for me to respond, as if she was worried that she might otherwise not be able to get away at all. "You don't mind, do you? I did write you a little something to assuage my guilt." She pulled a strip of paper out of her bikini top.

I smoothed it out. "What is it?"

"Poetry to ensnare the dream god, of course. Isn't poetry made of dreams? The perfect weapon, I thought. Although, he will have to be in the right place for it to work. Otherwise, any old person would be trying to capture him, and there's quite enough bad poetry in the world already." Her languid expression became more urgent. "Did you hear that? That's the library hurrying me along. It says you need to get a move on and that my mother's cake is about to burn in the oven."

I hadn't heard a thing.

"Good luck, Alisha. Good luck, werepigeon." She braced

herself for a moment then sprinted across the hall, where she disappeared in a blinding flash. A humdrum, who the library trusted enough to imbue with its magical powers.

"A woman like that travelling without luggage is quite something," Sahil said. "Most of the women I date pack three suitcases for a weekend."

"She's not big on stuff. Expensive dry-cleaning bills make her grumpy."

"My mouth feels like a cat's tongue. I'm going to grab some water, nail the trial and then slam-dunk this mission. Working as a team, of course." Sahil headed over to the fountain. "That's funny. There's only one glass. I guess we'll have to share." He picked up the glass and held it to the fountain.

The water dried up immediately.

A look of befuddlement crossing his face. He pulled the glass away and inched forward again.

The fountain started up and then waned again every time he neared it.

Sahil stared at the horse. "Well, you can tell the library it has a faulty fountain."

He grabbed his throat at the same time my own started to close up. I clutched it, gasping for breath.

Nightfall cantered over to me, neighing incessantly, and nudged me towards the fountain.

I staggered towards it, and the ring of fire suspended above split into five fiery rings of differing sizes. Realisation dawned, at last, as my throat continued to close.

This was the trial.

The fiery rings, the water, family under threat.

I wracked my brain. The library demanded selflessness and compassion for others above all else. What did it want from us?

Sinking to my knees alongside choking Sahil, my eyes grew blurry as Nightfall launched off the ground, plumes of black feathers emerging from his sides as he soared up to the rings, the whites of his eyes wild with urgency.

A cry wrenched from my throat. "We have to go through the rings."

Sahil gasped. "You're too big to fit. It's my trial."

His eyes shrank at an alarming rate, his body too, until he emerged from the folds of his clothes in his werepigeon form, his grey breast puffed out, spluttering still, his pink claws flailing as his wings lifted him into the air. My werepigeon brother flew through the fiery rings with steely determination, despite the embers falling onto his feathers. To and fro, back and forth, a frenzy of grey and red.

The fountain surged, water pouring out. I crawled on my knees to it, retching, and held the glass to it. Water flowed into the cup, and I tipped it half of it down my throat, my health immediately improved.

But my brother wasn't so lucky.

He plummeted to the floor, as the fiery rings fizzed out, his fall broken by swooping Nightfall's wings.

Crying out, I hastened to his side and cradled him in my hands. I hugged him to me. It couldn't end like this. My mind flashed to our childhood: hide and seek, running races, fights over who had the cheese sandwiches and who had the jam ones, stolen sips of fizzy pop, wrestling games that he always won, Sahil helping me with my maths, me determined to find a book that would make him a reader, the distance in our teenage years, the misunderstandings in our adult ones.

I startled as his heart leapt to life within his pigeon breast. Stomach churning, I reached for the half-glass of water and tipped tiny droplets of the water into his beak until the glass was empty.

Sahil—my infuriating, driven brother, whose decisions were often polar opposite from mine, but who shared my blood and my lifetime—opened his eyes and spoke in his thin, nasal werepigeon voice. "The boy did good. Am I right?"

I laughed, great peals of laughter, borne of relief. "I'd have you at my side any day. I was worried for a second."

He cooed. "You were?"

"Yes. Sahil, we have to press on. Can you manage it?"

My brother fluttered up to his weird upright standing position, tilted his head and rested his beady eyes on me. "I'm ready."

I turned to Nightfall. "Do you know where we can find a saddle?"

Nightfall directed his nose up with a suspicious glare.

I approached him carefully and laid my forehead against his muzzle.

"It's not for you, Nightfall, I promise. You can trust me. You knew my grandmother, Rajika Verma, remember? She created you." I tried to climb onto his back, but the horse skittered away, apprehensive still about the saddle.

But he was eager to please all the same, or maybe the library whispered to him as it did to the Custodian. The horse whinnied and beckoned us into the bowels of the Celestial Library, where he set off at a canter, past endless soaring, laddered bookshelves stocked with everything from encyclopaedias, biographies and feminist pamphlets to literary fiction, science fiction tomes, bare-chest romance novels and everything in between.

The Celestial Library housed more than books. It housed artefacts too, as Calypso had once told me: a Girl Scout sash that amplified practicality, worn by Mary Poppins herself; a key to fit any lock; Shakespeare's quill to ignite the muse of struggling authors and, of course, a stake from the cypress wood of Noah's Ark that could kill the strongest vampire or inspire the faithless gods to remember their better natures.

But I didn't need any of those artefacts. All I needed to find was the saddle.

Nightfall went faster and faster, his hoovers a clattering whirr. My heartbeat pounded as I tried to keep up. My sword bumped against my back. Worse still, my boobs bounced all over the place, and I resisted the urge to hold them in place. I should have worn a sports bra. I shouldn't have given up my jogging routine. I should have stretched out in Shanghai Moon to stop the stitches that plagued me after a few minutes of running. I flagged, as I got left further and further behind.

He was too fast for me but not too fast for a werepigeon.

"You've got to go on without me," I said.

Werepigeon Sahil hovered in the air. "I will come back for you."

I nodded and keeled over, hands on my knees to calm my ragged breath. Mirabel and Echo's faces loomed large in my head, but I blocked the grief out, or I wouldn't be able to function at all. Grief blinded me, and I needed to focus. Time passed differently in the Celestial Library. How long until Ezra held me and Mirabel in his arms and Echo begged for cubed salmon steak? How long before the halls became quiet and Sahil came back to me?

But he did come back.

He came back, grunting with exertion, his werepigeon body damp with sweat and smelling like old socks. Landing on my shoulder, he pincered me with his pink claws. "I'll guide the way."

Following his directions, I strode through the aisles, past obscured doorways of different shapes and colours, past laboratories, dead ends, shrinking ceilings, planetary viewpoints, living quarters that smelt of New York cheesecake and winding steps that led to God knew where.

"In there." Sahil used a bedraggled wing to point at a stable door.

The whiff of wet hay reached my nose. I shook my head. "That must be where Nightfall sleeps. It's not an artefact room."

"That's what I thought until I looked inside," said my brother. "Brace yourself. It's a bit creepy."

Crossing my fingers, I pushed the door open. Inside, the air was cooler than I expected. Bundles of hay were stacked against the wall. The vaulted ceiling gave the room the look of a chapel. Horseshoes hung on one wall and a lone horse-riding hat and whip. A pair of boots about my size stood in the corner. My brow furrowed at the shrine of Ganesha in the corner, a black-and-white photograph of a moustached Indian man and a flickering candle. There were paintings of creatures on the wall that tugged at the strings of my memory. Wombats and possums, giraffes and polar bears, stingrays and nightingales and a small study of horses that looked just like Nightfall.

But it was the trestle table that caught my attention, laden with polished armour. There were gleaming breast plates, chainmail, helmets with visors, silver gauntlets, sharpened spears and swords that had not rusted with age, though they lay here without care or use. All too small to fit a man.

My breath hitched in my chest at the sight of an age-worn English saddle in the middle of the table, made from pliable brown leather, with iron stirrups and D-rings stitched into it.

"I told you so," said Sahil.

"God, you're brilliant. You found it." I drew out Death's sword, sent a silent prayer to the universe that Gaia had been right and touched my obsidian blade to the saddle. My sword whispered to me, urging me caution, to use every avenue, every ruse if I wanted to achieve my goal of bringing Mirabel and Echo home.

The saddle jumped up.

Sahil and I bellowed with fright.

16

<hr>

Goosebumps swept up my neck and across my body as an apparition surged from saddle. Wearing a long dress coat in navy blue over fitted *churidar* trousers, he was of Indian heritage, with dark, shoulder-length hair that was parted sternly. His form was like gauze, an ethereal intangibility that would allow him to access the dream realm.

"Am I hallucinating?" Sahil perched on the riding boot. "Please tell me that's not a ghost. I avoid cemeteries to the best of my ability. Burial mounds, crumbling headstones, dead flowers and angelic statues give me the heebie-jeebies. If we've summoned a ghost, I might never sleep again."

"The pigeon talks," said the man in heavily accented English. "Is this another one of my wife's tricks?"

Gripping Transcender tightly, I stepped forward. "I'm Alisha, granddaughter of Rajika Verma."

The ghost circled me, leaving a trail of cool air in its wake. "I am Sohail Verma, husband of Rajika Verma, and I am no fool. Be gone, malevolent humans, and leave an old man to Limbo so I can await my passage to the afterlife."

Warmth radiated through my body. I spun to Sahil, eyes

widening in astonishment. "We've somehow managed to waken our grandfather's ghost. This room must have been part of Rajika's quarters when she was Custodian. It's like she died and nothing changed." I picked up a chainmail dress, keeping a wary eye on the disgruntled spirit. "This is hers. It must be. And that shrine of Ganesha is where she prayed for our grandfather's soul."

"Rajika Verma did not take her wifely duties seriously. I can count on one hand the number of times she knelt at that altar." The spirit darkened in anger. "You are imposters. Who are you, and what do you want?"

"I am your grandson," said Sahil. "I look just like you."

The spirit reared up. "I do not look like a werepigeon, you imbecile. A talking werepigeon cannot be my grandson. You are an abomination of biology and nature. If we are related, what unholy thing transpired with my bloodline?"

Sahil made a straining noise then fluttered with anxiety. "Why can't I shift into my human self?"

"Because you're a werepigeon," said our grandfather. "You must accept it like I had to accept I am a ghost, with no agency of my own. I am stuck here until I have fulfilled my final purpose."

My brother protested. "But I have lots of agency. I am powerful, Grandfather."

This was getting us nowhere. Locking horns didn't always solve problems. I placed my sword in my baldric and tried a different tack. Dad had told me that his parents had shared a great love story. "You must miss her," I said. "You must miss Rajika."

The spirit sighed. "She died in these walls, and I was trapped in the crotch of this ridiculous saddle. I couldn't even say goodbye."

I frowned. "Why did she trap you in the crotch of the saddle?"

"Rajika was a spontaneous woman, forward-thinking and action oriented. The other villagers thought I was mad to marry her. She roped in a witch to anchor my spirit to the saddle crotch. It was her little joke. She was lonely up here amongst the stars and wanted to ride me even after death." He harrumphed. "She was very loyal. She never married again. We had a son. He had only just turned seven when I died of malaria."

"I know. Joshi is our father." Every minute of passing time gnawed at me.

"You lie." The spirit flickered like a radio wave on an unstable frequency. "To be married to a woman who could animate jungle animals and ocean predators from the page and to be felled by a mosquito dented my pride, I must say. The villagers tittered at my funeral. They thought I had it coming. Rajika said that's why I couldn't move on to fulfilment. She said one day I would have another opportunity to salvage my pride."

"She didn't tell Joshi that your spirit was here…in the crotch?" I asked.

Our grandfather's moustache drooped. "I railed at her. The photographs she showed and the stories she told me weren't enough. But she insisted it would be unhealthy for a little boy to grow up that way. People always said that magic came first for her, but I knew it was our son. Everything she did was ultimately for him."

"I'm not sure he sees it that way," said my brother.

"We never see our parents the way they are. They are our first comfort-givers but also our first antagonists. We make everything their fault, even if it's not true. Even if they were a product of their upbringing. A good parent never complains about being a sponge for their child's insecurities and hurts. That was my Rajika. She was a difficult woman, never afraid of making hard choices." His eerie eyes became forlorn.

"When she died, I thought we'd have some time in Limbo together, but she bypassed me somehow. I suppose I should be proud."

I spoke with quiet authority. "I think your chance to reach fulfilment has come. The question is, will you take it, Grandfather? Will you help us?"

The spirit flickered, as if he might vanish.

"Let me introduce you to your son," I said with urgency. My grandfather had a part to play in our story. I just knew it. But if his spirit melted away, we might never be able to entice him out again. "Let me take you to our father. You will see that we tell the truth."

"I will not fall for this trickery," said the spirit.

Sahil flapped closer and tilted his green-tinged head. "How can we gain your trust?"

Our grandfather folded his hands behind his back and paced the floor. "There is one way. You must earn a dragon's trust. Rajika always said they are the most discerning creatures on the planet. If you can do that, I will waive my doubts and help you."

I nodded sagely. "I know where we can find a dragon."

"The werepigeon stays here," said the spirit. "As surety. Just in case you plan to purge me."

I shook my head. "I'm not leaving him here."

"It's okay. This is how I redeem myself." Sahil strutted across the hay bales. "It might not be glamorous waiting here. But maybe this is how our family reunites."

TWO DAYS UNTIL THE ECLIPSE. The air in my lungs thinned just thinking about it.

We stood at the periphery of Bansko, the Bulgarian town that was a safe haven for peculiars and where they tended kindly to my dragon, the first creature I had animated. We had hidden Tielbu here, aided by a local witch's glamour, back when Lavinia had wanted to use the dragon as a weapon in Phinnaeous Shine's convenient war against the elves. Even mired in my anxiety for Mirabel and Echo, I marvelled at the quaint chalets and a bell tower church against the background of ski trails and a gondola on snow-capped mountains.

Marina tightened her shoelaces and straightened. "Talk me through it one more time."

Ezra rubbed his forehead. "The plan is to convince your grandfather's ghost that you and Tielbu are strangers and then for you to pretend you're earning his trust?"

"I tried to tell him the truth, but he was stubborn. This is the only way. You heard your aunt. We can't access the dream world alone." I buried my head in his chest, and the scent of mountain air and roll-ups washed over me.

Ezra sighed and raked a hand through his hair. "I hope this works. You called your dad and briefed him? He's had a word with the dragon?"

Knots expanded in my belly. "The crunch point is going to be when Tielbu sees us. My grandfather will expect him to burn us to the bone, but he will be overjoyed to see us."

"You made the mistake of underestimating him once, but it took him mere hours to learn our language. You animated him, but he's not a newborn. Dragons are ancient creatures. He is capable of so much more than we know." Marina slung her veterinary bag onto her shoulder. "And if all else fails, we have meat, tranquilliser darts and my empath skills. Let's hope we can pull the wool over your grandfather's eyes."

I massaged my temples. "Alma did her flour seer thing this morning, and she said that it boded well, apart from a blip towards the end that will work out just fine if someone lets their inner beast out."

"No better than a loony with a fake crystal ball at a seaside fair." Ezra grabbed my hand. "Come on, we'd better get going if we're going to make sure we're in the cave before the ghost makes an appearance."

I nodded. "Not a word of our ruse until my grandfather has entered the dream realm."

The snow lay deeper than the last time I had been here, packed tight under our feet. Only a sole pair of tracks marred its crystalline surface, which presumably belonged to Dad and Alma. My heartbeat quickened with the sudden dimming of light as we entered the mouth of the cave. The stalagmites and icicle-like stalactites disappeared the further into the caves halls we entered. There was damage to the cave walls where the dragon had lumbered and where he had breathed his fire. The scent of barbecued meat came from the innermost cave.

We paused just outside it, noting how it was warmer here and how no icicles or snow could survive where a fire-breathing dragon dwelt. Curls of smoke shrouded our feet.

I jerked at a sudden swell of cold air at my ear, to find my grandfather's apparition there.

"So you found a dragon." He wore the same garb, the Indian coat with its high collar and cotton trousers.

I nodded, wondering if those had been his favourite clothes or the ones he had perhaps died or been cremated in. How odd to have the privilege of meeting my grandfather but for us to act like strangers. The pressures of Mirabel and Echo's predicament made me single-minded, but at another time, I would have peppered my grandfather with all the questions under the sun, from his worldview to his greatest happinesses and deepest regrets.

Instead, my heart a stone, I simply said, "Sohail Verma, meet Ezra and Marina."

"Though you masquerade as my grandchild, you have no shortage of companions. That speaks well of your character," said my grandfather. "But I tire of small talk. Let us proceed."

Amber eyes glowed in the gloom as we made our way into the cave. The dragon followed our every move. At one wall, two figures stood shrouded in shadows, illuminated only by a small crack of light from the ceiling of the cave. One held a torch. The other puffed a pipe that I thought had been confiscated long ago.

"Who are they?" said my grandfather.

I kept my voice even, though I had missed Dad and Alma, and my instinct was to run into their arms. "They care for the dragon, bringing him food and medicine."

"In my day, dragons were solitary, independent creatures. The world is not what it was," said the spirit. "Carers of the dragon, shine your torch hither so we may see the beast more clearly."

Dad did what he was told. The light pooled around Tielbu, and a sense of euphoria came over me at his splendour: iridescent scales the hue of the Pacific Ocean; sunken, amber eyes in a rounded, horned head; a sword-edged tail and colossal, bat-like, bony wings.

My grandfather frowned. "He doesn't seem very angry. A docile dragon won't do."

On cue, Tielbu's amber eyes flashed with malice. He blew out smoke rings that clouded our vision and unleashed clumps of debris from the cave walls by crashing his forelegs against the ground.

"Perhaps I spoke too soon," said my grandfather's spirit. "I bear no responsibility for injuries sustained or lives lost. Only the gods know why you accepted this challenge."

"Here goes nothing." I gritted my teeth, drew my sword and strode towards Tielbu. When I reached him, I whispered. "Just follow my lead."

Deep-set amber eyes regarded me with interest before he inclined his head just a fraction.

Our dance began. To the unknowing eye, a middle-aged woman pitted herself against a fairy-tale beast in a crumbling Bulgarian cave. The woman was on the curvy side but strong, her muscles clenched tight and her focus rivalling a knight's. The dragon's razor-sharp tail came dangerously close to severing the woman's leg, his jagged teeth and fiery breath terror-inducing, his menacing, black talons capable of blinding a battalion.

But to me and dragon, this was puppy play.

I faced him head on, my back to our onlookers and waggled my eyebrows to the left. The dragon misread my instruction and leapt to his right, blowing smoke rings that made my eyes sting. We collided, my face against his scaly throat. I rubbed my nose ruefully, but kept up the charade, like a pantomime villain. My eyes sore, I poked him with my sword, underestimating the distance between us and penetrated his tough skin.

The dragon shrieked and eyed me, first like a traitor and then a fool.

"Sorry," I mumbled, taking care that my grandfather wouldn't overhear.

We circled each other like bull and matador, and when I gave a signal for him to breathe fire, the flare leapt so close to me that the heat singed my eyebrow. I patted it out and put on a brave smile for the concerned dragon, worried that he'd give up the charade and this would all be for nothing. Tielbu took great, thumping leaps from side to side that threatened to collapse the cave or bared his beautifully flossed teeth or breathed out fire. I blocked him with my wind powers, diving out of the way or getting in a cheeky poke to roars of approval from my enraptured grandfather and polite applause from my loved ones.

My grandfather chortled. "Bravo, bravo. A thrilling battle and a fitting contest to win my help."

When the dragon tired and my breath came in bursts, I called out to Marina for the meat.

She tossed over the plastic bag of oozing, slopping flesh, keeping her distance to maintain the charade.

The dragon collapsed onto his forelegs in the thick, dense heat of the cave and eyed me wearily. When I offered him the deer meat, he snorted and inched closer until it was within his reach.

I laid a hand on his forehead and whispered, "Thank you, my darling."

Tielbu's wise, amber eyes rested on my face with absolute trust, and then he lunged for the meat.

I turned to my grandfather's ghost in triumph. "I have earned the dragon's trust, and now you must enter the dream realm and bring back my daughter Mirabel and the leopard."

"The leopard," said my grandfather. "Chanakya Gunbir Hredhaan of Maharashtra?"

"The one and the same," I said.

"That tiresome cat. As newlyweds, he thought he had as much right to my wife as I did." He softened. "Can it be you were telling the truth?"

"It was you who said that dragons are the most discerning creatures on the planet." I bit my lip. "I have someone to introduce you to. Dad, come here. Grandfather, meet your grown son."

Dad stepped forward, trembling with emotion, supported by Alma. His appearance was older than my grandfather's, and I realised how young he had been when he had lost his father and how he had learned to be a good one himself without his own father as a role model.

Dad stared at the spirit, though they couldn't hug and the emotions were too much for them to bear. "I missed you, Father. What we had and what we could have had."

"You have grown old and haggard, son. Maybe my love

would have protected you from life's hardships. Has it been a good life?"

Dad's eyes filled with tears. "It has."

"You had children? And great loves? And fulfilling work?"

"I did. I had it all," said Dad.

"Then all is not lost," said my grandfather. "And that gives me peace."

17

———————

My grandfather left for the dream realm, tasked with bringing back Mirabel and Echo. It was as Gaia said. Once freed, no borders and boundaries existed for spirits, unlike for those of us with souls housed in bodies. If they wished, spirits could roam from continent to continent, speed across the oceans, be guardian angels, conduct hauntings or appear in dreams to their loved ones.

I had faith that my grandfather would give his all to bring our family back together.

That was the thing about mothering. Sometimes, you couldn't step in to keep your children safe. All you could do was relinquish control and ask with a red-welt heart for the universe to bring them back to you.

We sat cross-legged in a circle in Tielbu's cave, as Marina held a stethoscope to the dragon's chest to check his health. Dad relived the moments of his encounter with Grandfather's spirit, as if repeating the details over and over again could enshrine the experience in the vault of his memory.

"I will never forget the moment you walked into the cave with my father, Alisha," hiccupped Dad. "Those few words he said meant so much to me."

He chugged his pipe, and I tried not to disapprove, although the whiff of cannabis was strong.

"Look at you, Joshi. Sweat and tears all mingled together." Alma dabbed his face with a tissue. "Don't be cross at him for the pipe, Alisha. He was so worried after your call with this great charade. It took the edge off. It really is wonderful to see you and Ezra back together."

Dad inhaled deeply from his pipe, in a pensive mood. "I always wondered if the scarce memories I have of my father were of my own making. Fathers were stern in those days, and over the years, I wondered if I had bolstered his affection in my head. I have no siblings to crosscheck my memories with. Those moments were a gift. He'll bring Mirabel and Echo home, you'll see."

Ezra, whose hand rested on my knee, went unnaturally still. He had taken his jacket off in the smouldering heat of the cave. Goosebumps raced up his arms. He looked around abruptly.

An empty, fluttery feeling in my stomach. "What's wrong?"

Copper sparked in his eyes.

"Someone's here. Or something." And then he was ripping off his clothes, with no regard for Alma's blushing or Dad's protestations to spare his eyes the sight of such manly prowess. Off came his jeans and his T-shirt and even his boxers, as he stood there starkers in the cave, wearing only his charm necklace. "Draw your sword."

His bones cracked as he shifted into his wolf, thick copper-brown fur threaded with silver on a muscular frame. When he turned his mournful grey eyes to me, I knew we were in trouble. A wolf's senses outpaced a druid. Maybe Ezra smelt their smoky flesh or heard the beating of their wings or felt the changes in the threads of the world, there beneath the surface where he felt so at home.

He bared his teeth before the first djinn arrived.

They materialised, filling every crevice in the cave. They hung bat-like from the walls and populated rows upon rows, behind and in front of us, until all I could see was slanted nostrils, sinewy flesh, horned heads and dead eyes. They pressed in on us, ridged tongues flicking, like heinous serpents from hell. A synchronised ambush of unthinking demons, fixated on serving the dream god.

The largest one eyeballed me. "You seek to outsmart Morpheus. It will not be done."

"Marina," I screamed, unsheathing Transcender. "Take Dad and Alma and get out of here. Run."

"Come with us." Horror coloured Dad's voice, although the marijuana made him sluggish.

"I'll be right behind you." I hoped it was true.

I slashed wildly with my sword to carve a path out of the cave for them. Ezra growled and threw himself bodily into the fray, leaping and tearing their flesh with his teeth. His size matched theirs, but it was me they wanted. Me, they hungered for. Their wretched, writhing bodies clawed at me even as I fought with my sword and my kicks and gusts of wind.

The dragon rumbled to life, sensing my plight, but when he breathed fire, the djinn fed off the flames becoming stronger still.

I called out. "No fire, Tielbu. It's water we need."

Was that how they had found us? Because of the heat generated by the dragon in this snowy wilderness? The cogs of my mind whirred. I needed to get them outside, where even one snowflake would cause them to shrivel and die.

How I wanted these soulless creatures dead that Morpheus magicked up to do his bidding.

I drew the ire of the djinn away from my family and friends with bruising determination, taking slashes to my face and neck and forearms from their gory teeth and thick, twirling tails. The dragon unfolded his wings to knock down the djinn like bowling pins, using his piercing teeth to tear off their heads or nibble their wings. I ducked and dodged the dragon's chaotic, veering body, while I chopped and stabbed and sent tornados of wind to crush the djinn.

I was stronger now than I had ever been. Stronger because of my talents and my training but also for the love that gave me purpose and the loved ones who fought at my side.

Marina wasn't a damsel in distress. She punched and kicked her way through, cursing colourfully all the while, her rainbow hair allowing me to track their progression to safety while I fought. All around me there was carnage. Marina's touch—or the cannabis—emboldened Dad and Alma, who giggled as they used lumps of meat as projectiles. Ezra, my brave Ezra, risked life and limb to barrel a path through throngs of djinn and over their fallen bodies into the cooler outer caves.

And suddenly, Marina, Dad and Alma were free, out in the snow, where the djinn couldn't follow.

My heart was lighter knowing they were safe, and I worked with renewed vigour. Then Ezra fought his way back to me, putting his wolf body at my back so we could fight in tandem, protecting one another.

I clashed with the largest djinn and frowned as he issued a command in Aramaic. Deep foreboding swelled in my stomach as a surge of demons scattered away from us to the dimmest corner of the cave.

Ezra howled, his call brimming with melancholy so heartbreaking that I jerked around.

Tielbu sank under the weight and thrust of the djinn. They clawed at him, springing up his body towards his amber eyes, and the dragon roared, convulsing, desperately trying to break free. Ezra charged into the chaos without a thought for himself. With a growl, he leapt, landing by the dragon so he could rip the djinn from the dragon's body one by one. But the djinn enveloped him too. They converged upon both wolf and dragon, and I knew that the djinn meant to finish them off so they could come more easily for me.

My stomach twisted. My own life didn't matter. It only mattered that I saved my loved ones.

Their leader, the largest djinn, continued his attack, his grin more gruesome than my darkest nightmare.

Giving my all, I slashed at him and ended with a kick to the stomach that sent him sprawling. Then I swivelled towards the convergence of demons. My breath burned in my lungs, and my grip tightened around Transcender's hilt as I raced to reach the dragon's back.

The djinn crawled like ants on top of him and Ezra.

Though my logic told me that faith in these gods made no sense, I prayed to all that was good in the universe that they would be okay. That evil wouldn't break them and that I could save them. Pushing Transcender into my baldric, I steadied my breathing and held up my palms to clear a path to Ezra's side then held my palms downwards to blast myself up and to my lover's side.

Then the djinn were all over me too.

They groaned with pleasure and hissed like reptiles and dug their talons and teeth into my arms and thighs.

But it was what I wanted.

"Hold on, Ezra. We have to get them to water. It's our only chance."

His fur was wet with blood, his body limp.

Heart hammering, I lassoed us with a rope of wind to Tielbu's back, and then I closed my eyes and remembered how it had felt to animate my dragon the first time. I remembered the lines of Dad's painting dancing beneath my fingertips, stretching and pulsing like veins full of blood. The iridescent blue of the painting oscillating, like it was a body of water. Blood and cells and fire and heat. The quiet power of his moment of birth when it had been just me and the dragon and his thoughts were my thoughts.

And even as the djinn tore at my flesh and began to devour Ezra, I leaned my head against Tielbu's scales and whispered, "Fly. Fly upwards through the crack in the cave. Fly, Tielbu."

The dragon unleashed a spine-tingling roar and shuddered. His wings, deceptively fragile with their bone structure visible through his skin, unfolded. Launching himself up, he breathed his fire on the cave ceiling and broke clean through it.

I clutched Ezra's fur, moulding myself to him as we caught the periphery of the dragon's heat, holding on for dear life as Tielbu took us and his djinn passengers—those greedy beasts who craved his fire—out into the sky above the ski village.

"Higher, Tielbu," I whispered. "Higher."

A chorus of grizzled screams around us as the djinn realised what was happening. A clutch of them dropped to the rubble of the cave below, their bodies hitting the ground with a sickening crunch. They were no stronger than humans and no more intelligent. Others slid on the dragon's back, desperately trying to cling onto his scales with their talons and their long tails. But Tielbu swooped and swerved on his way up to the stars, and gravity beckoned them to their deaths in the snow below. Only the stubborn, strongest and fiercest ones remained, clinging on.

But Tielbu's thoughts were in tune with me, and he knew what to do. The dragon pounded his wings, even as the air thinned. He set his sights on the clouds, those parcels of dust and water vapour that would mean the djinn's end.

As I blacked out, I hoped that the wind lasso securing Ezra and me would be enough to save us from death.

Or that the djinn would die first.

18

I dreamt of whooshing air and beating wings, of scaly skin and blue seas, of a wolf's damp fur against my cheek and loving arms enveloping me. I dreamt of fierce whispers, wrenching cries and the Jericho stone burning my skin. I dreamt of gossamer sheets, leaves pressed to my body and sips of water funnelled into my mouth.

When my consciousness returned, I tried to open my eyes, but my body was sluggish to respond. My eyelids were nebulous pink and my breathing thin. Voices talked low around me. My clouded thoughts were slow to unravel where I was or where I had been. Fragments came back to me, first by degrees and then in an avalanche. I wrenched my eyes open and tried to sit up, heart pounding, ready to fight.

A gentle hand eased me back against a pillow.

Rayna Willowsun loomed into my vision, a wreath of flowers in her grey hair. Her potion belt clanked at her waist. "Stay calm, Alisha. You're in the infirmary at Wildwoods. The walls have ears, so listen carefully. I will only say this once."

I nodded, my mouth dry.

She whispered in my ear. "Tielbu carried all seven of you here. He made better time than a Boeing 747. A good thing he did too. Ezra wasn't in a fit state to teleport. The Bansko coven's glamour seems to have held out. At least, the dragon's flight didn't result in the scrambling of any military jets. He's now tucked away in the woods you hid him in once before."

My voice croaked. "Is Ezra okay?"

"I'm here, hellfire."

"Thank God." I turned my head to the left, and there he was, not five feet away, in a neighbouring bed. His tanned skin had a pale undertone, and deep blue shadows of exhaustion circled his eyes. But his body, bare above the waist, had no gashes or welts. Relief flooded me, making my throat clog with tears. "The djinn?"

"All dead. It was an excellent plan," said Rayna. "With Lavinia now Prime Sorceress, I'm rather wondering whether you might want to consider stepping up as defence minister."

"Rayna, this can wait until later. She's barely lucid." Ezra rolled out of bed and tenderly swept back the tendrils of my hair. "I thought we weren't going to make it there for a second, hellfire."

Rayna nodded. "You've been through quite the ordeal. As has your father. I sent him, Alma and Marina to rest in my office. It's been a long night, but they'll be very pleased to know you're on the mend. You and Ezra are quite a pair. Without the Jericho and charm necklaces and the dragon's quick-thinking, you likely wouldn't have survived." She exchanged glances with someone out of my field of vision. "There is someone here who refused to leave your bedside."

Heeled shoes came forward. The man's voice echoed in my head before I saw his face, rasping and filled with sadness. *I came as soon as I heard. It's been hell watching you in that bed.*

Orpheus. Heat radiated through my chest, chasing away the lingering cold that had penetrated my body while riding the dragon. *Are we still friends? Aren't you angry at me?*

I told you once I respected your choices. I do. Even if it's me who gets hurt, said Orpheus.

I'm sorry. I should have realised sooner that your feelings had deepened. I could have saved you the hurt, I said. *I've missed your friendship. I was worried you'd disappeared from my life.*

His dark eyes glimmered. *Never. Your friendship saved me.*

He spoke out loud, pricking the balloon of our intimacy. "As I told Neuhoff, I'm angry at myself for not accompanying you to Bulgaria. I'm here now. We will deal with the dream god together. And punish him for—"

Ezra gave him a warning glance.

My mind reeled as I tried to get a handle on the facts. "Seven. Rayna, you said seven came home."

Rayna's expression faltered. She fumbled for words.

"It's okay. I've got it." Ezra scooted closer, his vibrant eyes unusually dull. "Seven people travelled back from Bansko. You, me, Marina, your father, Alma…Mirabel and Echo."

I listened, pulse pounding. A magnetic pull drew my head to the right.

Mirabel Elmstorm, fire fairy, my foster daughter and the bravest girl I had ever met, lay in a bed, the cotton sheets pulled up to her chin. Her eyes were prised open, feverish, over-bright and curiously empty. At her feet, lay Echo, curled up in a ball, his emerald gaze pinned to her face.

"My grandfather brought them back." I stumbled out of bed, propped up by Ezra and Orpheus, uncaring about my granny pants or the flimsy infirmary gown that gaped at the back. Kissing Mirabel, I hugged Echo, but he remained unmoved. "What's wrong with them?"

Rayna exhaled a pent-up breath. "The spirit did his best, but the mind is a tricky thing, and only one of them returned with their mental faculties intact. Echo is listless, but Mirabel…her body is here, but her mind is still trapped there."

"No, I won't believe it. I won't give up on her." I buried

my face in Echo's golden fur and sobbed. "You silly cat. I could have lost you both."

My tears broke the hold of his depression.

Echo lifted his majestic head off his paws and tore his gaze from my daughter. He'd grown thinner in the past two days, and his emerald eyes held none of their spark of mischief or passion. "I stayed with her through her nightmares and my own, but it wasn't enough, Alisha. What purpose do I serve if I cannot protect?"

My eyes blurred with tears. "Comfort. You comfort us. I would be lost without you. And I know that Mirabel is holding on because you were with her."

"The leopard followed the spirit out of the dream realm, carrying the girl on his back. He has more courage in one whisker than most peculiars have in their entire bodies," said Orpheus.

"You hear that, Echo? You are a marvel." I pressed a kiss to his head just above the scar he had sustained in the Battle of the Celestial Library. "You risked life and sanity to follow Mirabel into the dream realm when she isn't technically a Verma and therefore not part of your oath."

The leopard's eyes narrowed. "She is a Verma in spirit."

I gave a sad smile. "I think so too."

Ezra squeezed my shoulder as I shifted closer to Mirabel. Maybe she just needed to hear my voice to guide her home. Maybe it had been me she had been waiting for.

I cupped her face, stroking her soft skin, brushing her auburn hair from her forehead and tried not to internalise the horror in her open eyes. "Come back to me, Bel. There's a good life in front of you. Filled with love and friendship and purpose."

She didn't move or respond, and my heart broke.

Rayna sighed. "You've done more than anyone, Alisha. You gave her a home, and you fought to bring her back. But she's non-responsive. We've all tried, but there's not been a flicker. It hurts me to say it, but maybe it's time to let her go. We'll make it a gentle passing and full of love."

Echo snarled and inched up Mirabel's bedsheets, protecting his charge from both friend and foe.

I felt physically ill. I stroked her face, smoothed her sheets and turned, my body rigid. "It doesn't feel right. I won't let you do it. Gaia said love would bring her back. She'll know what to do."

"Alisha," said Orpheus gently, "the child is suffering. She is reliving her nightmares as we speak. Endless nightmares she can't escape from. You know what is in her past."

I clenched my fists. "But I also know what can be in her future. She is so good and so kind. And so very clever. And her laughter, when it comes, lights up the world. How can we let that go?" My stomach churned. "How long was I unconscious?"

"A day," said Rayna.

I blocked everything out. Everything except Mirabel and the tiniest glimmer of hope. I blocked out the aches in my body and the fear in my heart. I blocked out the looming threat of the dream god and the encounter I knew would inevitably come.

Inhaling deeply, I looked at my friends. "We have a few precious hours until the eclipse. Let's use them to save her."

Ezra's hand rested on the small of my back, imbuing me with strength. "You heard the eternal girl. We're calling the Earth goddess."

And so we called her.

We summoned Gaia with an altar of flowers, a tea light candle and a prayer in our hearts.

Then we waited.

The clock hands advanced relentlessly, the ticking mechanism a roar in my head. I kept vigil at Mirabel's bedside, applying cold flannels to her face, massaging her feet. I talked to her about my hopes for her future and our future as a family, about the continents for her to explore and the talents she had yet to uncover.

All the while, panic rose in me, and I gulped it away, willing myself to keep a clear head.

Rayna calculated that a total eclipse would take place at three o'clock, lasting a full seven minutes.

That gave us two hours to bring Mirabel back from her nightmares.

When Dad, Alma and Marina returned, they tried their hand again at coaxing Mirabel to a waking state. Neither Dad's grandfatherly chiding and pinching of her cheeks nor Alma's pocketfuls of flour to facilitate visions of the future nor Marina's empath touch could bring her back.

"I can't reach through the darkness," said tearful Marina. "I really wanted to. For you and for her. I feel so helpless."

"Go home. There's nothing you can do here. You all look so tired. I'll keep you in the loop, I promise." I turned my back on them, needing them to leave. I couldn't be strong when I saw the sorrow in their eyes.

There was a time for emotions and a time for practicality.

The druid headmistress pottered in the infirmary, tending to her patients and plants while we waited for Gaia. She surrounded us with carnations and chrysanthemums for protection and strength, tied heather to Mirabel's bedpost for luck and left a floating lily at the foot of the bed for healing.

Still, the girl's pupils remained fixed and dilated, and the horrors she swam in retained their hold.

Rayna adjusted Mirabel's nightdress. "We'll make her us comfortable as we can."

"We'll figure this out," said Ezra, grim-faced.

"Neuhoff is right," said Orpheus. "We will make every second count."

But their words rang with emptiness.

Only Echo remained quiet, as he kept watch on Mirabel's bed, his golden, rosetted fur swamping the girl's slight form, as if he suspected these were her last rites but couldn't bring himself to admit it out loud.

My memories taunted me. Mirabel, standing up to the teen wolf bullies when I first met her. Mirabel, floating in Kraglek's tank. Mirabel, terrified when earthquakes hit Wildwoods and coming to me for comfort. Mirabel, breaking curfew to sneak into one of my night classes. Mirabel, inconsolable after her parents' death. Mirabel, seeing the cottage for the first time and unpacking her suitcase. Mirabel, curled up on the sofa with Echo. Mirabel, twisted with doubts when the djinn inhabited her.

My insides contorted. It wasn't fair.

Time quickened, cruel and unrelenting, until the Earth goddess arrived.

Now all will be well, said Orpheus, but his fatalistic nature meant he didn't believe the words.

Gaia's sari was beetle-black, with no embroidery or sequins to bring relief, and her eyes were lined with kohl. Her hair sat in a neat bun at her nape, dark, threaded with silver and infused with pungent hair oil. She sighed at the sleeping girl, caressed the leopard, greeted Rayna and Ezra and gave Orpheus a respectful nod.

With her dislike for dead things, it was the most acknowledgement she had ever given the vampire.

Then, she held a papery hand to my cheek. "I told you once, Alisha, that mortals rarely meet my expectations. But you continue to surpass them."

I captured her hand and held it for a moment. "You told me my love would bring Mirabel back."

"And it may." Her sari rustled, and she lowered herself into a chair that Ezra vacated for her. "I stood in this infirmary once, right by that window, and gave you a weapon. A weapon gifted to you by an old lover. You barely knew your powers then."

Ezra picked up Transcender from where it was propped up against the bedside table and offered it to her

"Give it to Alisha, wolf." The Earth goddess's brown eyes flickered like the death of a distant star. "She will need that sword presently. Don't let it go, druid, though the temptation will be strong. It is the key to everything."

I accepted the sword from Ezra with an anxious glance. "But what about Mirabel? You are the mother of all things, Gaia. Surely you know how to wake her?"

She sighed. "Love is many things. It is heartbreak and pain. It is comfort in the darkest night. It is freedom and sometimes a prison. And always, it is letting go."

The goddess sounds like a quote on a gift shop mug, said Orpheus. *I was expecting more.*

Fury sparked to life inside of me. "No riddles and no hints. Please, Gaia. Speak plainly. Mirabel can't be collateral in this game between the gods. It isn't fair. She deserves so much more."

Orpheus nodded. "Tell us how to help the girl before it is too late."

"You will get your chance to help, vampire." Gaia's eyes flashed like lightning. "Quiet. She comes."

The quiver in the goddess's voice made me want to flee. My mouth went dry, and my senses became more acute. Time slowed, and I became attuned to it all. Mirabel's slow creaking breathing. The trees branches skating the window. The glimmer of winter sun on the pane. The pink of Lavinia's colours on the Wildwoods cabins. Ezra's pacing. Echo's statue-like vigil on the bed. The click of Orpheus's dress shoes on the infirmary floor. Rayna quietly folding bedding, unobtrusive but always caring. The rat-tat-tat of my own anxious heart. The rustle of Gaia's sari as she stood abruptly.

"I have been expecting you," said the Earth goddess coldly. "Although I thought I had cloaked my journey enough to prevent you from following me here."

I stood and held the sword aloft. My friends recognised the warning in the timbre of Gaia's voice, though neither god nor monster appeared. We all reacted, taking up position around Mirabel's bed. Six defenders of the sleep-ridden girl: Ezra, Echo, Orpheus, Rayna, me at Mirabel's head and Gaia at her feet, all determined that nothing would befall her. That any attacker would have to go through us.

When the stranger appeared, my gut twisted in horror. I had seen her at Stonehenge when she had commanded Ra to kill Gaia with the twin of my sword. Even at a distance from the ancient druid stone circle, I had known her to be the one in control. The one I should fear most. The one who would eventually come.

I just hadn't wanted to believe it.

I had wanted to believe in my happy ending instead.

She stood seven foot tall, with four arms, blue-black skin and a cascade of matted, black hair only partially obscuring her naked torso. In her mouth hung a cigarette. She wore a necklace of decapitated heads and a skirt of rotting human arms. Each hand held an item: a whip, a bell, a lotus bud and the bloodied twin of my sword. The sword she had named Surrender. And even though the sight of her made my blood run cold, she had a feral beauty and raw power, as if she would never kneel before the world.

Her coal-black eyes rested on Gaia, unyielding and bold.

19

Beads of sweat broke out on my forehead.

The stranger wasn't a stranger at all. She had been Gaia's lover.

She was a woman with whom we were all intimately connected in some way or another. Her name was Death, although she had held many other names through time and culture. Thanatos. Hel. Hecate. Anubis. The Grim Reaper. La Muerte. Styxx. We held our breath as the blue woman smiled and stamped out her cigarette on the white infirmary floor with her sandal.

Surely Lavinia would appear, with the full force of Wildwoods security alongside her—the coven, the sphinxes, creatures from the bestiary?

Ezra's breath burst in and out as he stared at the fag end. "I've seen that brand and smelt it before."

Gaia's eyes burned bright with intent. "Are you here for the girl or for me?"

"This is the perfect place for a tête-à-tête, my love," said Death. "You know how sickness draws me. I've been looking for you everywhere. How rude of you not to come and say hello when you awakened."

"I knew you'd find me." The Earth goddess sighed. "You always find me in the end, Kali."

Death pouted. "You make me seem like a stalker, Gaia. Did you like the twist when I ordered your killing? I know how you like surprises. With all your intuition, I suspect you didn't see that one coming."

Ezra's face turned ashen. He whispered over his shoulder. "This doesn't concern us. We have to concentrate on Mirabel."

"Neuhoff is right. Why didn't the Earth goddess tell us to run? Let the wolf teleport us away," said Orpheus.

Rayna shook her head. "It's too dangerous to move the patient."

Worry wreaked havoc with the compass of my intuition, but I knew one thing.

My voice was low and urgent. "The goddess always has her reasons. It's when I don't trust her that I go wrong. Let's hold our nerve."

Gaia and Death only had eyes for one another.

The Earth goddess trembled. "You and your sorry circle of bootlickers broke a sacred oath. You turned on me and spilt immortal blood. What comes next is not my doing. It is yours."

Spittle flew from Death's mouth. "Who, pray tell, is going to stand in my way? You quiver like one of your precious leaves, dear one. Pan, that sorry traitor who gave up the secret of the Rejuvenation Pool, runs scared with his stinking herds. You ally with mortals in your pathetic attempts to bring Him back." Her smile didn't reach the sunken pits of her eyes. "The scent of death mingles with the fairy girl's stale breath. I may as well take her now."

Echo rounded on the goddess, his tombstone teeth a whisker away from one of her many arms. "Touch her, and I will make sausage meat of you."

"Cerberus would adore you as a plaything," said Death.

I stroked Mirabel's hair, a primal scream building in me. "Gaia…"

Gaia tightened her fists and faced up to Death. "Tell me why you have come."

Death's gruesome skirt rattled as she threw back her head and laughed. "Isn't it obvious? All this time plotting and planning behind the scenes, when I've been dying to see your face at the moment of your downfall. I must say, you've been much better equipped during this game of the gods than I gave you credit for. You outsmarted…" She drew a tally on her arm with her sword in long, deep strikes. "Ra, Pan, Hermes, Mami Wata and even your old friend Cardea, although she got in a blow or two, eh? There are some rather grumpy gods on the prowl. Still, all this scheming you've done to avoid our traps makes Morpheus's triumph all the more delicious."

The Earth goddess's eyes flamed like molten lava. "He has not yet won. There is still time."

"He's on the brink of success, and you know it." Death's gaze narrowed on Mirabel. "It was a clever plan of his to target the girl. I never would have thought of it myself, but I've very much enjoyed watching it play out. The druid speaking to the spirit was an inspired move. It's rather annoying that he's at peace. I would have welcomed him downstairs, metaphorically speaking."

I ate up that good omen like I was spiritually starved and tucked it away to share with Dad if I ever got the chance.

Death continued. "I don't know why you're still putting up such a fight, Gaia. It's over, my love."

"It's not over until He is no more." The Earth goddess wrung her hands together. "You feel him too, don't you?"

"I feel nothing." Death scraped her sword against her bare breasts leaving a trail of blood.

Gaia shook her head in sadness. "Then you have learned nothing."

"Oh, I have learned. I have learned to sniff out love and snuff it out." Death's nostrils flared. "There is love in this room. I can smell it like a sickness. Have you told them that love is the precursor to death?"

Ezra moved closer to me, his protective hackles rising.

Was this why the rogue gods played havoc in the world? Because the Father of the Gods lay dormant and perhaps would never be the lighthouse they needed to guide them again? Because Death had once been in love with Gaia and her heart was broken? I knew the signs of heartbreak. I had suffered through it myself. Death's words represented a past hurt bubbling up, a bleeding wound sprinkled with salt. It felt like snooping to listen, so I dropped my eyes and so did my friends.

"I remember the first throes of passion," said Death. "When we talked through the night and realised how we complemented each other. How we grew more balanced from sharing our perspectives. How we couldn't take our hands off each other and would share our chores. Me, walking with you through the seasons and continuing your chores when your feet were sore. You, peeling the shovel from my hands when my back hurt to dig my quota of graves."

Gaia's voice was the quiet of a still lake. "I remember too."

"You told me we would always have each other, but it wasn't true." Death jabbed a finger at us. "So you see, love doesn't solve anything. It doesn't stay the same. It combusts or it fades away, and all that is left is agony."

Gaia frowned. "You're playing for time."

Death's full lips stretched into a smile. "Beautiful, clever and brave. That's why I loved you. And why I hate you now. It is true. I admit it. If a person is in the dream state for too long, they will die. And with the druid dead or mired in grief, all your chess moves, all your compassion, are for naught."

The sunlight dimmed in the room, as the new moon crossed the face of the sun and the solar eclipse began.

A cry escaped my lips as I jerked a look at Mirabel.

Ezra's voice was whiskey and sorrow. "Goddess, please."

"The sword," said Death.

I stood my ground. "No."

She rushed at me, her eyes pits of malice. Her large frame was unexpectedly agile, arms working with a spider's efficiency. She raised her obsidian sword in the air. The orange stone in its hilt—larger than Transcender's blue jasper —was shaped like the elliptical pupil of a snake. It mesmerised me.

I moved away from the bed just in time, anxious to spare Mirabel.

The swords met, and their clash shook me to my very bones, making the cabin shudder in its place amongst the trees in the ever-darkening light.

But Death wasn't finished. Our swords clashed again, and my friends sprang into action. Death was a warrior. Plant pots tumbled, the sink cracked in two, Mirabel's bed juddered as we fought to keep her and ourselves safe. When Echo leapt at Death's face, she let the lotus bud fall and slapped him away. With the other hand, she cracked the whip and sent Ezra and Rayna sprawling. Bone cracked as she slammed her foot into Orpheus's Roman nose, before three boxing fists floored him. A strong kick made returning Echo whimper.

It was as if she lived for these moments. As if this was when Death felt most alive. In the adrenalin-filled wrangling of a brutal fight. Knuckles sore. Spittle flying. Bodies hitting the ground.

Mortals were never enough to overcome death.

And maybe the earth wasn't either. Maybe death always won in the end. Maybe that's why Gaia hadn't fought. Why she remained quiet and still.

The Earth goddess's wise voice cut through us all. "Enough. For all that is good, stop."

Not all of Death's arms stopped. With a spiteful cry, she lunged towards Mirabel.

But Rayna was there, with her clanking potions and her trusty dagger. She stabbed Death in her blue thigh, twisting her dagger through muscle and sinew to protect her patient.

Only, Death's obsidian blade was longer and her will stronger. To Death, injuries meant nothing. They were just another blow. Her sword went clean through the druid headmistress's stomach.

Rayna fell with a cry, buckling and wrapping her arms around her middle.

Gaia was there in an instant, cradling her, rocking her like a baby. The day was almost night, and the infirmary was filled with wails while Death admired her handiwork.

My chest emptied of air.

The sun was almost gone. Was this a nightmare or was it real? I couldn't tell.

Orpheus and I fell to our knees beside Rayna, leaving Ezra and Echo to guard Mirabel.

Only when I touched the warm blood and held my hand up to a pool of lingering light did I understand that she might not survive. That Rayna had risked her life to defend her pupil and charge, despite knowing that Mirabel might not pull through.

Rayna's hazel eyes had already clouded over, her voice weak. "My diaries are in my office, Alisha. You must complete your learning."

I held her limp hand. "Do something," I said to Gaia.

"Death has touched her." The Earth goddess shook her head sadly and murmured a prayer as Rayna faded before our eyes.

There was a great heaving as tree roots sprouted in the floor of the infirmary.

Rayna gasped in wonder as the roots become a willow tree there in the encroaching darkness.

Orpheus stroked the dying druid's hand, stoically disregarding the shadow-soaked warrior just beyond. "Rayna Willowsun, you are the most accomplished headmistress and healer that Wildwoods has ever known. You died as you lived, in service to children."

Gaia stood. "You didn't need to do that, Kali. It was not her time."

"Time is not a given." Death hovered, waiting to take Rayna's soul.

And as she had done thousands of times before, at the moment of death, Death rang her bell. A sob ripped from my body as Rayna's soul departed her body and settled into Death's cupped hands.

Death's dark eyes shimmered, her hands finally still. "Say your goodbyes. I will return for the girl."

The Earth goddess nodded. "You will return, Kali, and I will make a flask of chai, and we will ride out this eclipse in civilised discussion to see if can come to a reasonable solution."

Death considered her old lover for a long moment. "Very well, for old times' sake. Be sure to make the chai just as I like it with the right balance of cardamom pods and cinnamon."

She disappeared, taking Rayna's soul with her.

20

Ezra touched the moon charm on his necklace to turn on the light in the gloom. We stood beneath the newly grown willow tree, each of us cowed and beaten. Then Orpheus lifted Rayna's cold, bloodied body onto an empty bed and tidied her hair. Orpheus, vampire who struggled with belief and belonging but who stayed in this fight for me.

My heart was a broken-winged bird in my chest.

I had done this by not walking away from the Otherworld. I could have lived a quiet life in a small cottage with Ezra, baking bread and helping our girl navigate the world.

Instead, I had ruined it all.

Gaia shuffled over to me. Her shoulders slumped, and her sari hung limply on her frame as if the centuries had finally taken their toll. "I know this is hard. But I want you to know that there is still a sliver of opportunity for us. A small light in the darkness."

I wanted so much to believe her.

All cherubic plumpness had gone from her face, leaving worry wrinkles, haggard shadows and a smattering of newly sprouted chin hair. It indicated that every encounter with Death had the reverse effect to the Rejuvenation Pool. "Death will return, but if we all play our part, she won't win. I will do everything in my power to keep her from your daughter. Nothing is more important to me in this moment. Neither the ravenous children at my doorstep, the avalanche on French ski slopes, the grinding of tectonic plates below the ocean nor the *laddus* being stolen from my fridge."

I tracked the solar eclipse, as panic built to an unbearable pressure in my chest. "But how? How will you stop her from taking Mirabel?"

In the periphery of my vision, Orpheus gently closed Rayna's eyes.

"We will drink chai, and I will tell Kali what she longs to hear from me. About how I love her and how I was wrong to leave her," said the Earth goddess.

My eyes widened. "Gaia—"

She waved away my concern. "I have survived many ordeals across the centuries and will survive many more. What is important is that you go into this fight with your mind at peace." She placed a hand above my wounded heart. "I can sense your torment, druid, just as I sense the torn wing of a butterfly or the crushed leg of a stallion." Her eyes were a movie reel of memories, and I thought I glimpsed my grandmother there, resplendent in her chainmail armour and her hands decorated with henna. "You are like your grandmother in so many ways. She, too, struggled with the question of what was more important to her, family or magic. But she honoured them both and never wielded her power selfishly. She found a way to be there for her family and her community."

My throat scratched. "But Dad said—"

The leopard's emerald eyes shone. "It is hard to undo a childhood belief. Joshi always believed that Rajika put magic ahead of family, but there's no truth to that. She died protecting you. On the night of the Battle of the Celestial Library, she delayed joining the fight to ask Gaia to protect the Vermas. And in her dying breath, it was family she thought of."

The Earth goddess inclined her head. "So you see, Alisha, you can choose magic *and* family. Sometimes, the only way forward is to heal the wounds of the past. It is darkest before the dawn. And you were born to chase away the dark."

The pangs of guilt in my belly evaporated, leaving deep resolve.

I met Ezra's copper-grey eyes, there where he stood glued to Mirabel's side. All this precious time I had been mired in self-doubt when I should have embraced what I wanted all along. All the wasted time harbouring doubts about my grandmother, when our values and destinies and been irrevocably entwined all along.

I wanted all three: Ezra, Mirabel and my magical identity.

I pushed back my shoulders. "We're going to get the Book of Names, and I'm going to put an end to this."

Gaia gave a nod of satisfaction, tucked the trail of her midnight sari into her waist and wiped away the smudge of kohl from underneath her eyes. She summoned coiling vines and winter flowers to cocoon Mirabel. They flowed from her wrists, building layer by layer. When she had finished, only Mirabel's face could be seen, like she was a fairy-tale princess waiting for her prince to come.

"It won't be easy," said the goddess. "This cocoon will protect her from residual harm when Death comes. The rest will be up to how much talking I can do and how fast you can be."

I pressed a kiss to Mirabel's forehead, the vines cooling my hands.

"Now I must make some *chai*. But you have a much more vital task." Gaia closed her eyes for a fraction of a second. "Morpheus's dust already spreads across the city. The full solar eclipse is almost here, when the dream god is strongest.

Already, his nightmares breach the waking world, turning minds everywhere into terrifying landscapes."

"We need to get back to the Celestial Library." How had it only been a day since I had left Sahil there?

Gaia pressed her parched lips together. "Ezra, you must teleport your friends to Shanghai Moon. Keep ahead of the sandstorm. The others must make it through the tarot portal before you and the foxes succumb to the sleep sickness. Hurry."

A vein throbbed in Ezra's jaw. "Won't I be accompanying them?"

"You will be asleep in minutes, fighting your own nightmares. But Alisha's Jericho necklace, more potent than the one your witch aunts fashioned for you, keeps her safe. The leopard's exit from the dream realm means he had gained immunity to the dream sickness. And the vampire never sleeps. They will be her travelling companions." Her fingers brushed the map of my scars, focusing on five points within it. "Beware, Morpheus will be able to reach the Celestial Library while the eclipse rages."

The vampire's dark eyes were sombre. "The leopard and I will keep Alisha safe, Neuhoff."

Ezra's mouth twisted. "If my experience is anything to go by, it's more likely *she* will keep *you* safe."

He held out his calloused hands and signalled us to make a circle. I stole one last look at the Earth goddess and Rayna's body just beyond. Then Ezra jolted us across the city towards Shanghai Moon.

I'd travelled in Ezra's arms dozens of times. Though teleporting still muddled my insides, I'd never felt in peril. My trust in him was absolute. But this time was different. He jerked in and out of the monochrome world, and the four of us gasped for breath as swirls of sand drifted into the slipstream from towns along the way, where the dream god had already enveloped Londoners in their nightmares. We zig-zagged, dipping in and out of the folds of the world—like teabags dipped in lukewarm water—catching glimpses of victims.

The path of Morpheus's sands unleashed nightmares on the world. Citizens waded through their mental anguish, embattled and breaking. Some stood paralysed in the midst of their daily routine, eyes bulging. Others thrashed and pulled out fistfuls of hair. More still, retreated into a fetal position on the frosty ground, moaning and whimpering. A few squeezed their eyes shut and clawed at their cheeks.

Streetlamps flickered in the semi-darkness as we emerged in Balham, despite it being a quarter to three in the afternoon. We had minutes to make it to Shanghai Moon, but Ezra had landed with a jerk some distance away. The four of us catapulted apart, each heaving with motion sickness.

My palms were sweaty as I turned to Ezra. "Are you okay? What happened?"

His breath rasped. "I thought for a moment we weren't going to make it. I couldn't stay beneath the surface. The sand kept catching up."

Orpheus vomited bile on the ground, his skin as paler than ivory, and drew his shirt sleeve across his mouth. His voice was droll when he straightened. "You're out of practice, Neuhoff. All that riding alongside Lavinia in Otherworld taxis."

I scanned the street, alarm growing. In the distance, a dust cloud brewed, and it billowed our way.

"Run." Echo spun in the direction of our destination with a growl.

The leopard and vampire raced ahead to the shop, with Ezra and me close behind. Headlights looming, drivers halted their cars in confusion at the sight of the sky, alongside perplexed passers-by. By now, I understood that sands would turn their reality into nightmares too. My heart wrenched for them, but we didn't warn them of their impending fate. There was no time, and explanations to humdrums would be fruitless.

They would never believe us.

When we reached the tea and occult shop, the door sign read *Open*, but inside all was quiet. The bell tinkled as Orpheus pushed the door, and we tumbled inside, exhausted by our pace and adrenalin. A thin layer of dust lay over the shop, although the foxes usually kept it meticulously clean, save for their takeaway boxes. With fear snaking up my spine, I rushed to the tarot table and pulled back the thick, velvet sequinned curtain.

The foxes lay slumped at their tarot table, Fei Yen mouthing a voiceless scream. Next to her, their sides pressed together in terror, Faeza had covered her eyes with clawing fingers.

"We're too late." I shook them, but just like Mirabel, their nightmares had trapped them.

Echo leapt up onto a chair to survey the table. "Maybe not. The cards are dealt. Let us choose."

He was right. Faeza's hand lay open next to a curved line of her Ryder Waite tarot cards, as if she had been expecting us and had already dealt them out.

"Hurry." Ezra leaned on the tarot table, dread rising. "The sands are not far behind."

I wiped clammy hands on my jeans. "You should choose, Orpheus."

The vampire shook his head. "The three of us have all travelled to the stars before, Alisha. You drive this offshoot of destiny, first and foremost. You must pick the portal card."

I leapt for a card—a single card—as the door to Shanghai Moon flew open and a river of sleep dust flowed our way. With white spots of panic floating in my eyes, I flipped the card to find the Queen of Wands. She sat on a throne surrounded by a black cat and sunflowers and held a wand.

It would have to do.

"Go. Go now." Ezra stuffed a roll-up between his lips and lit it with shaking fingers.

The sands neared, and the Jericho stone burned my chest. With a deep inhale, I secured my sword on my back. Ezra sank to the ground as I dove into the card, with Orpheus and the roaring leopard a split second behind me.

We fell like thrill seekers without parachutes.

We fell through ice and fire and sediment and sky. We fell, tumbling like acrobats through the universe, paws and limbs and fangs all muddled up together, cursing and spluttering and dry heaving with alarm. And when my stomach could no longer cope with the free-wheeling angst of it all, we crashed into the Celestial Library, where a battle was already in full flow.

Despite the eclipse, there was no darkness here. The Celestial Library was lit by a sky of luminous stars and swirling planets. But the great hall, with its marble pillars and paintings of angels and cherubs on the ceiling, was already overrun with hundreds of djinn.

Their number was greater than in the Bansko cave, where Ezra and I had almost died defeating them.

Everywhere we looked, wild djinn frothed and seethed, determined to penetrate the inner halls of the library. I hated them. Their horned heads and fiery bones, their decaying flesh, monkey limbs, ridged tongues, stunted wings and heavy, twirling tails. I hated the dense, sticky heat that accompanied their arrival and hung like vapour in this sacred place.

At the centre of the hall, Calypso spun, her dreadlocks loose. She was dressed in tracksuit, her coconut bra and her hula skirt confined to her wardrobe once more. She delivered a powerful kick to a host of djinn, before using her blade runners to bounce off the group and slice into another section of their heaving mass.

The leopard snarled as he surveyed the carnage. "This was

the home Rajika fought to keep safe, and Morpheus has opened the gates of hell into it."

Orpheus dusted himself off. "I have seen this sight once before on the night of the Battle of the Celestial Library almost forty years ago, when I was a young, ambitious vampire."

I glanced at him in shock as I drew my sword. "You were there?"

He gave a wry smile. "Excuse my vanity, Alisha. I didn't want you to think of me as an old man. I was saved from a staking by the intervention of a rhinoceros your grandmother had animated."

"Let's hope we are as lucky tonight." I scanned the room. "We need to get into the inner halls. That's where the book will be. But we have to help Calypso to thin the crowd before we get through. Agreed?"

Echo's emerald eyes widened as a coat of silver-plated armour flew through the air and moulded itself to him, leaving only his paws and the expanse of his wide face unencumbered. His chest puffed with joy. "It's enough to make me sing. I didn't think I would ever feel the weight of this armour again. It is what I wore when I fought alongside Rajika."

"Let's put to good use, shall we?" Sword aloft, palms ready to call the winds, I led the way into the fray.

Echo roared past, glorious in his coat of armour. He landed and immediately sank his teeth into a foe.

Orpheus bared his fangs but seemed to have second thoughts. Instead, he used his lightning fists and speed instead to wound, disorient and evade the djinn.

"Nice of you to join us." Calypso darted me a glance, her metallic eyeshadow matching the silver of her dual blades. "What the hell is going on?"

"The dream god has unleashed the nightmare realm." I fought alongside her, my sword carving shapes through the hoards. In between killings, I centred myself and imagining terrifying winged creatures in my mind's eye. I pulled them from my head and flung them across the great hall like marbles rolling across a table.

At five foot tall when full grown, the shoebill storks were as tall as the djinn. They were prehistoric creatures, descended from dinosaurs, with predominantly grey feathers, yellow button eyes, a tufty crown and a wingspan of eight metres. Capable of overpowering crocodiles and decapitating their victims with ease, they had enormous beaks. Creepier still, they moved slowly and quietly. Their rare call sounded like a machine gun. Though they were my creations, I shuddered at the sight of them fanning out across the hall.

"Forget the djinn." Calypso winced. "I am never getting over those things and their death con stares."

"You should be all right. Their purpose is to defend the library at your side." I hacked the head off a challenger and, in a fit of pique, sent a whirlwind through the lines of the djinn.

"Now you're showing off." Calypso threw her daggers into the breast of two djinn and ran to collect them, her energy and determination a wonder to behold. "If you must know, the library and I have this very much under control." She stretched out a hand like she was beckoning someone.

Sure enough, the library responded. A stream of paper boats flowed into the great hall, made from the inner pages of books. They carried pockets of water within their folds, and once in position, they tipped their contents onto the djinn below, vaporising them. Spine-chilling shrieks erupted across the battlefield as the demons perished.

Thirsty for more blood, the library kicked up a gear, encouraged by the knowledge of the djinn's weakness. The floor of the great hall became an entirely new terrain, a lake with hidden depths and bubbling jets, from which the djinn shrank. Echo swam within the growing waters, taking bites out of anything within his reach. Bony wings took to the air as the djinn flew out of the danger zone, only to be met by the fleet of paper boats. I sensed the library's anger in its onslaught, how it retaliated against those that had bypassed its entry measures. For the Celestial Library, pure intentions mattered above all else, and it would defend itself, even if that meant soggy or ripped texts.

Calypso grinned. "I told you I have this under control."

I sloshed through the water, landed a punch and followed up with Transcender. "Echo will stay and help. I have to get inside."

The map on my arm burned. *It is time, Orpheus.*

He waded over to my side, bloodied but unbowed. Together, we pushed past floating bodies and into a dividing corridor that remained dry. There, the library defended itself with arrows made from the frayed spines of books. We ran into the bowels of the inner sanctum itself, farther and farther, until the sounds of battle became a distant rumble. I stalled between the myriad of bookshelves, hands on my knees, spluttering from the heat of my burning lungs.

Orpheus squeezed out his wet trousers. "How long do you think we have?"

I grimaced. "I don't know. Time moves differently up here."

Then I heard the sounds of hooves against the gleaming floors. The stallion that had once been Rajika's loomed into vision. I wondered if what the elf queen had said was true. That Nightfall knew the whereabouts of the secret book. He clip-clopped towards us, whinnying in greeting. On his back lay my grandmother's armour, the leathers and chainmail dress I had found in her hidden quarters.

"Hello, Nightfall." I stroked his muzzle. Then I picked up the armour and hugged it to me. "This belongs to Rajika Verma. But you want me to wear it?"

Nightfall snorted in agreement, prancing on the spot.

The vampire sighed. "I don't suppose the horse thought to bring me any armour? A codpiece, perhaps? Not even a cricketer's groin guard?"

I dressed quickly, addressing the horse. "Have you seen my brother?"

Nightfall rolled his eyes and pushed his gummy lips at the map of my scar.

"You know it's time," I marvelled.

The horse bowed, and when he stood tall again, I leapt onto his back and pulled Orpheus up behind me. The vampire wrapped his arms around my waist as Nightfall galloped into the depths of the library, charging past buckling shelves, hidden doorways, secret tulip gardens, rooms that catalogued all the delicious smells in the world and those which stocked every imaginable flavour of tea. The horse's hooves pounded the floor, making spoken conversation impossible, so Orpheus and I slipped into our old habit of communicating in our minds.

This saddle-less jiggling is woeful for my meat and two veg, said Orpheus. *Luckily, I've had a lot of use out of my nether region recently, or it really would be a shame.*

My head whipped around to follow a flurry of paperbacks heading at warp speed towards the great hall. *I hate to see books as weapons. It feels wrong.*

But books are always weapons. They are weapons against ignorance, boredom and close-mindedness, said Orpheus. *I think it's quite beautiful to see them repurposed here as defenders of a revered place. Just like old ladies with handbags and umbrellas, I think there's a place for using books as blunt-force objects to hammer home points.*

A female voice chuckled. *A wise woman once said that all rules go out the window in battles.*

Disconcerted, I frowned. *Orpheus, are your balls so shaken that your baritone voice has become a soprano?*

What in the world are you talking about? said Orpheus, grizzled as ever.

Warmth filled me as I understood that, though I wasn't the Custodian, I was the grandchild of one, and the library was speaking to me. This was how my grandmother spent so much time amongst the stars without feeling alone. The library had talked to her, just as it talked to Calypso.

It gave me confidence to know that I was worthy of this connection too.

Perhaps I could pull off this feat for Mirabel's sake and for the sake of us all.

I didn't know if minutes or hours had passed by the time Nightfall slowed. Remaining mounted, I patted his neck and looked around. The book aisles seemed wider and the ceiling higher here. Frowning, I studied the raised braille dots of my childhood scar and the lines I had acquired at Stonehenge, like I had studied the scar a hundred times before. Gaia had lingered at five points on my skin.

Awareness dawned, making me lightheaded. With the planets spinning above us, the map suddenly took on new meaning.

"What is it?" said Orpheus.

I held out my arm to show him. "These five points. Do you think they could have been mapped on the solar system?"

I looked up at the planets and at my arm again, brow furrowing.

Orpheus nodded. "It's a pentagram. Maybe the points of the pentagram are certain books in the library. Important books. We should avoid the pulp fiction aisles and check histories and biographies first and maybe first editions of classic novels."

I chewed my lip. "The library is a wily place, prone to mischief and manipulation and hidden crevices. What if the pentagram points aren't books?" I caught sight of an arched door, painted in the same hue of green that Gaia liked to wear. "What if they are doors?"

Clever girl, said the library. *Now repeat these three words to the winged horse. The one who has roamed these halls in solitude for decades to fulfil this very task.*

I whispered the words—perhaps Gaelic in origin—syllable for syllable.

Nightfall reared up. The vampire cursed as we barely held on, and the horse extended its plumes of black feathers. He launched into the air, soaring on a path etched into his memory forty years previously. Swooping and swerving, his hind hooves touched each point of a pentagram: the arched green door, a crumbling door, one splashed like a Jackson Pollock, a stumpy narrow one decorated with children's handprints and lastly, one painted the colour of a summer sky with a cloudy, round doorknob.

The Celestial Library quivered in response.

My stomach somersaulted as the winged horse whizzed forward to reach a newly visible door at the centre of the pentagram. It was an ordinary door compared to the others, made from unobtrusive weathered timber with a baby's christening robe carved into the door. The door had no lock.

Orpheus slid off Nightfall's back and helped me down.

I leaned my forehead against the horse's flank and breathed in the scent of him. "Thank you, Nightfall. When this is over, maybe you'd like to see the rest of the world? But for now, go. Be safe."

I patted his bottom. He sped between the aisles of ancient tomes.

The door with the christening robe on it waited patiently, as it had waited all this time.

The vampire's expression full of dread and terror. "There could be anything behind that door, Alisha. Anything at all. Centuries have passed since the Chameleon Tale was first told. And now we find ourselves here, and I am, quite simply, terrified."

I bit my lip. "But, Orpheus, whatever is behind that door, I must enter. Because Mirabel needs me, and without the Book of Names, the nightmares plaguing this city do not go away."

Holding my breath, I pressed my palm against the weathered wood. It was jammed, so I sent a sliver of wind around the rim and tried again.

The door clicked open.

21

———

The door creaked open.

Orpheus and I stepped into a room no bigger than a camper van with a hearth at its centre. A vast expanse of glass panes instead of slit windows caught my attention. My mouth slackened at the view. Pools of shadow and reflected light. Cratered planets and frothy seas. Dwarf planets in orbit, black holes, distant galaxies and a comet a mile wide. And the sense, somehow, that my grandmother had walked this path before me.

But it was another sight that made my blood run cold.

Morpheus sat quietly on a chair in his original demon form.

Orpheus gripped my elbow in warning, but we were already in the demon's trap.

"Did you think I wouldn't come?" The dream god's voice slithered like a snake. He was black as the night, a towering height with dense muscle and laser-sharp wings, reptilian skin, with one unblinking blue iris and one green. "Did you think you could turn your nose up at my ultimatum, kill my army and seek to control the gods and that I would go gently into the night? I *never* go gently into the night. It was always going to end here, with my hands on the Book of Names."

My voice was steel. "You schemed, Morpheus. You created diversions and caused injury to innocents. You preyed on my affection for my loved ones. You accessed the Celestial Library at the height of the eclipse. But it was all for nothing. You don't have the book."

The dream god opened his leathery palm to reveal a small mound of sand and blew hot breath in our direction.

The vampire grabbed my hips and swung me around so he took the brunt of the dust. After all, Gaia had told us that he had nothing to fear, that the dream god couldn't induce him to sleep or nightmares. And she had been right. But much as Orpheus tried to shield me, dust had a way of sneaking into every nook and cranny.

It swept into my nostrils. Still, I believed the Jericho stone could protect me. But the necklace was untested at close proximity to a god. And the gods differed in power and intent. As the sleep dust mingled with my churning blood, I wondered if Jericho would keep me lucid or lessen the effects of Morpheus's will or only keep my body intact while my mind suffered. We had entered the room on faith alone, and a handful of knowledge, but faith wasn't always enough.

My mind warped. I clutched my temples at the flood of images that overwhelmed me. My ex-husband riddled with alcohol, jabbing a finger in my chest. Sahil smirking as he chose someone else over me again. Dad tearing out clumps of hair at Mum's bedside. Gaia toothless, her face a shrunken pit. Fei Yen and Faeza losing all language, unable even to console each other in the face of life's ills, translate the tarot or open the portal to the stars. Marina, lying in sweet repose in a coffin as I wailed at her side. Ezra, pulled apart by the forces of teleportation. Mirabel, an empty shell of herself until she rotted there, where she lay, cocooned in the infirmary. Echo, Tielbu, Kraglek and Nightfall, lying at the bottom of a trench with all the creatures I had ever loved or animated. The elf queen Meriel Naehorn cackling, telling me that I had failed, just like she had. The gods roaming an empty planet, with civilisation and our greatest feats wiped from existence.

The nightmares came, relentless, one running into the other, as the Jericho stone seared my chest.

Somewhere the dream god laughed.

And a vampire pleaded for my life.

I fell to my knees. But at my back, tucked away in my baldric that the foxes had made, Transcender whispered. And though the library was quiet within this most secret of rooms, voices of the departed spoke to me.

I heard my mother's voice, my grandmother's voice, Juniper Elmstorm and Rayna. Strong women, who had stood for right and who urged me on. And their voices pushed back the swell of my nightmares, acting like a tide breaker. Enough that I found the resilience to reach below my grandmother's chainmail and find the poem that Calypso had written to ensnare the god.

After all, as she had said, wasn't poetry made of dreams?

I thrust the crumpled strip of paper at Orpheus, my vision blurred.

The vampire knew what I wanted without words. He read as the dream god revelled in my suffering.

"Tangled mists, tightly woven, juniper trees, blue erosion," chanted Orpheus.

Squeezing my eyes shut, I held onto to the rhythm of his words, even though their meaning couldn't penetrate my overwrought mind. And as he continued apace, the energy in the room grew still and my mind with it. And when I opened my eyes, the dream god's mouth had been sealed and his clawed demon feet rooted to the floor, his sinewy arms straining against an ephemeral hold.

"I don't know how long it will endure." Orpheus tugged me up. "You must find the book, Alisha, and use it. Quickly."

The sword whispered to me. *Hurry. He breaks free. Hurry.*

I looked around, the air in my lungs thin, tingling all over. There was no hiding place in this room. Only walls and windows to the stars and the hearth. The hearth.

Yes, breathed the sword.

A new kind of whispering called to me. Dark and primal, like the first fires of hell and the crystalline lakes of heaven. The whispers seduced me. They spoke of powers unknown to any mortal.

The power to control the gods.

Mouth dry, I veered past the dream god to the hearth. His furious, straining rage told me that he hadn't known how to find the book. I looked up the hearth to the hollow at its middle, but I could see nothing there. Only darkness and a draft that called me out to the stars.

I swivelled to Orpheus. My voice wasn't my own. "There's nothing there."

His head jerked, eyes like flint. "There has to be."

Unsheathe me, whispered the host of women through my sword.

I pulled it out. Obsidian and blue jasper and a mammoth tusk hilt. I had drawn it a hundred times before without cutting my own skin, despite its double-edged blade, but this time, it slashed deep into my palm.

Orpheus cursed and hastened forward, tearing a strip from his own shirt to bind the wound.

But the blood drops rose into the air and drifted into the centre of the hearth. Heart pounding, I followed their ascent and placed my bleeding hand up the hollow. Deeper, deeper, until my shoulder was almost completely up the shaft.

It didn't matter that the dream god toiled still against his constraints. It didn't matter that my hand flowed with blood.

The primal whispers called to me, and I responded like a magnet.

I gasped as my hand closed around something cold that fit

into my palm. I pulled out the Book of Names from where it had been entombed amongst the stars, lightheaded with relief. A rush of power flowed over me. I looked at it with wonder. It was a notebook made from cowhide and covered in stardust. Sapphire ink covered its unlined, crumbling pages.

"You did it," said Orpheus. "You brilliant woman."

In our rapture, we didn't see the dream god break free. Morpheus slipped his bonds, a whirring mass of teeth and claws and spiked tail. A god, who had once been a dreamer but had long since succumbed to nightmares. A god, who feared me and the book I held in my hands and wished me dead.

I'd had enough of deadly dreams and the advance of death.

I dropped the book and lifted my sword. But the dream god performed his party trick of fading and dematerialising, and even Orpheus with his speed couldn't stop him.

Then came the blare of disco music as a grey blur of thrusting chest and scruffy wings flew into the room, beak first straight into the dream god's re-materialising black eyes. Sahil pecked Morpheus's eyes to the beat of "Night Fever" by the Bee Gees and I'd never been prouder of my brother in my life.

The disco-loving dream god screamed.

I scrambled for the Book of Names, turning instinctively to where the black, internal ribbon had marked a page. I read the words on the page with quiet authority, power coursing through me.

Then I plunged Transcender into Morpheus's stomach and twisted, with not one iota of guilt for this violent reckoning. We'd even played him out with a song.

The dream god faded from sight, his face a nightmare landscape of its own.

I sank into a heap on the floor.

A hand on my shoulder. "It's over, Alisha. He is gone."

"Come back, werepigeon. You can't outfly me." Echo burst through the door in full armour, his emerald eyes widening at the sight of me in Rajika's chainmail and the Book of Names in my hands. "What did I miss?"

Happiness burst in my chest. Planets swirled around us.

When I looked down, the scar on my arm was gone.

22

———

Ezra's copper-grey eyes sparked with the focus of an athlete as he tossed a pancake into the air and caught it. He threw a hand up in the air in celebration. "The indisputable champion of pancake-tossers. Who cares if it's not February? In this household, we eat pancakes whenever we want. Right, girls?"

He grinned like a loony as he slid the pancake onto a plate for Mirabel and slathered it in raspberry jam.

When he brought it to the kitchen table, she looked at him in awe. "How did you know that raspberry is my favourite jam and that the apricot one makes me want to vom?"

She took a big bite.

Ezra hid a smile. "Because I notice things. Especially when it's you. Like how you're okay with Alisha brushing your hair now."

She shrugged and shovelled in another mouthful. "It's no big deal."

He and I exchanged glances as I put down the hairbrush. We knew differently. We knew that the road to contentment had been a bumpy one for Mirabel and that we had almost lost her. We also knew that her happier moments outweighed her sad ones now and that her fire powers had become less volatile. Maybe coming through our ordeal had made us bond as a unit, or maybe I had Gaia's cocoon to thank for Mirabel's progress. It didn't matter what the reason was. Only that every day Mirabel got closer to the girl she had been before her parents died, even if she might never be entirely that girl again.

Together we had done it.

The Book of Names was buried in a tin box in the grove in the garden. Sometimes the wind carried its whispers to me. We had seen off the dream god. Death, sensing failure, had skulked off when the eclipse had passed. And the world had returned to its equilibrium. Although the BBC reported an extensive clean-up operation after the Saharan sandstorm and an anonymous donation of shoebill storks to London Zoo.

Ezra tidied up. He was barefoot, wearing only his boxers and the new Beatles T-shirt I had bought him. I peeled the sponge from his hands and curled my arms around his waist from the back, enjoying our domestic harmony. The family life I had waited so long for.

"I've been thinking." He drummed his fingers on the countertop. "In all that time that Death was in the infirmary, my aunt didn't make an appearance."

"Did you ask her about it?" I leaned my head against his back.

He pulled my arms closer around him. "She was a bit cagey. It's probably just a Prime Sorceress thing. She can't tell me everything. You know how it is. The car rides are the only time we really get to speak alone these days." His voice tapered off.

"What is it?"

"That cigarette Death smoked. I keep thinking it was the brand I saw in Lavinia's office."

I frowned. "You're overreaching. We've just not come back

down to earth yet after the anxiety of the past few weeks. How about we forget about work for a while?"

I scooted around him and pressed a lingering kiss to his lips.

He opened his mouth, allowing my tongue to—

"Ugh," said Mirabel. "You're ruining my breakfast. What's the point of making it for me if you're going to go and do that just when I'm trying to digest it?"

Ezra pulled away but not before he slapped my arse. "Get used to it, kid. And get a move on. I know this family saves journey time, but we can't be late."

The leopard prowled into the kitchen, tail swishing. "What about my breakfast? These days, it's like you only have one kid."

I raised an eyebrow. "Echo, you've been out all night hunting. And judging by the smeared blood on your jaw and the size of your belly, you've had your fill and probably stashed a carcass up a tree in a city car park somewhere. Yes, the detective has been keeping me informed of your antics. That glamour you wear only goes so far. A Bengal cat doesn't leave a trail of blood and gore behind on his escapades." I paused. "But here's some salmon I prepared for you."

He purred and nuzzled his head against my leg. "I love you, Alisha. As much as I loved your grandmother. I told Gaia as much this morning when we visited the dragon. That any pull she had on my affection had been far outpaced by my adoration for you. She was surprised, but she let me live."

My heart jumped. "I love you too. Finish up and wash your face. We're leaving in ten minutes." I held out my hand to Ezra. "Help me change?"

His smile lit up my world. "Yes, ma'am."

QUIET REIGNED IN THE ARENA. There were no chairs. No music played. The sound of rustling leaves and howling wind seemed a fitting musical score to the final journey of Rayna Willowsun. There was no weeping, only solemn contemplation about a woman who had given so much to Wildwoods.

Peculiars travelled from far and wide to pay their respects to the druid headmistress on her final journey. The women wore crowns of flowers in her honour. There were students, old and new. Parents who maintained she was the teacher who had known their child best and how to motivate them. Friends she had grown up with. Elves she had nurtured even when they had been outcasts. Contemporaries she had taught about the power of plants. The rats she had been kind to. A niece all the way from Edinburgh. Senators she had served with. And us, a family forever grateful for what she had sacrificed for us.

The leprechaun Cillian began the procession, holding a wide linen cushion. On it rested Rayna's dagger and her potion belt. Next came Ezra, Orpheus, Erelim and Helio. They carried Rayna's body in, to a collective intake of breath.

She lay on a bamboo stretcher with four handles and looked as beautiful in death as she had in life. Her long, grey hair was flowing, and she wore a simple, grey shift dress with her bare feet turned out. When they placed her on the ground atop a pile of dry sticks, I imagined her breath mingling with red earth, but her lungs had long been empty.

The pallbearers bowed their heads and walked around Rayna's body to allow the congregation to pay their last respects. We filed around the body for one last glimpse, and the children placed a flower at her feet and at her temples and above her heart space.

When the last member of the congregation had paid their respects, Lavinia stepped forward. In the treetops, the witch's pink colours fluttered. Her voice swam with true emotion.

"Rayna Willowsun instinctively knew where this community was hurting and how it needed to learn. She was simple and kind, with a deep well of compassion. We will never see her like again. She was my friend, and she loved Zumba."

Next to me, Marina spluttered.

"The witch would have been wiser to say she loved plants. Who wrote this meagre speech?" purred Echo.

I shushed them.

"It is time for the final goodbye." Lavinia lit a match, and the body flamed.

The congregation huddled together as the flames rose, and as Rayna's body became ashes, I reached up to call the winds and sent them spiralling higher and higher into the sky.

When it was over, the Prime Sorceress approached Rayna's niece to offer her condolences and present her with the cushion of Rayna's belongings.

Lavinia returned to her place at the head of the congregation to address the crowd. "Rayna was not only a great pillar of this community. She was a fierce advocate of equality and of looking to the future. It seems fitting, on the day of her funeral, to announce our continuity plans for the senate. Let it be known, that Flinar the elf will be taking up his position as the new defence minister, filling the position vacated by me. And my sister Isadora will be the new headmistress of Wildwoods School of the Wondrous. Flinar and Isadora, please step forward to join our ranks. We wish them good luck."

Behind her, Ezra and Orpheus exchanged puzzled glances and made room for Flinar and Isadora. A rumble went through the crowd, followed by a smattering of applause, incongruous with the grieving atmosphere a moment before.

Lavinia's voice soared across the arena. "Those who serve on the senate do not do so for their own advancement. We are here to serve you. To serve this community. To shape it in a way that benefits peculiars for generations to come." She paused to gather her breath, and not a pin drop could be heard, such was her power. "As the eternal girl's escapades have just shown, we live in a world where shadows vie with the light. Where those in power, in the halls of Westminster and in the palaces of this country, even those in Wildwoods, sometimes have feet of clay. But with me as your Prime Sorceress, a new day has come."

Marina frowned. "Can she do that? I mean, Flinar is a wonderful appointment, but it seems a bit sus adding another witch to the senate, and her sister at that."

I shrugged. "Judging by Ezra and Orpheus's expressions, they had no idea. But if Lavinia had the votes without them, she can do what she likes."

So much for making Otherworld governance more transparent after Phinnaeous's reign.

After the ceremony was over, Ezra and I slipped away for a few minutes' respite at the foot of a bare oak tree. I leaned against the thick trunk, the scent of damp wood in my nose and Ezra's spicy soap on my tongue.

He kissed me, long and hard. "She had a good send off."

"Yes, she did."

A frown. "My aunt is up to something."

I nodded. "A battle for another day."

We'd already been through so much. I'd stepped into the Otherworld as a blinkered humdrum. I'd learned about my magic and heritage and been heralded as the prophesized eternal girl. I had grown in confidence and trained hard. I'd tussled with immortals and overcome threats to my loved ones. There had been losses, but I had the Earth goddess as a mentor, Death's sword in my hand, my mother's Jericho necklace to protect me and the Book of Names. Most importantly, I had loyal allies.

Death and our enemies would come for us.

But I had everything I needed for the coming fight.

Every cell in my body fizzed with destiny. I was ready.

Ezra murmured in my ear. "It will all be okay as long as we have each other."

Warmth spread through my core as I looped my arms around his neck. We meandered through the trees some distance away from the arena, bodies heavy with the need for rest but relieved to have each other. Ahead of us, in an alcove hidden from plain sight, Lavinia stood deep in conversation with her sister Isadora. Her bubble-gum pink yoga wear teamed with her brown umbrella stood out against the dull winter grey.

The red-haired witch kissed the Prime Sorceress on her smooth cheek.

Then Lavinia Drach—who had long coveted Ezra's teleportation powers—disappeared between the folds of the world.

Ezra and I exchanged dismayed glances.

Then with wordless agreement, he grasped my hand, and we teleported after her.

ACKNOWLEDGMENTS

A big thank you to my readers. To the ones who devour the stories, the ones who preorder my novels, the ones who leave reviews, the ones who quietly turn the pages, the ones who tell their friends about my books and the ones who message me. Readers of Paranormal Women's Fiction are some of the kindest, funniest, kick-arse readers I have met.

A special thank you to my wonderful reader group, who aided my research when choosing the shoebill stork for Alisha to animate and especially to Elizabeth, who gave me the perfect description for it.

To my author friends and colleagues: Lynn Morrison, Louisa West, the Fab 13 and my Divining Tales crew. Thank you for being welcoming to writers new to this genre.

To my wonderful editor Jeni, who was flexible when I realised I had stretched myself too thin on the deadline for this manuscript, thanks for being wise, firm, supportive and oh so very skilled with your red pen. I learn from you with every interaction. To Maria, my cover artist, this book art is so beautiful it made me consider making hardbacks. Thanks for bringing Druid Heir to life so vividly.

To my beta readers Debbie and Sherry, who have become voices in my head when I am writing. Thank you for always making time to read for me and cheerleading. This story world has your imprint on it. I'm so grateful that I found you all those months ago at the start of this journey.

For our children, it's the summer holidays, and I won't be working as much. There'll be sand between our toes, wet towels on the floor, fun fairs, duvet days, movie nights and endless hours to read for pleasure. I can't wait to make memories with you.

To my Jan, who can read my every thought and makes me laugh every day. With each novel, I wonder if I can repeat that magic, and you tell me I can. And that small act of faith is enough for me to start another story. Thank you for holding my hand through our winding path.

FREE SHORT STORY

If you enjoyed this book, please leave a review online to help other readers find this story.

The Druid Heir novels are written in Alisha's perspective, a 40-year-old teacher living in London. The short stories explore the world from an alternate character's viewpoint.

You can get the Druid Heir short stories for free by signing up for my fantasy newsletter at www.nillunasser.com.

MIDLIFE BATTLE: DRUID HEIR BOOK 7

Death is coming for me, of that there is no doubt. My hair greys quicker than before, as if she already has a grip. Life with Ezra and our daughter is joyful, but the city is strange. Footsteps trail in the snow where no man has walked. An unexpected migration of birds clouds the London sky. The book buried in the grove of the cottage whispers to me, even though I ignore it.

When the Wild Hunt sounds its horns and the blue goddess rides, the drumbeat of doom fills the Otherworld. Gaia is jittery, more bride than warrior. I am her champion, though I have no experience of leading an army. Though I prefer compassion to my obsidian blade. As magical factions take sides, the only constant is treachery. The new Prime Sorceress wants an alliance, but after her betrayal of Ezra, how can I trust her?

As my power curls within me, Rayna's diaries illuminate a way out of the darkness and I dare to hope destiny favours me. It all comes down to this. Blood, graft, loyal friends and a handful of multivitamins. Together, we'll stop the rogue gods from reforging humanity in their hateful image. Together, we must find a way to cheat Death or lose it all.

If you're a fan of Paranormal Women's Fiction and magic-wielding heroines over forty, grab the final Druid Heir book today.

ALSO BY N. Z. NASSER

DRUID HEIR

Midlife Dawn, Book 1

Midlife Tremors, Book 2

Midlife News, Book 3

Midlife Drift, Book 4

Midlife Portals, Book 5

Midlife Eclipse, Book 6

Midlife Battle, Book 7

Druid Heir Collections

MAJESTIC MIDLIFE WITCH

To Save a Sister, Book 1

To Curse a Rival, Book 2

To Trick a Raja, Book 3

To Hunt a Foe, Book 4

NEWSLETTER EXCLUSIVES

The Magical Grandmother, Druid Heir Short Story 0.5

A First Date in Paris, Druid Heir Short Story 1.5

Midlife Battle, Druid Heir 7 Bonus Epilogue

To Become a Witch, Majestic Midlife Short Story 0.5

Biryani Junction, a Majestic Midlife Witch Cookbook

ABOUT THE AUTHOR

N. Z. Nasser is a writer of paranormal women's fiction. Her stories are about women who change the world, filled with magic and rooted in friendship.

A lover of barefoot walks along the beach, she is glad to have left behind her career in the civil service and to never wear heels again. Whether she is writing in her garden office or wrangling laundry, she is happiest with a cup of tea at her side.

She lives in London with her husband, three children, two cats and a fox-mad dog.

For new release alerts, you can follow her at Bookbub or Goodreads. For a more personal touch, join her Facebook reader group Nasser's Book Nymphs, say hi on social media, or visit her online store at www.nillunasser.com.

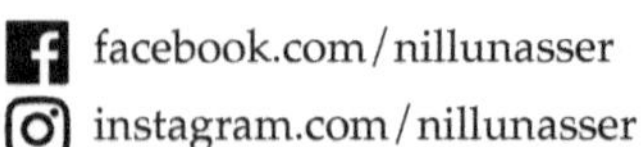

facebook.com/nillunasser

instagram.com/nillunasser